To Katherine e
Pete

with much love
to my dear friends
x x
16-1-17.

Penny Estlin

THE BOOK OF MIRRORS

AUSTIN MACAULEY
PUBLISHERS LTD.

A CIP catalogue record for this title is available from the British Library.

ISBN 9781786290007 (Paperback)
ISBN 9781786290014 (Hardback)
ISBN 9781786290021 (eBook)

www.austinmacauley.com

First Published (2016)
Austin Macauley Publishers Ltd.
25 Canada Square
Canary Wharf
London
E14 5LQ

Dedication

This book is dedicated to my husband, Keith, for his constant love, patience and support whilst I studied theology alone at home for nine years in Normandy, France. He struggled to understand my studies, which he often didn't and never understood my allegorical *'Book of Mirrors'*, that is, until he helped me with my dyslexia problem. Now he sees the dual role of my work for Jaycee – Jesus Christ.

I also thank my granddaughter Jubilee, with her love of reading from the cradle, who has been enthusiastic and encouraging from my very first notes, helping me with proof reading.

Acknowledgements

I am particularly grateful to Reverend Christopher Probert, B.Theol., M.Th., Dip P.S, here in Normandy, who has helped me with understanding the interpretations of Christian theology while I was studying for my Theological degree with Middlesex University, the London School of Theology.

I give my grateful thanks to Art-SoulWorks.com for giving me permission to use the painting of Jesus, the Prince of Peace, by Akiane Kramarik. She was only eight years old when she painted it!

I also wish to thank John and Jackeline Blunt for giving me permission to print a picture of their family home, Staunton Harold Hall, where I spent time nursing the incurably sick when it was part of Group Captain Cheshire's homes in the late 1950's. I was just sixteen years of age, and this experience helped me to see the souls of the patients by looking in their eyes – not by looking at their bodies.

PROLOGUE

THE ARRIVAL OF THEIR FIRST child thrilled Jane and Stuart. Born with a full head of sable hair and pale blue eyes, Jeremy always had a gentle smile and a peaceful gaze. Even as a baby, he always seemed to be wondering about something.

When he was five years of age, his father once asked him, "How many times do I have to tell you no?"

After a moment's silent thought, Jeremy replied, "About seven?"

He is now 15 years of age and thinking about going to university   after sixth form. He is quite tall, slim and musically gifted. Being naturally charming, he is gifted with excellent communication abilities. He is also a natural leader with strong ideas and very protective of his family. He tends not be realistic or practical, in his idealistic thinking – but he is determined to make a difference in the world.

Lydia was born eighteen months after Jeremy and was a dainty green-eyed girl. Similarly, she was also born with a full head of sable hair like their mother. With a boy and a girl, each blessed with a healthy set of organs, their parents felt content.

Jeremy's baby sister delighted him, and he looked after her with great care. When he was only three years old, her plaintive crying one afternoon concerned him so much that he carefully lifted her out of her crib and carried her out of their shared bedroom. He then hooked her head under his right arm so he could hold onto the stair railing to get down to the kitchen. Grandma nearly swallowed her teacup at the sight! Jane gasped in horror when she saw her baby hanging by her neck, but she stayed calm to avoid agitating the situation. She slowly took her now docile baby daughter, who didn't seem to mind being carried in that position.

"Baby crying, Mummy," said Jeremy, gently.

Unharmed, Lydia grew into a beautiful girl with an angelic smile; in social situations she tipped her head to one side to smile up at people. But she soon made it clear that she had a fiery temper when she pressed her lips together and gave a determined stare. Lydia had no difficulty in making her wishes known, in fact her very first word was "No!"

Lydia is now just over 14 years of age, a second mother to the babies. She is of medium height and has grown up with the ability to comprehend a situation immediately. Like her mother; she can summarise a position in six words – while others around her are still trying to work out what's going on; consequently, she is practical and sharp. However, she tends to be emotionally unsure.

Life rolled on happily for the young family until Stuart lost his job as a kitchen designer when the company made changes. Unfortunately, the cost of renting apartments rose and they lost several properties, one after the other. Jane made amends by taking in other people's ironing to earn a little money at home.

Jane and Stuart thought that Lydia and Jeremy would complete their family until Jane fell pregnant, and they discovered that another baby would soon join them. Some months earlier Jane and Stuart had been introduced to a Christian church where they discovered their faith and as their newfound faith continued to grow, Jane became convinced that everything would be alright. "How can you say that?" asked her mother.

"You already have two small children, and you are expecting your third child in a few days."

"Everything will be okay, Mum." Jane smiled with confidence.

That was all she would say. Grandma couldn't understand her daughter's certainty, but it seemed that Jane's new faith in God had given her an incredible peace.

Frustrated, Grandma tackled Stuart, during a discussion. "Stop being like an ostrich and get your head out of the sand. Put your priorities in the right order. You need more money; that'll solve your problems!"

How wrong she was! One week before the baby was due, a three-bedroom house became available for them to move into, arranged by the local government authority. Neighbours and friends at church came to help Jane and Stuart. Some decorated and cleaned the house while others worked hard in the garden. At last, the family with two children and one unborn child was complete and safe.

Sam was the name given to the new baby; he had fair hair like his father. His schedule involved a lot of time grinning and sleeping. He spoke his first word when he was one year of age. "Help!" he cried from his bedroom. Jane hurled herself up the stairs, wondering what on earth was happening and being amazed at his first word! She found Sam hanging upside down from the top of the wardrobe with his left foot stuck in the jammed door that had closed as he tried to climb back down.

Samuel is now 12 years of age; he has a strong physique and loves street dancing. He is pure in mind and sees the good in everyone, which makes him vulnerable. He is always optimistic, helpful, charming and 'boyish'. He has amazing ideas with good intentions, but his spiritual side is more important to him, which overrides his earthly reality. He is nearly taller than his mother and is always hungry.

The three children grew up as close friends while their parents continued their struggle to provide for them.

Seven years after Sam was born, one night in a difficult November, Jane called her mother with some exciting news. "Mum, I'm pregnant again."

"What? Good heavens, Jane, will you be able to cope?" her mother replied in shock.

"You know that I've been praying for another little girl, Mum. I had begun to think it would never happen! I'm thrilled to bits. The children and Stuart like the idea of having another baby in the house," she excused.

"That may be, but it will make things a lot harder for you both," her mother argued.

"I know, Mum, but this is what I've wanted for so long. And it may be my last chance; I'm nearly forty years old, you know. And Sam's a big boy now. He spends most of the day at school. Do you think God has heard my prayers?" She asked her mother, searching for parental approval.

Of course, Lydia was thrilled to have a sister— another girl in the family.

Jubilee was also born with lots of dark hair, but hers curled slightly and, as she grew, hung in soft waves, unlike Lydia's. She had amber eyes set in elegant and graceful features; they clearly looked like sisters.

Often, when they ran home from school, the three older children fought over whose turn it was to look after the baby. One-day Grandmother popped in to enjoy a cup of tea with her daughter.

"Where's the baby?" she asked with curiosity.

"Oh I'm not sure," replied Jane, laughing. "She's upstairs somewhere, with one of the children. I hardly get the chance to hold her these days," she said with her head in her hands.

Jubilee is now 6 and a half. She is a cute child who will be a beautiful woman, similar to her sister. She is calmer than Lydia, shy, thoughtful, and a deep thinker. She weighs up everything in her heart and would be the first one to see what the cause of someone's problem was. Although she is delightful in her manner, her fragile appearance hides a healthy and robust character. She has a good sense of humour and desires to please everyone; this means her innocence needs to be protected, probably by the more adventurous Lydia.

When Baby Jubilee was six months old, Grandma received yet another surprise phone call.

"Mum," said Jane in a small, quiet voice. "I'm pregnant... again!" She waited for a reply.

"For heaven's sake, Jane! I'm happy for you all, but five children will certainly keep you busy, my girl," she exclaimed at her daughter.

Joel, born seven months later, came with darker, straighter hair. He developed a quick wit to go with his laughing grey eyes. He had an ability to say what everyone else was thinking, but didn't dare say.

With his inquiring mind, he was the one who wanted to understand how their parents knew for sure that Jesus was God's son?

Joel is now 5 years of age. His sharp wit delights in questioning everything, even if it's embarrassing. He sees the obvious, doesn't understand sarcasm and translates everything literally. He's cute, often needs to be told to be quiet, probably because his mind goes straight from A to B without any deviation; this makes everyone laugh at his innocent comments – which he finds puzzling. He might build an empire.

Chapter 1

THE NIGHT OF THE STORM

In the beginning there was "Light and Life"
cf. Genesis 1:3-5

LYDIA FLICKED HER LONG HAIR over her shoulder as she sat on Jubilee's bed. At fourteen, she often took a motherly tone with her six-year-old sister.

"I know you don't like storms and lightning, especially at bedtime, so I'll stay with you until it goes, okay?" She comforted her younger sister.

Jubilee looked up from under the edge of her duvet and nodded silently.

Five-year-old Joel sat up. "Oh goody, we can play games," he giggled.

"No, we can't. You, young man, are supposed to be asleep," Lydia responded.

"That's the point—I can't sleep with all this noise going on," he explained, shrugging his shoulders and holding up his hands as if to prove his point.

The door opened, and Sam stuck his head around the door.

"Everything in here alright?" he asked.

Lydia grinned as she looked up at him. Though two years younger, he had grown taller than she. He was certainly not the fair-haired baby of the family now.

Joel leaped out of bed and grabbed his brother's hand. "You can sit on my bed!" he pleaded.

Sam tried to push his younger brother's dark hair back into place, but it stood up like a shoe brush over his sparkling grey eyes. Sam lightly laughed as he sank into the space Joel had made for him.

"I'm not here for all night, Joel, just until the storm is over," he warned him.

"Why don't the lights work? Has a power line been cut?" Joel quizzed him.

"That's two questions in one! And the answers are I don't know, and yes. There probably has been a power cut because of the strong wind. It's not just us; the whole street has no electricity," he explained.

"Is Jeremy going to come in here?" Jubilee asked in a quiet voice, uncovering her eyes and pulling down the duvet; she peeped over the top.

Jeremy stepped through the open door, grinning.

"Did someone mention my name? I thought I would find you all in here," he laughed, shutting the door behind him.

"Will Mum and Dad be able to get home alright?" Joel persisted.

"Oh, yes. They probably won't stay with Auntie Joan very long since she's sick and needs to rest, but they may wait until the heavy rain stops. The roads may be flooded," Lydia explained.

The first crack of lightning flashed through the bedroom window, filling the air with blue light but leaving the corners of the room in dark, frightening shadows.

"Oooooooh!" trembled Jubilee. "I don't like this." Lydia pulled her into her arms.

"It's alright. We are with you. Let's say our prayers," she instructed.

"Why do we have to say our prayers every night? They don't work," said Joel.

"What do you mean, little man? Who says they don't work?" asked Sam.

"Well, Jubilee prays not to be scared of storms, but she still is. I hate being told to go to bed early, but I still have to." He looked across at Lydia. "Lydia doesn't believe that Jesus is God's son because her boyfriend says he's just a wise man, like Grandad," he continued.

"That's because her boyfriend is studying modernism and other things like that," said Jeremy, ducking to miss Lydia's hand swatting at him.

"He's not my boyfriend but he does know a lot about prophets," she said raising her eyebrows.

"Mum says that Jesus isn't only a just prophet, he's God's son, so there!" added Joel.

"Does that mean, you think that God did send His son down here to live with us?" asked Jubilee, curling her lip.

Joel's face lit up.

"You mean he came as an alien from another planet?" He grinned.

A loud roar of thunder rattled the window.

"That was loud! Is it getting closer to us, do you think?" asked Jubilee.

"It sounded to me like it's on the edge of the village," said Lydia. "I know what we'll do. Let's push the two beds together. That'll be fun. Come on, Jeremy and Sam. You stay there, Jubilee. No need for you to move," she said, taking the lead, to make fun out of what could be a long evening.

"Can I stay in bed as well?" asked Joel, his eyes wide with excitement.

Sam playfully pushed him back onto the pillow. They moved the beds together, then lay on top with Sam in the middle, their arms wrapped around one another. The thunder and lightning crept nearer and nearer as the children huddled together. Jubilee squeezed her eyes shut and Joel shrieked with delight. The room filled with flashes of blue light, time and time again.

"Wow, that one was the biggest. Do you think it was right over our chimney?" Joel marvelled.

"That thunder sounded very close to me," said Sam, looking a little surprised. "I hope the TV aerial is okay," he wondered.

Each flash of light grew stronger and stronger as the corners of the small room danced with light instead of shadows. Suddenly, without any warning a brilliant flash of blue light filled their room, blotting out any darkness.

The children could see into every corner fully, there were no shadows. It was strange, so unusual they should have felt fear, but they did not. The peace that came with this strange light stayed for a few moments as they marvelled at its strange brilliance, their faces shining with joy as they grinned at each other. Instinctively they each knew that they had to hold hands in readiness for what was about to happen. They leapt out of bed and stood in a circle beside the beds. As they waited, each of them began to glow, giving off different colours like a rainbow spectrum.

"What's happening?" asked Lydia, who felt uncertain. Flashes of dark red sparked out of her sphere like a small burst of fire.

"I think we are beginning to see our magnetic energy field," suggested Jeremy.

"Wow," said Joel. "I don't know what that is, but I feel great!" he said, looking like a sparkler about to burst.

"Me too!" said Sam. "Jeremy, your colours are not the same as mine, and you Jubilee, well most of your colours are quite pale; beautiful," he noticed.

Slowly, together, they began to float up towards the ceiling. They were so surprised no one spoke. Lydia thought she was going to fall in a panic; she gripped the hands of Joel and Jubilee tightly. But before anyone could take in what was happening to them, they slowly passed through the roof and into the open sky. There was no wind. No rain.

No storm. The stars passed by as they began to fall asleep to the words,

"You must find the *'Book of Mirrors'*," being whispered around them.

CHAPTER 2

THE HALL OF WRITINGS

THEY AWOKE IN A STRANGE, dark hall. It looked like an ancient library of a forgotten temple covered in the dust of time. Joel rubbed his eyes, and they all gasped at the huge collection of writings. They saw dead spiders hanging from broken cobwebs, which slowly wafted to, and fro as the children moved, as if only they, breathed fresh life into this place of the dead past. The huge domed ceiling above them disappeared into the gloom. Everything smelled musty, like a dirty, damp cloth in a bucket, forgotten in a closet.

"Where are on earth are we? I'm not an alien, am I?" Joel asked Jeremy, convinced that his older brother knew everything.

"I don't think so." Lydia slowly answered him.

She watched in horror as the skeleton of a dead bird started to move between the shelves and then it stopped, as if it had been caught doing something it shouldn't. Was it coming back to life again? She blinked hard trying to fix her gaze on the stiff, now still, bones. The light came in from small slits along the edge of the floor. Shelves lined the high cedar walls and sad, ancient books filled them. Were the books fading in and out of sight?

"We were told to find the *Book of Mirrors*, weren't we? Maybe if we do that, we'll find out what's going on," Jeremy said quietly and suspiciously.

"The last thing I remember was floating up near the stars, and I don't remember anything else," Sam replied.

Jubilee's face crumpled slowly, and she began to cry, so Sam picked her up to comfort her. Joel, who found the whole thing intriguing, quoted the family's standard joke for unusual happenings,

"This is amazing, Grandma!"

The joke had started when Lydia was about four years old. She and her grandmother had gone on a ride with large teacups to sit in. The ride went round and round, and then the teacups themselves also went round and round. As the ride came to an end, Lydia turned to her grandmother with wide eyes filled with awe and said,

"That was amazing, Grandma."

Joel liked to remind them of this story, and it usually comforted them when life got strange, but they had never experienced anything like this before.

"Oh, be quiet, Joel," said Lydia.

She frowned down at the large stone slabs on the floor of the library. Now that their eyes had adjusted, they could all see that the stones floated around. The writing on them made them look like very old grave stones, recording the past, gathering moss and dust and growing clusters of fungi. The stones were cold, uneven but slightly shiny, like large slabs of black treacle toffee. Mum loved toffee. Home? The yearning in their hearts strengthened as they remembered home and their parents.

"I want to go home," Jubilee whispered, trying not to cry as she rubbed away a tear.

"We all do," said the rest of them, except Joel.

"Are we aliens or aren't we? That's all I want to know," insisted Joel.

He began to jump from one moving stone to another, which was only possible because each slab froze when his foot touched it.

"Stop it, Joel! You'll hurt yourself," said Lydia, "and that's the last thing we need right now."

They all stood in silence, looking around, squinting at the titles on the books. Jeremy casually walked down the hall into the darkness, paying close attention to the inscriptions on the spines of the large, heavy, leather-bound books that had faded. There were also parchments rolled up together with crumbling twine.

Suddenly Jeremy stopped. "It says here, The Valley of the Shadow of Death,[1] " he said.

"What does that mean?" asked Sam, wrinkling his nose.

"That describes our walk on earth before our spirits ascend to heaven," he replied.

"Humph. I don't like the sound of that," replied Sam, running a clammy hand through his matted brown hair.

A sound of shuffling made them turn to look up at the thickly carved shelves.

"Jeremy, come back over here!" Lydia called, her voice bouncing around the hall.

They slowly became aware that the books were watching them.

"We'll never find the '*Book of Mirrors*' in here; there are so many books it would take us years and years," said Jeremy under his breath, scheming a way out.

"How many of the books here have mirrors?" asked Lydia, still watching the books suspiciously. "Surely there can only be one?" She hoped.

"I suppose so," said Jeremy, "the Bible alone has sixty-six books in the Old and the New Testaments. There are also many thousands of books, letters and records written about

---

1   **Symbolic meaning: –** [walking through our life on earth with its problems, loves and losses – yet our needs will be met, we have no need to fear evil – We will live with God and enjoy His peace.] *NBC. D.A.. Carson. p.500 'The providence of God, appointing life's experiences, His protection over life's pathway, [with] His provision now and always.'*

the Bible, so we could be here a long time!" Jeremy sighed, anticipating the work involved.

"Oh, this is going to be awful." Lydia groaned.

"No it isn't," said Sam. "All we have to do is believe that we can find the Book, wherever the Book is..." Sam's voice trailed off as his eyes scanned the high walls of books in dismay.

"How do you know we can find it, just like that?" asked Joel.

"I just do," replied Sam.

Books of Major & Minor Prophets²

Joel, distracted, ran up and down the hall, jumping from stone to stone as he slapped out at the books he could reach as he went past. Puffs of dust rose up from the books, creating thick clouds of dust. Joel went into a frenzy of coughing. One book fell off the shelf, landing open upside down on a

---

2   This is where over two thousand years of early Biblical period scripture rests. This includes the Mesopotamian chronology – and the 12th – 18th Egyptian dynasties – [writings relating to the Son of God and His coming to earth to save us].

stone slab. They all heard a distinct tinkling sound. All the stones suddenly stopped moving.

The children looked around, desperately searching for an explanation. Lydia snapped at her young brother,

"Stop it, Joel, and come here. Now look what you've done," she said.

She bent down to pick up the small book and turned it over.

"It's not a book, it's a looking glass," she said quietly, "And… it's broken in two," she explained, holding it up so that they could all see.

All the books shuffled on the shelves as if in response. More small puffs of dust fell into the gloom and floated down slowly as if wanting to wait for the next thing to happen. The newer books seemed to be trying to look past each other to see what the old books were going to do. From the far end of the shelf marked 'Major and Minor Prophets', a small voice was heard.

"I told you this was all going to happen," one book said dryly.

"I can tell what things will come to pass as well," said a smaller book from the section on Minor Prophets. "Me, too," said another minor prophet.

"And I," said several others in the section.

"I want to go home," Jubilee said softly as another tear slowly trickled down her grubby cheek.

"Oh come on, this is going to be fun!" Jeremy reassured here.

He was looking over Lydia's shoulder at the badly cracked looking glass. The glass showed Lydia, a distraught but brave teenage girl. She smiled at Jeremy sympathetically and placed her hand on his. She turned to look back at the looking glass and stopped, shocked.

"Look! There's an image coming, but it's only in one-half of the looking glass. I can see a dense forest of trees all touching one another. There is one large tree, much taller than all the others, with small white flowers all around in the grass beneath it." Lydia described, holding the looking glass at a distance, in case it did anything dangerous. Sam, looking into the glass, realized that the trees were cedar trees, like the panels in the room they stood in.

"It's a cedar tree—a cedar of Lebanon," Sam concluded.

"That means like a good strong person, doesn't it?" said Jubilee, suddenly becoming interested.

"What does that mean?" asked Joel, ignoring his sister.

"It is symbolic of goodness and truth," said Lydia quietly.

"That must be a sign," said Jeremy, sounding much more confident. "Come on, let's get out of here," he said.

He led the way, and the rest of them traipsed after him; Jubilee bouncing along and Joel dragging his feet.

"Wait—what about all the other mirror books? We need them to explain what's going on," Jeremy paused, exasperated.

"There's hundreds and hundreds of books here. It would take the rest of our lives finding the right one," Jubilee complained.

They stood for a moment, looking at each other, searching for an answer. They hadn't moved much more than ten yards from their original spot.

"Why don't we ask the books?" said Joel, shrugging his shoulders as if this was obvious.

Immediately the books all jumped up and down, nodding excitedly.

"Me, first!" said one.

"No, no, ME, first," said another.

"It's not your turn," said another.

The louder they spoke, the more the dust fell off them and the shelves. The cacophony of their excited arguing filled the 'Hall of Writings'. Joel stumbled and fell over backwards in surprise, but a stone slipped quietly into place to catch him.

"Wow, that was neat," Joel said, smiling and Jubilee couldn't help grinning, too.

Suddenly it all seemed so funny; as Sam's mouth fell open, Lydia took control of the arguing books. She snapped at them with authority, saying, "Stop that nonsense this minute. We need your help and wisdom. Now, where is the 'Book of Mirrors'?" she asked.

A sudden silence fell. The cracked looking-glass in Lydia's hand began to shake.

"The mirror that you hold only answers your questions," said one of the books in Minor Prophets.

"Pity it's broken", the same book continued.

All the books began to sigh asking, "Will it work now, will it? Will it?" the books asked.

The other books gently shook their covers making small puffs of dust. One of the Major Prophets seemed to look kindly at Jubilee, saying,

"*The Book of Mirrors* tells the story of humanity through the ages. You have to be very, very special to hold that one," the book said quietly.

The books then all began to sing, "Holy, Holy, Holy…"

They sang the phrase over and over again. Jubilee and Joel began to smile; it was all beginning to be such fun. Grinning, they joined hands and began to swing their arms as they danced to the delight of the books who never seen anything like this before. Shrieks of laughter echoed around the great hall as Joel's thumping footsteps and Jubilees light skipping steps shook the shiny floor slabs of stone, which seemed to anticipate their movements as they spun around. The happy floating dust became bright white specks of light; that floated around like tiny fireflies dancing at sunset on a midsummer's evening. As they watched, the tiny lights joined to form an arrow that slowly moved across a row of books. When it stopped, the books snapped to attention. A hush fell. The older children stopped the little ones' dancing. They all looked towards the shelf where the arrow of light was pointing at one book at the end of the row. It was the size of a small box of chocolates. In the semi-darkness, the beams of light from the slits high in the great domed ceiling above them suddenly became much brighter.

"Wow," said Joel, now sitting on the floor.

Jubilee, no longer afraid, smiled.

"I'll get the book," said Jeremy, reaching up.

"You won't need to do that," said Sam with quiet confidence.

At his words, the book appeared, in a purple cover with distinct red letters, spelling, 'The Book of Mirrors.' It floated down and landed in the hands of Jubilee. She was the one chosen to be 'The keeper' of the God king's book. She took it, smiled again and looked up at her brother Sam with starry eyes. Instinctively, she clutched it to her chest. The book disappeared from her grasp, and Jubilee was seen to be hugging thin air.

"Now what? I thought we needed that!" exclaimed Joel.

Sam laughed at his small brother as he helped him onto his feet.

"Don't be silly!" said Sam. He patted Joel's head, explaining. "Don't you understand? Jubilee is the one who thinks about things first, not like you and me, we rush into trouble all the time, don't we?" he asked calmly.

"Hmm," Joel sputtered, "You're right, and she loves me, don't you Juby."

Jubilee laughed, grinned and nodded saying,

"I promise to keep it safe in my heart, with you," she whispered.

Joel gulped.

"That's so cool, but how do we get it back?" he inquired, furrowing his eyebrows.

"We don't need to. I'm sure it will appear when we need it," Lydia chimed in, still holding the looking glass with the broken mirror.

"Find the Seven Signs. They will help you find the answer and get you home," the children heard it say.

Lydia closed her looking glass, which resembled a small ladies face compact that they carried in their purse. She made a special note of the words, 'Help you find the answer and get you home'. She placed the precious looking glass in the zip pocket of her tee shirt. It didn't disappear. She kept her hand on her pocket, then, dropping her head slightly and squeezing her eyes tight shut, she wished, 'please help us to find the Seven Signs so we can get home'. She took a deep breath before opening her eyes. Then they continued ambling down the corridor until they found a pair of humongous wooden doors with iron plates on the front. Jeremy and Sam placed their strong hands on each door, pushing with all of their might. A few moments of struggle passed, and Joel even joined in, finally, the doors gave way and opened up a brightly sunlit scene. They saw that the Hall was floating in mid-air! But it was slowly going down towards the thick grass in a small valley.

"Come on," said Sam, "we can jump."

"Oh no you don't," said Lydia. "We're not jumping anywhere," she continued as she clutched the little ones to her side.

"I can jump Lyd," said Joel. "I can, I can." He reasoned.

The hall slowly drifted a little lower. Jeremy took control.

"When I say three, we all jump," he said, raising his eyebrows at Lydia.

He took Joel's arm; Jubilee went to Sam. Sam grabbed Lydia's hand to make sure she jumped.

"One... two...three NOW!" Jeremy shouted at the top of his voice.

They tumbled onto the soft grass at the foot of a tall Cedar tree. They looked around and saw that the hall had gone. Tiny white flowers in the grass smiled up at them as if to say, 'hello'.

"Look, these flowers are like the daisies on our front lawn back home," said Jeremy smiling at the memory.

They all turned their faces towards them. Lydia was the first to look up at the great cedar tree they now stood beneath.

"We must always look for these trees. They will keep us safe," said Jeremy, not certain how he knew that, but certain that it was true.

"We have to find the 'Seven Signs' as the broken mirror told us," said Lydia, reminding them all.

They turned to look into the forest, filled with trees that reflected images as if they were mirrors. Their flashing pictures were reflected back from other trees that produced a dazzling and confusing scene. It all reminded Lydia of people showing others only their best side instead of who they were. There were many different colours of green, brown, and golden leaves making the whole scene resemble a crinkled silk scarf at a fair. Jeremy frowned. How on earth was he was going to be able to lead them through that maze? Then he saw the thin line of tiny white flowers. He knew he and the others would have to stay strictly on that path of flowers if they were ever going to find their way home.

"I'm hungry," said Joel rubbing his tummy.

"Me, too," said Jubilee rubbing her face with tiredness.

"Hang on!" said Sam, "I see a fig tree full of ripe figs, I'll get you some. Jeremy, can you help me?" he asked.

Jeremy nodded, joining Sam at the fig tree.

"I think we're going to need to get food whenever we can," Lydia suggested.

"I'll leave that to you, alright?" Sam nodded back.

Lydia stayed with the little ones beneath the cedar tree. They felt safe there, and she decided that they should spend their first night in this strange, confusing land right there. They cuddled up together ready to go sleep beneath the stars. Jubilee became aware of a perfume coming from the tiny flowers. Instinctively she breathed in deeply, smelling the fresh soft aroma that made her feel relaxed and sleepy.

"Can you hear that tinkling sound, Jubilee?" asked Lydia.

Jubilee nodded and smiled. They lay together listening. She thought of asking the boys if they could hear it, but she decided they wouldn't be interested. It was then they discovered that the tunes were coming from the flowers around them. Amazing. Jubilee wondered why they hadn't noticed that before, in the garden at home.

Sleepily Lydia asked her, "Do you think the 'Book of Mirrors' will come to you if you ask for it?"

Before Jubilee could answer her, the Book appeared on its own? It stood on the ground surrounded by the tiny white flowers, who seemed to be smiling up at them. Then the book grew bigger and bigger?

"What's happening?" asked Jeremy, sitting up with a start.

The book became so big that it stood high before them, proud and inviting. A page appeared showing a picture of a table laid with food of all kinds. There was fresh bread, fruit and meats as if they were being invited to step into a new world to discover all they needed know to complete their journey. For a few moments, they just stared at the bewildering sight in front of them.

"What's going on?" asked Joel now fully awake. No one spoke. "Are we supposed to go there?" he asked again rubbing his eyes with his small fists.

Still no one spoke.

Then Jeremy stood up. "I think we are being invited to go there. It is as if the book is asking us to decide what we want to do?"

"We all want to find our way home," answered Sam, "so… we need to be brave and have confidence that this is the way to go."

Quietly they all stood up. Instinctively they all held hands giving each other moral support. Sam sounded confident but inside he was worried. Lydia wasn't sure. Jubilee smiled, and Joel thought this was a great idea.

"Well, are we going to or not?" Joel asked impatiently raising his free hand in a question.

Jeremy turned to look at the others. They all nodded. Slowly they walked towards the open book and the feast that lay before them. As they stepped into the page, they immediately felt loved as if they were all very precious. Joel ran straight to the table, slowly followed by Sam, who was still hungry. Lydia had to admit this place certainly felt wonderful. Jeremy smiled, he knew he had made the right decision. Glancing down at Jubilee he saw that she agreed with him. They were starting the journey of discovery, through *'The Book of Mirrors.'*

CHAPTER 3

THE WEDDING IN CANA AND THE CLAY JARS

The First Sign: Faith – Water into Wine, according to John 2:1-12

THE NEXT MORNING, THEY WERE back beneath the cedar tree. They awoke to bright sunshine surrounded by what seemed like hundreds of smiling white daisies. Lydia smiled back, wondering if they knew something she didn't. She waited for the rest of them to rise from their slumber, then asked Jubilee if the *'Book of Mirrors'* would come to her to show them what was going to happen next. Sleepily, Jubilee held out her hands and asked for the book to come to her. The pages flicked over then stopped at a wedding scene.

People were laughing and greeting one another. In the middle of the courtyard stood a confident man. He was a little taller than the other twelve men around him; he also looked physically stronger, as if he'd done hard work. Maybe he was a builder or a carpenter.

Lydia smiled at the picture. Jubilee somehow knew that the man was different. His smile was so sincere and his stance so confident as he listened carefully to the men as they spoke to him. He had the aura of someone caring, someone everyone would want to have as a friend. She decided that she liked him.

"Is that where we have to go?" asked Sam.

"It's a wedding party," said Lydia.

"Look at all that food," said Sam beginning to get hunger pangs again.

They followed the daisy path into the dark forest. Jeremy suddenly stopped.

"I see people; they look like trees walking around," [3] he said, confused.

Each of the trees appeared to contain many mirrors flashing their images from branch to branch, with each of the mirrors trying to reflect out the others. The erratic rays from the sun made it difficult to see where the pathway was. Keeping their eyes on the white daisies they tried hard to remain focused on moving through the forest, to reach the 'House of Wine'. Sticking cautiously to the path, they walked through the trees, although they found this difficult. They kept their eyes alert; at last they caught a glance of the village, through the thick bullying branches and squabbling leaves. Then they saw people arriving for the wedding celebration. Finally, they came out of the shadows into a bright sunny day; feeling the sun's rays on their faces as they approached the wedding party. The sun was beating down on a crowd of joyous people. None of the adults seemed to notice them emerging out of the forest, but the local children all stopped to stare as they joined the wedding group.

The house ahead was larger than their house at home and looked very different. It stood in a dusty clearing between the tall palm and smaller banana trees, which hung heavy with ripe, colourful yellow fruit.

Jeremy nodded to Sam as if to say "we'll remember to pick some of those on the way out."

The outer walls, made of dusty, dull red clay bricks, were uneven and badly built as a child's unfinished and forgotten building game. Two large wooden gates protected

---

3   **Mark 8:24.** NIV Study Bible note p.1479 'A blind man seeing tree trunks moving about' **Meaning:** – [does not see the truth].

the entrance to the inner courtyard and main living area. As they joined the people walking through, the children noticed that many rooms faced the inner courtyard, so the surrounding outer wall provided protection for the whole family within.

Inside the enclosed area, the bricks were smooth and painted white. More banana trees with huge leaves gave shade to the low clay seats built up from the floor. Solid brick steps led to the roofs, where sun shades had been built of palm leaves. Over one corner of the roof hung brilliant red, purple, orange and white bougainvillea that were hanging over the roofs mixing with sweet smelling jasmine, making an area of colourful harmony.

A row of six deep red clay jars stood in the shade beneath the many coloured flowers as people passed by these ceremonial jars to wash their hands before eating in an act of prayer and preparation. The long table in the centre of the courtyard held dishes of spiced rice with red tomatoes, cucumber, and green olives, as well as several bowls of meats and oils; constantly being refilled by the servants, as the guests helped themselves. The wine too flowed from jars to glasses and cups which some people mixed with water. People were dashing everywhere in and out of the crowds but never bumping into each other, like a spontaneous dance, they all seemed to move gracefully. Sam nudged Jeremy and pointed towards empty seats at the far end, in the shade near the clay jars. Jeremy nodded. They all followed him, carefully sitting down. No one looked at them.

"Are they speaking English?" asked Lydia, trying hard to listen to the conversations around them.

"I'm not sure," replied Jeremy.

Joel seemed distracted; he didn't hear Lydia's instructions to be quiet due to the loud hubbub of conversation. Sam seemed distracted, too. The boys' eyes focused on the food, their mouths watering in anticipation of their first real meal since their journey began.

"Are we allowed to help ourselves?" asked Joel.

"I don't know, but it's funny that only the children are taking any notice of us," observed Lydia.

Joel picked up a banana. No one reacted, apart from the two very small children who had stopped eating to stare at them. Jeremy, Lydia, Sam and the little ones ate happily for some time as they watched the people greeting one another. Lydia gradually realized there was a problem. A small, slim, older woman seemed to be pleading with the tall man; holding her hands out to him in an expression of concern.

Then things began to change.

CLAY WATER JARS
Who have their water turned into wine!

Jubilee had been looking intensely wondering why the big jars stood empty. She started giggling and pointed towards them pulling at Joel's sleeve. Faces began to be visible on the smooth rounded sides of the jars, and they winked at her, looking very excited. Jubilee nudged Joel with her elbow.

"That one's looking at you," she said, her eyes gleaming.

Joel's jaw dropped open, and he then burst out laughing, and then he slapped his hand over his mouth. Lydia looked at him sternly but then he jumped up and down on his seat and continued pointing until Jeremy and Sam turned, to see what was causing such a ruckus.

"Don't point, Joel!" said Jeremy. "It's rude to point at people;" he reminded him.

"They aren't people; they're jars," Joel explained.

He looked at Jubilee. She shrugged her shoulders; then she nodded towards the jars. Jeremy assumed that they were playing some game, so he turned his attention back to talking with Sam and Lydia.

The little ones grinned, then quietly slipped away from the table leaving the others to continue their conversation. As they approached the first jar spoke to them. "Who are you calling a jar?" retorted the nearest jar to Joel. It had a smooth surface with firm handles and a perfectly moulded opening. "I'm just like you!" it exclaimed.

"No, you're not!" Joel argued with hands on his little hips.

"Oh yes, I am. You're full of water, aren't you? Well, I'm special like you, and I'm about to be filled with water for a very special reason," the jar hinted, wobbling a little on the slightly uneven earth hardened floor.

"What's so special about that?" Joel went on confidently, "I'm nearly all water already; my father told me."

"We know that, but we are going to be filled with—," said the second jar.

"Don't!" exclaimed the first jar sharply. "We're not allowed to tell them yet!" the third jar argued.

The second jar blushed and clamped his mouth shut, pressing his lips into a thin line.

"Not allowed to tell us what?" asked Jubilee with resounding curiosity.

The third jar smiled comfortingly, leaned forward, and whispered, "We can't tell you because we are symbols of you!"

Jubilee nodded as if she knew what they were talking about, her hazel eyes wide and eyebrows high, but she didn't have any idea.

Joel retorted, "What do you mean that you are symbols of us?"

"Tsk, tsk. They don't know much do they?" one jar said to the others, making all the jars mumble with concern and disbelief.

The first jar puffed himself up, his handles pulling him up to his full height of nearly six feet. They were much taller that the children who gazed up at them. The jar explained, looking pleased with himself. "We represent the King's children—you! The God King is going to change the world, through you! You are His jars that will hold His most precious treasure inside you,"[4] he explained.

"We are his jars that hold his most precious treasure, inside us?" repeated Jubilee in bewilderment.

Lydia and Sam had overheard this.

"We are?" asked Lydia turning to look at the little ones, who seemed to be talking the jars? Do I hear things?"

Then they heard, "Why us? I'm not special," said Jubilee.

"Well, you might not be, but I am!" confirmed Joel.

"Don't you know anything?" asked the second jar.

"Err, no, not really," Jubilee said, apologetically.

"Tsk, tsk," said the third jar, "well, all will be revealed in good time."

"They must know because they were made in His image!" Enquired the third jar, nodding up toward the heavens.

"Do you mean God the King?" asked Joel, beginning to understand.

"Of course!" said all the other jars, now listening to every word with excitement.

---

4   2 Corinthians 4:7 *'We have this treasure in jars of clay'*

Jeremy, Sam and Lydia sat in stunned silence as the little ones continued their conversation. They seemed quite safe and happy, they must be pretending – perhaps a game.

"Are they alright?" asked Sam.

"I think so, but they seem to be talking to someone."

The second jar was saying, "His son, Jaycee, used to make beautiful things with wood when he was a boy." He gestured to the work of a carpenter.

"They don't need to know that!" said the first jar, shoving the second jar until he blushed and stopped talking.

"You are made in His image," said the third jar, nodding to the children and smiling broadly.

"We all recognized your family and who you were when you came into the courtyard, didn't we?"

All the jars nodded enthusiastically agreeing, yes, everyone has been waiting for this they bickered amongst themselves.

"What?" Jubilee asked again.

"You! You're going to have your insides rearranged! That's what!" the first jar said, slapping his side with his handle and trying to stamp his base at the same time, which made him wobble and nearly fall over.

The two young children stared at the jar. They didn't know what to say. At that very moment, Jubilee noticed something in the sky. Pointing upwards, she said, "Look".

The angels are descending! [5] On something that looks like a ladder?"

"What's descending mean?" asked Joel.

"It's The God King's angels who go up and come down on it,[6]" said the excited jars altogether. Joel looked up, dropped

---

5   **John 1:50-51**, see also *'Jacob's Dream* – **Gen: 28:12** and notes. [Thus marking Jesus as God's elect – the chosen one – who will bring us salvation].

6   **Genesis cf.28: 12-14** – *'a stairway resting on the earth... its top reaching heaven, and the angels of God were (going up and down on it, as they do for us).*

his mouth open, and said enthusiastically, "That is amazing, Grandma!"

"Why are the angels going to that tall man in the middle of the servants?" asked Jubilee.

"That's the chosen one," said the first jar with a slight bow, honoured to know such a thing.

"He's the one called Jaycee," the jars explained.

Jubilee stood quietly, taking all of this in. Joel slowly moved closer to his sister, taking her hand in his as they looked across the crowded courtyard at the tall man who was laughing. They had listened to what everyone said.

Now Joel's eyes widened. "Are you telling us that He is the God King's Son?"

"Exactly!" said all the jars. "He's royalty!"

"That's right. Today will appear the sign which shows His hour,[7](meaning the right time,) has come to begin his work on earth. He will do wonderful things," the first jar explained.

They stood silently, trying to understand how long this hour was going to be and what amazing thing might begin that would make the jars so excited.

"Uh-oh," said Jeremy, "the servants are coming this way. They must be coming to collect those jars where the little ones are.

"I'll get them," said Sam as he sprang into action. "Come on, you two, looks like you need to move out of the way." He turned them around to return to the table. "Come over there with us so that we can keep our eyes on you".

"What are they going to do?" Joel asked Jubilee, dragging his heels as Sam pulled him a few feet away from the jars.

Sam thought Joel was talking to him, so he replied, "We think they're coming for the jars." Joel did a double take at the jars, which now glowed with excitement.

---

7   **John 12:23** – *'The hour has come for the Son of man.'*

One by one, the servants carried away the empty jars, who looked very proud, grinning and winking at the children on their way out. The servants filled them to the brim with clean, ordinary water.

Jubilee whispered, "I wonder what he meant when he said our insides will be changed?"

Joel hunched his shoulders up in bewilderment, shaking his head. The worried small lady who had been speaking to Jaycee earlier watched everything that was happening. Then they saw a distinguished looking man with a small cup come over to the filled grinning jars. The end jar whispered to them,

"He's the master of the ceremonies. He's coming to taste the water from the first jar.

"Brilliant!" said the master of ceremonies as he tasted the wine. "Thank goodness for that! Now we will have enough wine to last until the final guest has gone; and may I say," he said as he tilted his head to one side, "a magnificent wine, too."

Jaycee smiled at the banquet master.

"What's going on? That's water, not wine," said Jeremy.

"Not now," said Jubilee with a very broad smile.

The older children looked down at her, and then at Joel, their faces questioning.

"We'll tell you later," the little ones said.

"Now," said Lydia putting her hands on her hips.

"Huh-hoe!" said Joel taking a deep breath. "Well, it was the jars, they told us that the tall man over there is the God King's Son, and he is going to start doing wonderful things on earth. We don't know what."

"Or why," said Jubilee joining Joel. "It looks as though he has just turned the water into wine. I saw his mother asking him to do something because she noticed they were running out of wine for the wedding guests." She shrugged her shoulders high, holding out her arms with her hands open, as if to say, 'I don't understand how he's done it either.'

Joel cocked his head to one side and looked at the tall man curiously. "Why is He bright and shiny?"[8] He said.

"Who is bright and shiny?" asked Lydia, not understanding.

"The tall man talking to the other man about the wine—the one dressed in white, the one who is going to be here for only an hour," Joel said, raising his arms for emphasis.

"He isn't all in white!" argued Lydia.

"Yes, he is," insisted Joel, turning to Jubilee. "Isn't he?"

Jubilee nodded, frowning and wondering why Lydia couldn't see it.

"I'm thirsty!" Joel whined, rubbing his tummy.

"We all are," said Lydia, now smiling. She knew that thirst wasn't necessary anymore as she gazed at the man in the middle of the group of men. He looked confident, calm, and peaceful. There was a certain something about him.

What was it that the young ones could see that she and Jeremy and Sam couldn't?

The first jar, who was now full of best quality wine, coughed, cleared his brim, and got ready to speak; he would have to tell the children.

The other jars whispered, "He's going to tell them." "He's not! Is he allowed?" asked another jar.

"I don't think that will stop him," another concluded. ——

Then all five jars turned to see what was going to happen. Joel squeezed his eyes tight shut and prayed, 'please, let my older brothers and sister see and hear the jars.' As they all stood staring at the full jar of wine, the jars started to change right in front of them.

"Wow, that was quick," said Joel. The jars became visible to the older children.

---

8   **John 1:14**; – 'The Word became flesh [Jesus] and [lived] among us'.

17:5, 'And now Father glorify me in your presence with the glory I had with you before the world began'. Jesus was (called 'The Word' in Genesis) who was with his Father in heaven before He came to earth.]

Making sure his unique wine wouldn't spill out, the first jar said. "The water that filled us, 'the ceremonial jars', meant that we were ready to be used for the God King. His Son has started his work for his father today by turning that water into wine. He is the only one in all of this land who can do this work."

The jar's eyes welled up with tears of joy. Joel opened his mouth to ask another question, but the jar frowned at him. He closed his mouth.

The jar continued, "This wine has incredible powers. It makes people see things more clearly, instead of 'looking through a glass darkly.' [9] It brings them peace inside, and they begin to live in a new way. They feel loved by the King, but if they are too busy to look properly or don't believe in its power, it won't work."

"Don't forget to say that this was foretold in the writing of the *'Book of Mirrors'*,"[10] the second jar chimed.————————

The older children stood in silence; mouths held tight in complete surprise as they looked at the jars. Lydia was suddenly terrified that they would be in trouble if the jars knew that they had the *'Book of Mirrors'*. The jars stared at them expectantly.

"Golly, that's amaz—," started Joel.

Lydia clamped her hand over Joel's mouth, making him gulp for air. She quickly changed the subject. "So, is the water in your jar like the fountain of life?" she said perceptively.

---

9   **1 Corinthians 13:12** (King James Version) – *'Know we see but a poor reflection as in a mirror... but will see [him] face to face.'*

10   **Isaiah 25.6-8** – The future feast of God. *'Rich food for all peoples... best of meats and the finest wine... The Lord will wipe away the tears from all faces.'* [The wedding at Cana and its celebration, is symbolic of what is to come for His children]. **John 15:1-6**; – *'I am the vine ... you are the branches'.*

"It's called the living water,"[11] said the jar with a proud nod.

"I'm still thirsty," said Joel, pulling Lydia's hand from his mouth.

Jeremy looked around and saw a water-skin hanging on the wall near the well. Taking it, he quickly filled the skin with water from a jar that had not yet been changed. Still confused by what the first jar had told them, Jeremy checked to see if Sam was still holding Jubilee's hand. Of course he was. He also had the bananas he had picked. So Jeremy lifted Joel, who was yawning and suddenly exhausted, onto his shoulder and led the way out of the village. The stars began to shine in the early evening sky. They continued to walk for what seemed like ages, back up the daisy path because Lydia thought they would all be much safer spending the night back under the cedar tree.

As they walked, Jubilee snuggled up to Lydia, saying, "The angels were beautiful weren't they?"

"Hmm. They reminded me of Mum," she replied. "She's gorgeous as well."

"Yes, me, too, Lydia, I miss her terribly," Jubilee said, her large green eyes searching for comfort from her older sister.

"Yes, but we'll be home soon, and she'll be so pleased to see us again!" Lydia changed the subject. "I wonder when the '*Book of Mirrors*' will come back to us."

"I don't know. I just get this warm feeling in my heart when it arrives. Anyway, the grumpy head waiter seemed a nicer person after he tasted the wine, didn't he?" said Jubilee.

"Hmm." Lydia smiled. "Maybe the wine was working on him already?" Jubilee smiled.

---

11   **John** 7:38-39 – *'Whoever believes in me, as the Scriptures said, streams of living water will flow from within him.'* [That is, the Love and knowledge of God].

"I do love you, Jubilee," Lydia laughed. "Do you think you could try to get the *'Book of Mirrors'* to come back later?" asked Lydia, holding Jubilee's hand tight in hers.

"I think so," Jubilee replied.

"I'm just wondering if it will tell us what's going to happen next," said Lydia, raising her right eyebrow brow in wonder.

"I like the idea of being a clay jar, don't you?" asked Jubilee, skipping as they picked up the pace again.

Lydia was quiet as she remembered the last thing the broken mirror had told her about the Seven Signs.

"Jeremy?" she called, looking back at the three boys, all walking in a cluster. "Do you think that the First Sign of turning water into wine could mean that 'with faith' we can begin to understand His world?"

"Yes and just as important, that Joel and Jubilee could see how glorious he was," Jeremy confirmed.

The forest of mirrors seemed a lot quieter as the sun began to set over the distant blue hills. On entering the trees, they were thrilled to see that the white flowers were now luminous, clearly lighting the way in the near darkness under the full moon. Holding hands, they walked in single file through the darkened mirrors. With not much light to reflect their way, the children soon come through and finally found the cedar tree waiting for them on the small hill in the valley. They gratefully collapsed onto the soft grass covered in white flowers.

"Before we all fall asleep; I think we should ask Jubilee to see if the *'Book of Mirrors'* will come back so that we can make sure we go where it wants us to.

Jubilee closed her eyes, squeezing them tightly together, and asked for the book to come to them. With a quick flash of blue light, it was in her hands, open just where they needed to look.[12] This time the blue light from the book

---

12 **John 3:16.** *'For God loved the world so much that He gave His one and only Son, that whoever believes in Him shall not perish but have eternal life.'* **Daniel 12:1-3.** *'Everyone whose name is written in the book [of life] will*

stayed with them, lighting their faces as they gathered around to read it, except Joel, who was fast asleep.

They read about the prophets of many years ago, who told how the God King's Son would come hundreds of years into the future and what he would do for them if they believed. They looked at one another.

"Golly," said Jubilee, "that's amazing—"

"—Grandma," they all said together, laughing as the full moon disappeared behind a soft grey cloud.

The book went. Smiling at one another they settled down for the night amid the tiny closed white flowers, who had already folded their petals and gone to sleep.

"It's time for us to get some sleep, sweetheart," said Lydia looking into Jubilee's tired eyes.

Turning to Jeremy, Jubilee asked, "Do you still have the water-skin? I think we all need a drink before we settle down for the night," she suggested.

They passed around the water for the four of them to have a drink.

"Sweet dreams, everyone," Lydia said as they lay down.

The book disappeared from Jubilee's lap. Finally, contented Jubilee stopped to think over the plans for the next day, and then she curled up alongside her big sister, quickly falling asleep.

"I will keep the first watch! Sam, you take the second," directed Jeremy.

Sam, nodded, nestling down next to his inert younger brother. Lydia looked back at the daisy chain path, like a silver ribbon of life, which wound itself down the hill into the stream at the end of the valley. The mirror trees, now looked like a thick blanket, each stitch tired of struggling to get the best position. Sam and Joel were already asleep. Jeremy watched over them all as they cuddled together,

---

be [saved.]' **Luke 24:27** He [Jesus] explained to them what was said in all the Scriptures [in the *Hall of Writings*] concerning Himself.

unsure of what would happen next. He looked up at the stars and scratched his head in wonder. 'I must make sure to plan each step we take,' he thought knowing that they all relied on his calm and steady decisions.

CHAPTER 4

THEIR FIRST STEPS IN THE VALLEY OF DEATH

The Thistles and the Stone of Ages

JEREMY WOKE TO THE SOUNDS of Joel swinging on a branch of the cedar tree.[13] Suddenly, the branch broke off and Joel fell to the ground with a thud and a squeal.

"Oh, Joel," said Sam, grinning as he walked over to his young brother. "Tell me where it hurts?"

He sat down next to him and rubbed his knees gently. Just then, the slim broken branch slid across the ground, to rest at Sam's feet. Lydia looked up from braiding her hair in time to watch the branch move.

"There's something about that branch, Sam. Pick it up," she instructed.

Joel, who had stopped crying, stood transfixed as he watched his big brother bend down to touch the branch. As Sam's fingers lightly touched it, the 'stick' immediately turned into a strong, straight sword. Flinching, he dropped it. It hit the ground and changed back into a simple piece of branch again, just as ordinary as before.

No one spoke, except Joel. "Wow, pick it up again," he said, intrigued.

---

13   **Psalms 92:12 cf..** "*The cedar of the Lord.*" The growth of a strong cedar is a symbol of a righteous man.

Sam did pick it up, and the wooden branch once again changed into a luminous sapphire sword, with a silver light shining from the point. The sapphire-stoned handle had scriptural carvings on it, which emanated white light that shone through his fingers. He nearly dropped it again, but this time he knew that this sword was given to him to have confidence; to be used only when they were in great peril. Gently he bent down and placed it on the ground. This time it turned into, what looked like, a wooden shepherd's crook – a staff.

He grinned. "I have a special staff and no one will know what it is."

Lydia jumped up to go and hug him; so did Joel and Jubilee, as they admired the magnificent sword he had been given.

Grinning, Jeremy strode over to join them.

With a firm military stance and his fists on his hips, he announced, "It looks like you are going to be our warrior."

Sam grinned. He felt so proud of his new position within the group.

"I'm glad about this," said Jubilee, "because I've been afraid of going down into the forest again. I don't know why, but I just had a feeling."

To celebrate, Jeremy smiled as he passed the water skin around. Everyone now felt much safer, and Sam couldn't stop being amazed at his wonderful gift. Lydia handed out the bananas.

"Do you think we should look in the *Book of Mirrors* again before we leave here?" Sam asked, eating his third banana.

"I wonder how many times we can request the book to tell us where we are going?" asked Lydia.

Jubilee shrugged her shoulders saying "Maybe we ought to wait until we need it."

"Mm-hmm," said Jeremy. "I agree. We have the broken looking glass that will give us half an answer, so perhaps we ought to try and find our way home on our own. As we came up here last evening, I noticed a signpost on the bottom road, perhaps that will help us."

Jubilee whispered to Lydia, "I hope the angels will be nearby, just in case we need them."

"I'm sure they will be, sweetheart," Lydia said with confidence.

When they reached the signpost, one sign pointed to the left and said, 'From the House of Wine'. The other sign pointed to the right and said, 'To the Temple of Water'.

"Well, that doesn't leave us much choice, does it?" commented Jeremy. "We have to go to the right."

The large trees in the forest started whispering as the children approached, as if a rumour passed among them; the branches flapped and twitched as though they were squabbling in the light breeze. The leaves now looked shiny as if they wanted to stick to the passing children for some reason. Instinctively Lydia gently took Joel's hand. The girls linked arms and Sam gripped his 'staff' as he bravely strode forward with Jeremy to lead the way through the menacing, waving branches of the glowering watching trees. They could see no more cedar trees! It seemed that something hidden in this forest didn't like strangers in the neighbourhood. As they followed the path, they saw more and more large, purple-headed thistles with spiky leaves swaying towards them.

"Don't get too close to those," said a large white stone.

Joel swung around. "Did you hear that?" he asked the others.

"Hear what?" asked Jubilee.

"That stone over there, the one that looks like a boundary stone," he replied.

"What is it?" asked Sam.

"That big white stone—it's talking to me," said Joel.

"Like the jars, I suppose. I can't hear anything," commented Jeremy.

"Neither can I," said Lydia and Sam together.

"Don't worry," said the stone to Joel.

"Only you can hear me though maybe your little sister still can. If you get too close to those thistles, they'll spit at you and then you will become one of them."

"I heard that!" said Jubilee, who couldn't believe her ears.

What was going on? She felt afraid of spiteful people; she'd had enough of that at school, being bullied by two girls in her class who thought she was prettier than them.

"Why would they do that?" asked Joel innocently.

"Because they are jealous of you, that's why," said the stone smiling showing a long, thin cracked mouth as he rocked from side to side. He seemed to be enjoying himself. "My mouth is stiff. I haven't spoken to anyone in ages and ages," he giggled.

"How do you know about the thistles?" Joel wanted to know.

"That's simple. I'm a boundary stone of ages." The thistles crackled with exasperation.

Jeremy stopped to see to whom Joel was talking. "What's happening?" he asked his little brother.

"That stone. It's talking to me. Can you hear him too?" Joel replied.

A light immediately shone from Sam's staff. Jeremy and the older children felt a ringing in their ears.

"They know who you are and where you are going!" said the stone.

Joel as he raised his hands and eyebrows in an expression of surprise saying, "They know us and where we are going?"

"That's good," said Jeremy, "because we don't know where we are going, except to the Temple."

The leaves stopped shaking with rumour, and the branches stopped swaying with intrigue. The nervous little animals in the trees stopped chattering and quickly rushed to hug one another.

"The temple?" asked Sam.

"Hmm, that's bad, but... it may be good," said the stone.

"Why?" Jeremy asked as the others came to stand around to watch the little ones talking to the stone.

"Because there are many bad people there. All they care about is cheating. Everyone who buys doves and other things to make a sacrifice to God for the things they've done wrong, is cheated."

"Killing little doves? That's horrible!" said Jubilee. "Why do that?"

SPITFULL THISTLES –
Because they spit hate and jealousy!

"It's their tradition. Life-giving blood is spilt as a sign of saying sorry to God, who gives life to every living thing. The merchants have moved into the temple area to sell doves and animals, for profit."

"Why?" asked Jubilee again. "Isn't the temple meant to be for praying?"

"I know," said the stone sadly. "The merchants come from this forest of sin and evil intent."

The stone dropped his gaze and then said, "This forest is known as the Valley of the Shadow of Death." Joel slips his hand into Jubilee's; he was afraid.

"How sad," said Jubilee. "But I don't understand. Why are they so selfish and evil?"

"That's easy," said Joel innocently. "It's because they are still full of water. They need to drink some of the water Jaycee made into wine."

"I still don't understand," said Jubilee.

Joel turned to Jeremy, who was listening intently to what his little brother and sister said. "Tell her. You know, don't you? Tell her about the wine in those funny jars that's now in your water-skin."

Jeremy grinned down at his little brother. The little ones both looked up at him in anticipation. "This unique wine comes from the God King. When people drink it, it makes them see things more clearly, and that makes them kinder to other persons, but some are too busy doing things for themselves."

"So they are blind," said Joel as he flapped his arms to his sides in exasperation. "They don't see what's happening."

The stone spoke again. "So don't take any notice of the thistles. Whatever you do, don't look straight into their eyes. That's when they begin to spit."

"Spit?" gasped Lydia. "Who's spitting?"

"The thistles. They are dangerous," said Jubilee. "We mustn't look at them. That's when they want to hurt us; because they are greedy and mock the God King."[14]

"They don't have respect for anyone," the ancient stone continued. They pretend to be nice and seem friendly, but they spit out unkind words about others to their fellow thistles, and it hurts. And then whoever gets hurt starts spitting back because they are upset and then that one becomes a thistle too. And..." He hesitated. "Many of the merchants in the temple are thistles." "How do you know all this," asked Lydia.

"He knows everything because he is a stone of ages," said Sam with a gentle smile, beginning to comprehend.

Lydia glanced around to see if any of the thistles were nearby, and they were! They were huge thistles, taller than the children. She had seen thistles like these before, at the bottom of her grandmother's garden.

"By the way," said the stone, "They are deaf because they only hear what they have to say. Just look at their feet—that will help you to avoid them."

"We have to go through here? There's no other way," insisted Lydia.

She felted exasperated trying to understand what the little ones were doing. Hopefully, she glanced up, looking at the sky high above the canopy of suffocating branches, wondering if they could find another cedar tree to rest beneath while they sorted out how to cope with this. A thistle began to shift, moving its roots through the ground.

The stone looked sorry, then slowly began to fall into the hollow made by the moving thistle. As he sank, he managed to whisper, "You should pass by the spring water of the Seven Fountains on the road to Capernaum. Jaycee often goes there with his followers to refresh themselves and others. You'll be safe if you stay by the living water."

---

14   **Psalm 69:9** – *'The insults of those who insult you fall on me.'*

"The Seven Fountains," repeated Jeremy. "Great." "I'm thirsty," said Joel.

"Oh, for goodness sake, Joel!" said Lydia. She turned to Jeremy. "Is there any water left?"

"Not much. We finished most of it this morning." He pulled the water-skin from his shoulder to pass it to Lydia. "Oh. That's odd…. It's…still full."[15]

"It can't be," said Sam taking the skin and passing it to Joel, who didn't care, just so long as he had a drink.

No one made any more comments. They were beginning to get used to unusual things happening. For the rest of the day, they stayed close together on the narrow path that seemed to remain on the outskirts of the forest. They all kept their eyes open for any swaying, grinning thistles.

The Road to Capernaum and the Seven Fountains

The daisy pathway finally led down a gradual slope and out onto open ground just as the evening sun misted over and dimmed. Their tired eyes, from concentrating not to look at thistles, now strained to take in the view ahead of them. They stood just below a ridge of hills where a road led down to a sapphire blue lake. They saw a tiny port in the distance, alive with lights flickering like stars in the growing darkness. In the twilight, they could see a long, slow moving row of sandy coloured camels carrying boxes of goods down towards the port. They crawled like a tired and crusty snake, sick of struggling with thirst towards the blue sea of hope.

"Look! Look," said Jeremy. "Isn't that a spring over there, coming from that rock? It doesn't look much further for us to go. Come on, maybe we can find some food. We're here," announced Jeremy, "and this water certainly looks cold."

"And somewhere safe for tonight," added Lydia.

---

15   **1 Kings 17:16** – idea from *'For the jar of flour was not used up and the jug of oil did not run dry'*

"I'm tired," said Joel.

"Me, too," said Jubilee.

Jeremy looked towards Sam and nodded. He picked up Jubilee and put her on his back. Sam did the same for Joel. Half an hour later they finally arrived, just before the sun set.

The sleepy little ones rubbed their eyes, then slowly took handfuls of sparkling water to wash their hands and faces, before paddling in the stream to cool their tired feet.

"This must be the spring water of the 'Seven Fountains' the stone told us about," said Joel.

"That's right!" said Jubilee.

"Then this must be Magdala, near Capernaum," said Jeremy, who had studied maps of the Holy Land in Sunday school.

"Which means," said Lydia thoughtfully, "this is where we spend the night."

Sam could just see enough to pick several juicy, ripe, brown figs for their supper, and then he stooped to wash them in the bubbling water, before handing them round.

"Oh, thank you. I'm so hungry," said Joel as he bit into the ripe and slightly sticky fig.

After they had eaten, Lydia led them all over to the shelter of a large fig tree, with huge leaves forming a protective canopy. As they settled down beneath its branches, Jeremy and Sam discussed taking turns on guard.

Smiling a tired smile, Lydia asked Jubilee, "Shall we look in the 'Book of Mirrors'? I think perhaps we need to know where we are heading. What do you say?"

Jubilee nodded, held out her hands and the book appeared on her lap. The pages flicked over then stopped at a page showing cattle, sheep, and doves in the outer courtyard of the temple. They saw that Jaycee, who was outraged, was shouting and waving a whip to move the animals out of the temple courtyard, the only place where the Gentiles were allowed to pray. The merchants all looked furious because

Jaycee was also turning over their money changing tables. Piles of carefully counted coins cascaded onto the floor, spinning and bouncing in all directions. The distressed and angry merchants had fallen onto their knees desperately trying to pick up their spinning coins.

"Golly, that looks terrible — they are struggling to save their money as if it's the most important thing, just like some of our neighbours back home," whispered Sam.

"Maybe it's an image of what is going to happen in the future," said Jeremy, who knew everything.

Some people ran away others looked shocked, and still others stood in groups with their mouths open with complete surprise.

"Oh dear," said Jubilee. "The Thistle merchants the Stone told us about, look very upset. I wonder what's happening."

"Whatever it is, it seems shocking," said Sam, wondering if he was going to need to use his staff.

They all fell quiet, each with their thoughts but this created a troubled atmosphere that hung over them like a thick cloud about to burst with tears. The leaves of the fig tree began to sway, fanning them from above trying to disperse their collective sad thoughts, which had caused a change in their force fields. Gloom and doom swirled around them. Jubilee was sensitive to this atmosphere. The other trees joined in fanning them to sleep by causing a breeze that slowly became a strong wind. At least the wind was warm, and in a strange way – comforting. Without being aware of what was happening, they each drifted away in their dreams feeling as though they were floating on the wings of large white birds. 'Sweet dreams,' the birds whispered as they gently lay down the sleeping children on the grassy outskirts of the temple courtyard.

Chapter 5

THE TEMPLE OF WATER AND THE EVIL SPIRITS

The Second Sign: God's House Is for Everyone—
John 2:13-22

THE NEXT MORNING BEGAN IN total confusion. How did they get here? They were near to the courtyard they had seen in the '*Book of Mirrors*' the night before.

"That's funny," said Sam, "I had a funny dream last night that we flew here on the backs of huge white birds, like the swans back home on the river?"

"Me too," exclaimed Joel looking shocked in complete surprise.

Lydia and Jeremy shook their heads in agreement, saying, "Us too."

They couldn't believe they had all had the same dream. Their thoughts were broken by the noise of people hurrying all around them, buying and selling animals for sacrifices to the God King. Men with full bags of money rushed by, looking important while others paraded donkeys in front of customers. Escaped doves, who had been waiting to be sold for sacrifices, flapped around everywhere, leaving a trail of pure white feathers amongst the dirt and animal fur. A loud buzz of conversation filled the air between customers and sellers. There was barely any room to move in the crowded and dusty courtyard.

"Wow. How did we get here?" Jeremy murmured scratching his hand as he gazed at the sight.

"This is amazing!" Joel said, his eyes aglow as he looked around at the business of the temple. "I recognize it, don't you?" Lydia asked, but she didn't get a reply.

"What's going on?" asked Jubilee, looking concerned.

"Don't you remember, in The Book they are buying animals for sacrifices," Jeremy concluded.

Then they caught the gleam of a silver plate filled with the sacrificed meat. It was handed to the priests, to eat for their supper. The sacrifice to the God King was meant to ensure forgiveness for their mistakes and sins. The older children knew that the tradition required the spilling of blood[16] of an innocent animal that had had no sickness or weakness.

The spilled blood seemed to be everywhere, but somehow the children instinctively knew that the life giving force of the animals had gone back to God in heaven. The Jewish merchants didn't seem to care about anything else, except their ill-gotten money.

."This is horrible!" Jubilee sobbed burying her head in Lydia's stomach.

"Not as horrible as insulting God by using His house to cheat people and make money in!" said Sam, indignantly. Obviously, he felt very strongly about it. No one else spoke. They had read about these things in the Bible with their parents.

They turned to see three men walking urgently toward the Temple. As the men strode forward, Lydia, Sam, and Jeremy could see that they were important. The taller man, walking in the middle, had a glow all around him,

---

16   **Ephesians 5:1-2** – *'just as Christ loved us and gave himself up for us as a fragrant offering and sacrifice to God.' (Because of his love for us).*

   Philippians 4: 18-19 – *'and God will meet all your needs... according to his glorious riches in Jesus/Jaycee].*

and light shone brightly from his hands.[17] His aura made the tax collectors, frantic mothers, and babies expectantly stare as He walked by – as if they sensed his aura. The children recognized him; he was Jaycee. He had turned water into wine at the wedding in Cana. There, people had been happy to be together. He had been relaxed as he spoke to his friends and all the guests; he had spoken slowly and looked kindly into the eyes of the people to whom he spoke. Now he looked angry, very angry. In fact, He looked furious with righteous anger over what people were doing here, because they were acting with disrespect in His father house, the home of the God King.

THE SERPENT OF DECEIT

---

17   **John 1:5** *'The light shines in the darkness'*.
   Ephesians 5:14 *'It is the light that makes everything visible'*. [so that we can understand].
   2 Corinthians 4:6 cf. *'My messages...were not with wise and persuasive words, but with a demonstration of the Spirit's power.'*

Suddenly, Sam's wooden shepherd's staff turned into the bright sapphire sword. Guided by the light from the tip, he knew he could protect them. The air around the shining tip trembled. Sam gripped the sword with both hands, wondering what would happen next. As Jaycee strode over to the cheating money changers, the children moved to hide behind a thick round pillar. They saw Jaycee lay his strong, capable hands flat on the table before him as he stared at the merchant counting his money. Then, he began to flip over all of the tables with great force. Everything went flying and crashing to the floor: pots of money, piles of temple coins, capsized displays, open cages, and jugs of water.[18] Hysterical animals escaped their cages, vanishing into the crowd. –

"Take these out of here! How dare you turn my father's house into a market?"[19] Jaycee's shout echoed all through the temple.

Silence fell all around them as the animals scattered out of sight. Everyone gasped, slapping their hands over their mouths in horror. Some people turned pale at the shock of such a sight.

"Who is he to be doing all this?" people murmured under their breath or to each other.

"Who is he?" they asked and pointed.

"Who is that man? Look! He's even setting the doves free!" one man exclaimed.

"He must be someone very important to do such a thing in the Temple!" someone shouted at the top of their voice.

The twelve men who were with him also looked shocked at His behaviour yet they did nothing to stop Him. The Jews screamed wanting to know by what authority He was doing this, as they rushed to the front of the crowd, pushing and shoving until they made it. They stopped when they saw

---

18   John 2:15 cf.– 'He scattered the coins of the money changers'.
19   John 2:16 – 'Turn my Father's house into a market'.

Jaycee. He ignored their questions but told them the truth in a puzzle.

Destroy this temple and I will raise it again in three days,"[20] He said with truth in His eyes." He meant His body, but the people didn't understand.

Many people were still on their hands and knees on the sandy earthen floor of the temple area, scrabbling around for their money. Others stood in silent shock, watching Jaycee intently. Doves flew everywhere though some of the birds sat wide-eyed bewildered on the top of the temple, looking down at everyone shouting. The goats, oxen, and lambs all squealed and squawked as they fought their way out between long straggly legs, running feet and flapping robes. The noise was terrible; confusion swirled about as the devil's demons raged and swirled overhead in anger as Jaycee's actions destroyed their evil plots. Joel and Jubilee put their hands over their ears, their eyebrows furrowed as their faces crumpled with dismay. Sam and Jeremy stood on either side of the young children and Lydia to protect them. Lydia still put her hands over her head; she didn't want the demons to get caught in her long hair. More than anything right then, she wanted to be at home in her mother's arms. Sam's sword was now glowing brightly. Slowly, Jeremy and Sam backed the children and Lydia away from the merchants. Then, one fat, red-faced, furious, and profusely sweating merchant saw them moving.

"What are you looking at?" he yelled at them, pointing.

Lydia blinked hard, pulling her hands away from her face.

"He can see me!" she gasped.

"What do you mean, he can see you? Of course, I can! I'll stop you staring at me!" he said striding angrily towards them.

---

20 **John 2:19** – *'Destroy this temple and I will raise it again in three days'.* **Meaning:** – [not the church of stone – but himself, for he was the temple of God's spirit.]

Several demons came out of the man's two ears and advanced towards them. Then a hideous slug crawled out, covered in thick, sticky slime with white fly grubs, crawling all over it, the same kind of maggots that they had seen in their uncle's fishing bait tin. The grubs whispered 'white lies, white lies, we live on white lies.' The blue-green demon slug rose above the head of the merchant and smiled a wicked smile as slime dripped from its ears. Lydia let out a shrill scream and threw her head into her hands again. She just couldn't look. Jeremy and Sam instinctively stepped in front of them. Sam held his sword in his trembling hands, the light glinting on the sharp edge of it shot through the heavy air of anger. Another merchant joined in.

"Yes!" he snarled, "Get away; you're not going to get our money! Why are you here? You have no business. Leave at once!"

THE BUBBLE OF PROTECTION

The merchants spat; Jeremy and Sam flinched as the spit hit their faces. Jubilee and Joel stared in horror at the fat slug and the crawling grubs. Suddenly, they noticed that a large crowd of men shuffled towards them, getting nearer and then nearer; they started to run towards them. Jeremy raised his fists to fend off the merchants. Sam raised his sword, a blue beam of fluorescent light now cutting through the angry crowd. Then... they were suddenly inside a large pink bubble.

The first merchant raised his fist to punch at them, but before his fist struck Jeremy, the merchant froze like a statue. As if in slow motion, they watched his skin slowly harden into salt and begin to crumble away. The demons looked bewildered and angry. Jeremy, Sam, Lydia, and the children had become untouchable.

"What happened? Marius, what's the matter?" cried the second merchant, more concerned that they would not win this conflict rather than his friend turning into a pillar of salt.[21]

Then the family faded from human sight, person by person until all that remained was space in the crowd where they once stood.

"They were here! I saw them. I did. I did!" the merchant raved as people began to marvel at what just happened.

"They have disappeared!" cried another merchant, turning to face the crowd.

"Yikes—that was close! I almost got scared!" laughed Joel, showing off.

Sam gave him a playful little slap on the side of the head. "I saw you screw your eyes up when he almost hit Jeremy!"

---

21 **Genesis 19:26** (idea taken from – pillar of salt). Her disobedience brings folly.

"Are we invisible?" Jubilee asked, stretching her arm out to feel the field of protection around them. It was like something she'd seen on TV back at home.

"I'm not sure. Are we?" asked Jeremy, looking at Sam.

"If we are," Joel asked, "can I punch that horrid merchant back?" His tiny fist was ready to take a good swing at him.

"No!" the others exclaimed loudly together.

They were now on the pathway leading to the temple just outside the village. As they looked back at the scene in the marketplace, a lamb, and a young donkey came running towards them, their eyes wide with fear.

"Look out!" yelled Sam.

They jumped to one side to dodge the animals, but the donkey and the lamb ran straight through them and the bubble without a second glance.

"Wow, that was close! We are invisible," said Jeremy, who laughed with relief, looking back at the escaping animals.

"This is amazing, Grandma," Joel gasped in surprise.

"Not now, Joel," said Jubilee exhausted. She sat down cross-legged and rested her chin in the palm of her left hand. "Can we please get away from here?" she asked, her voice trembling as tears began to roll down her flushed cheeks.

"Well," Joel insisted, "what I know is, we are we aliens. I told you so!" He nodded his head adamantly to confirm his suspicions.

"Let's just hope that this bubble stays with us until we are safe; that's all I want right now," said Lydia, kneeling beside Jubilee and embracing her.

At that moment, they turned to see Jaycee and His followers coming towards them. A white cloud that looked like tiny snowflakes sparkling in the brilliant sun floated all around Jaycee.[22] The children froze as one when He walked

---

22   **Daniel 7:9** – *'white as snow.'*

Matthew 26:64 – *'the Son of Man sitting at the right hand of the Mighty One.'*

past them. His friends looked bewildered and shaken, but they quietly followed Him.

"Did He smile at us?" asked Lydia.

"Yes, He did! I saw it!" Joel said adamantly looking back at Lydia.

"He can't have, though. We're invisible, remember?" said Sam, he gestured with his arms to the bubble around them.

"We're not invisible to Him," said Jeremy. "No one who has drunk the living water is invisible to Him."[23] He looked at Lydia and then at Sam. "What is going on? I don't understand any of it."

He sat down next Lydia and Jubilee.

"Well, it seems," said Sam after a few moments of thought, "that all the merchants and money changers are still full of water. That is why the sign said, to 'The Temple of Water!' They have no wine in their souls."

"That's why Jaycee banished them all from the Temple because it's where the God King lives in spirit," continued Jubilee.

"And... and He is invisible on earth like we are in the 'Land of Mirrors.' That does not change that the Temple is the only place where everyone can pray, including Gentiles, like you and me," Jeremy explained.

"I feel that I am beginning to understand a little better. You mean that they don't understand the spiritual world and... and how important it is?" Sam quizzed, trying to understand, too.

"That's right!" Jeremy confirmed.

"Why is it important?" insisted Joel, stamping his little feet.

Jeremy struggled to find the right words.

"I think it's because our spirits inside us, err... have perhaps seen by our force fields; as we saw in our bedroom

---

23 **Jeremiah 2:13b** – *'They have forsaken me, the spring of living water'*
John 4:14 – *'whoever drinks the water [spirit of life] I give him will never thirst... to eternal life.'*

at home. They can tune into the God King and His spirit kingdom world,"[24] he finished, feeling pleased that he could explain it in such a way.

"Grandma said our spirits can speak to God like that, and she ought to know because she's so old!" Joel said with enthusiasm, turning around to see everyone's response.

They walked in silence for a moment or two, the bubble remaining with them, still protecting them. Then Jubilee burst into tears. 'What's the matter with me?' she asked herself. Lydia rushed to her side and instinctively put her arms around her little sister.

"Those demons were awful, really scary," burst Jubilee between her sobs covering her eyes with her small fists.

"I didn't know things like that existed," said Joel thoughtfully, trying hard not to cry.

His eyes filled with tears and he looked flushed now that it was all over, and they were safe. Jeremy and Sam looked at them as they, too, began to feel the effects of shock after encountering the gruesome demons.

"I know, I know," whispered Lydia, comforting them. "In this place we seem to be able to see things in the spirit world as well."

A lump came to her throat as she also tried to recover from the living evil they had seen. Sam picked up Joel while Jeremy gave Jubilee a piggyback ride.

Holding each other tightly, they walked away from the temple.

"I agree," said Sam, kicking the dust as he walked. "While we are here, we can see both sides of the 'Land of Mirrors', can't we?"

"I'm thirsty!" Joel complained.

"And I'm hungry," said Sam.

"Can we stop somewhere and rest?" Joel persisted.

---

24 **John 7:38 cf.**- *'whoever believes in me...streams of living water will flow from within Him. By this, he meant the Spirit'.*

"I want to stop as well," Jubilee chimed in, now that she'd stopped crying.

Jeremy spotted a lone fig tree with large leaves in a clearing just ahead; another tree that would give enough shade for them all. They all slumped down on the hard ground at the foot of the tree.

Sam studied the tree, hoping to climb it and pick enough fruit for them all. "Huh, this tree is hopeless. Not a single fig on it. Not one." Sam frowned.[25]

"That's funny," said Lydia. "The other trees have had fruit on them."

"There are a lot of funny things around here," Sam said as he lay down on his back in the dry dust, placing his hands behind his head as a cushion.

"I wonder why there is no fruit on this one?" questioned Jubilee, who always wanted to know why; she was curious like that.

No one answered her. She brushed her long hair off her pink-flushed face and waited for an answer – which didn't come. So she asked, "Can I have a drink of water, Jeremy?"

Jeremy shrugged the water-skin off his shoulder and passed it to her. She tilted it perfectly to drink from it. As she raised the water-skin to take a drink, a few drops of water spilled onto her hands.

"Oh!" she gasped "It's—it's pink!" She held her hands out to show everyone.

"Pink?" asked Lydia. "Have you cut yourself by accident?"

"No, I don't think so!" she said, looking at her hands all over to check. She hadn't.

Jeremy took the water-skin back from her. Slowly he poured some of the water out into the palm of his hand as the others watched. It was pink definitely.

---

25 **Matthew 21:18-19** – *'seeing the fig tree he went up to it but found nothing on it.* [Symbolic of this branch of people – the Jews – not bearing spiritual fruit for God].

"Now what's going on?" asked Lydia, getting sick and tired of all the confusion.

Sam answered first, grinning. "It's Jaycee! It's a symbol that His wine has been poured into the water of our bodies, which means we are beginning to understand who He is!" Sam sounded excited; things like this often excited him and he became joyous.

"Well, I'm still thirsty!" said Joel, rubbing his head.

"I don't care what colour it is; I need a drink! I'm dying from de—," he stopped and started again. "Dehidri—?" He stopped again, looking confused.

"Dehydrated!" Sam finished.

Joel pulled the water-skin from Jeremy and quickly lifted it to his open mouth before anyone could stop him, he took a huge gulp. The others watched intently to see if the pink water had any nasty side effects. No one spoke for a moment; they sat in silence watching him.

He grinned. "Mmmmm," he said. "Tastes like strawberries to me!" Then he wiped his mouth on the back of his hand. Seeing their worried faces, he added, "It doesn't taste any different, but I feel great!" He gave them a thumbs up sign.

"Hey! The bubble has gone! Maybe we are safe again," Sam noticed, standing up and waving his arms.

"Perhaps, but I think we should stay inside the same area just in case," Lydia replied, worriedly.

Sam sat down again. After they each had a drink of the pale pink water, they talked about the events in the temple that they had just experienced.

"Why was Jaycee so upset? I was so surprised to see Him angry. He doesn't seem like that kind of person at all!" Jubilee exclaimed, then waited for a reply.

Jeremy decided that he should explain it all because he was the oldest and knew more about these things than they did. "Well, he was obviously mad that the merchants had taken the only place where the Gentiles could pray."

"Couldn't they go into the Temple?" Joel asked, thinking it was as easy as that.

"Oh, no, only Jews are allowed in there. They call themselves the chosen children of God," Lydia explained.[26]

"You mean it's sort of like a club?" Sam asked frowning.

Jeremy spluttered then coughed, cleared his throat, and answered. "Well, no, but they do keep themselves separate because they believe and feel certain things. God gave the stone tablets with the written Jewish law to Moses," he reminded them.

They all nodded in agreement.

"So? That's not fair. Where can everyone else pray? There wasn't much room as it was, with all the merchants and animals in the outer court of the temple," Jubilee argued.

"Not only that, but the Jewish Leaders were making them change their money into temple coins, which made it easy for the merchants to cheat and steal from them!" Sam pointed out trying to figure what had happened that day, almost answering Jubilee's question.

"And all the people wanted to do was to pray?" questioned Lydia.

"Exactly!" said Jeremy.

"The animals made it smelly," put in Joel, who had been listening intently and wanted to join in. "There was poo everywhere; did you see it, Jubilee? That's not nice in God's house is it? Mum and Dad wouldn't like it, would they? They would be very upset if they wanted to pray, and the animals made it messy."

With blood being splashed everywhere in our house as well," said Jubilee making a face of disgust.

"Yes, they would be upset," said Sam, laughing with his little brother.

Lydia raised her eyebrows as she looked at Joel.

---

26   1 Peter 2:9 – 'a holy nation, a people belonging to God.'

Jeremy couldn't help grinning as well. Crossing his arms, he said, "The point is, I think, that those in authority were worshipping money more than they worshipped God in heaven."

"Exactly," said Joel, copying his older brother folding his arms, although he didn't fully understand.

"I wonder what will happen in the future? I mean, if this Temple was ever destroyed for some reason, where will everyone go to pray?" asked Lydia, raising her right eyebrow and frowning in wonder.

Silence fell on all of them like soft dew, invisible but sad and heavy. Jubilee cuddled up to Lydia and Joel snuggled up to Sam. Jeremy kept watch, making sure that they were safe touching his staff that lay by his side.

"I think they are missing Mum and Dad," Lydia whispered to Jeremy.

"Yes, we are," said Joel, who had heard her.

He whispered back to Lydia, "When are we going home? Those demons were horrible, especially the one with white bugs crawling all over it. It made me feel terribly sick." He pretended to vomit, putting his finger in his mouth.

"I was scared of the slug covered in maggots, too," said Jubilee. She began to cry. "I'm going to have nightmares every night forever!" she complained, her bottom lip wobbling.

Suddenly, the leaves above them rustled, and Sam snapped to attention. "What was that?" he said, looking up.

"What was what?" asked Jeremy getting ready to fend off another attack of demons. He quickly following Sam's gaze who didn't seem worried at all!

"That!" said Joel, pointing with his grubby finger, then wiping his nose and tears on his arm again.

A pink streak shot past them, very fast, like the kingfisher bird that lived on the river bank back home. Another streak of pink shot back the other way.

"What on earth is it?" asked Lydia as they all swung their heads around, shifting to see what it was.

"There are two of them," said Jeremy.

"Three?" said Joel.

"No, two. Only two!" Lydia confirmed.

Suddenly, the fig tree shook vigorously making leaves fly everywhere. "Argh-h-h!" said a little voice.

They all looked towards the tree trunk. A small, plump, pink cherub slid down the tree trunk holding his nose. Thud. He landed on the ground right where they were sitting.

"Hello. Who are you?" Joel said, now wide-eyed and curious.

Another pink streak shot past them. "Oh, nooo!" said another small voice as a second cherub climbed to his feet rubbing his behind. "I still can't do it—I just can't do it, and I'm getting very sore."

The first cherub giggled at the second cherub then looked up at Joel and said, "He's only Grade Two, you know."

"And you are only Grade Two and a quarter!" his friend finished.

"Who are you?" Jeremy asked again though he didn't get up since the cherubs didn't seem dangerous.

The one in blue said, "Well, I'm Thumper —I keep thumping into tree trunks and things, my aim still isn't too good. He's Bumper—he hasn't learned the landing technique yet. He bumps along on his bottom!"

He was giggling so much that he nearly fell from the branch where he now stood. He then fluttered over to his companion. They stood side by side, each only about two feet tall, with their little hands on their hips as they viewed the startled children.

"Don't just sit there! Don't you want to know why we are here?" Bumper asked, frowning still rubbing his behind.

Jeremy laughed and so did Sam. Jubilee giggled, Lydia raised her eyebrows, and, for the first time, Joel was speechless.

"Yes, please," said Jeremy quietly looking amazed.

"We've been given the task of looking after you while you are on this journey!"

"That's right! Me and him," Thumper said, pointing first to himself and then to Bumper.

"It's not 'me and him', it's 'him and I'!" Bumper corrected him, elbowing his tummy with his left arm.

"No, that's not right either!" Joel argued standing up and looking down on them.

"It's 'he and I'," Lydia interrupted.

"Okay, okay," said Jeremy, laughing. "It's both of you!"

At this, the cherubs jumped up to fly, round and round in circles above the children's heads, managing not to bump into each other.

BUMPER AND THUMPER

"Did you like our bubble trick?" asked Bumper, landing with only one bump.

"That was you? Well, it was brilliant!" said Sam, understanding now. "And only just in time. We thought we were going to get into real trouble with those evil devils."

"Yes, they are evil, but we are good spirits," Thumper explained, landing successfully.

"Oh, I didn't know that. You mean that there are bad and good spirits as well as angels?" Jubilee asked, sitting up on her knees.

"Of course there are; why shouldn't there be? You have good and bad people on earth, don't you?" Bumper asked, tumbling into the centre of the group.

"Yes, but...I just never thought, that's all," Jubilee excused herself.

"Well, I suppose you haven't. You don't know very much, do you? And you are built-in His image,[27] you know!" said Thumper with a frown

"The jugs told us that—I remember!" said Joel, turning to everyone else.

"Have you met them? They're fun, aren't they?" said Bumper, kicking around in the air.

"Err, can you come to us a little bit quicker next time we need you? We were all very scared. You see, we have never seen anything like that before," Lydia joined in.

"That's because you are in the fourth dimension, and you would normally be in the third dimension, where time is stable. Well, for you," informed Thumper, wiggling his feathery wings on his back.

"I don't understand! What do you mean the fourth dimension?" Jubilee asked.

---

27 **Genesis 1:26** – *'Let us make man in our image, in our likeness.'*
Meaning: – [Spiritually, i.e., in our souls/hearts]

Galatians 5:22 in our souls/hearts – love, joy, peace, patience, goodness, faithfulness, gentleness, tolerance and self-control. Against such things there are no laws.

"It's simple. You will keep slipping in and out of the fourth dimension because of your thoughts and fears. Even we have trouble at times; that's why we are still learning how to travel through the gaps from one sphere to the next. I can't quite work out how to slip through at exactly the right moment, and Bumper can't get his feet down in time," he said, smirking at the end.

"That's why we are only in Grade Two!" said Thumper, frowning and shrugging his shoulders.

"Oh dear. But being in the fourth dimension must be good for something," Lydia wondered out loud.

"It is. We can sometimes see why things happen, and sometimes we can see what is going to happen in the future!" Bumper boasted.

"That's brilliant! So can you tell us why this fig tree hasn't got any fruit on it? Because we are all very hungry," Joel asked indignantly.

The cherubs looked at each other and giggled. Thumper asked Bumper, "Will you tell them or shall I?"

"You want to, don't you? That's because you passed your last test with high marks?" Bumper said as if he wished his marks were much better.

Thumper puffed up his chest, drew himself up to his full height of two feet, fluffed his wings, and put a confident smile on his little face. Then he cleared his throat. "Ahem. This fig tree is famous because it is the symbol of Israel not producing any fruit, which means Israel produces no good actions or deeds of the heart for the God King."

He ended with a bouncing nod and a sudden leap up, bringing his face within just a few inches of theirs. Startled, the children suddenly leaned backwards.

"Oh!" they all said, nodding all together.

"And...and will there be a new Temple soon?" asked Jubilee innocently, interested in the conversation if she could learn about the Temple.

Go to Page 86

"That's right," pondered Lydia, "It will have to be a new and different kind of Temple. The God doesn't live in temples made by human hands[29] – does he?" she said, making sense of it in her head but still not sure.

---

29   **Acts 17:14,** [God is a personal creator, he doesn't live in brick houses]

1 Corinthians 3:16 *'Don't you know that you yourselves are God's temple and that God's spirit lives in you?'*

1 Corinthians 6:19 *'Do you not know that your body is a temple of the Holy Spirit, who is in you...by the Spirit's presence and power* [you can] *be helped to* [conquer sin-selfishness].

CHAPTER 6

THE NOBLEMAN'S REQUEST AND THE CAMELS OF PRIDE

The Third Sign: The Word, According to John 4:43–54[30]

'The man believed the Word...[who] had become flesh,'[31]
—and found faith.

THE NEXT MORNING, WHEN THEY woke, the children were surprised to see a large bowl of fruit and five loaves[32] of bread waiting for them. The food had been placed neatly in a basket, in the middle of the reeds and green grass near the cedar tree.

"Look! Look!" squealed Joel, always the first to wake up in the mornings as he gleefully skipped away from them.

Climbing to his feet, Jeremy rushed to join Joel, in case he may be in danger. Sam followed, clutching his staff tightly in his right hand ready to fend off any dangerous creatures.

"What's the matter, Joel?" asked Jeremy, looking around to see if he had missed something.

"Look, food!" Joel said, grinning and pointing.

---

30   **John 1:2** *'In the beginning was The Word, (Jesus) and The Word was with God.'*

31   **N. T. Wright p.53** 'John for Everyone', part one.

32   **John 6:26-27; 6:9, cf.** *(6:35 – 'I am the bread of life'* – Meaning: – [food for thought -wisdom-knowledge for the spirit.]

"That's all?" questioned Sam his voice rising in hope with mock surprise.

His eyes widened in delight as he surveyed the meal before them. Lydia sat bolt upright when she heard there was food. Rubbing her eyes and repeatedly blinking, in case she had heard incorrectly. Lydia gave Jubilee a gentle nudge, but she didn't stir.

"Jubilee?" Lydia called softly.

Jubilee opened her green/brown, hazel eyes and smiled up at her.

"Did you say food? I am so hungry," she said slowly sitting up then leaned back on her hands to support her as she looked around. Then she saw the picnic laid out before them. "It must be the cherubs," Lydia decided, biting into a piece of fresh bread.

"Mm. The bread is still warm. It's funny bread, though. It's only the size of my hand and flat, not like the sliced bread we have at home," Jeremy pondered.

"Who cares? It tastes wonderful," Sam pointed out.

Their hands all reached together into the baskets and pots to take the food.

"I hope they bring food every day," said Joel with his mouth full. He turned to look at big brother Jeremy asking, "Is the water-skin still full, Jeremy?"

Jeremy passed the water-skin and they each drank from it. After they had eaten all they could, Lydia carefully packed together what was left, folding it into a scarf she had scrunched up in her pocket. However, as she tied the knots, the food faded from her hands. It disappeared![33] She looked at the place where the food had been and waved her hands around to look for it, but it was most definitely gone!

"It's all gone. Oh, dear. I wanted to keep it for later in case we get hungry again," Lydia muttered, concerned.

---

33 Exodus 16:19-20 cf. *'no-one is to keep any of it until morning'* **Meaning:** – [God will provide for us each day]. N.B.C. – We need 'to demonstrate our faith in God's provision.'

Jubilee knelt beside her and took hold of her hand. "Don't worry, Lydia. God will provide. I know He will; let's have faith," she said, smiling at Lydia, to encourage her.

Jubilee could tell Lydia still felt a little nervous. "Perhaps we ought to read the *'Book of Mirrors'* before we leave here?" she suggested.

"Exactly!" said Jeremy and Joel together, making the rest of them laugh at Lydia's surprise face at the quick dual agreement.

They gathered in a circle around Jubilee. She said, "I have a feeling, Lydia that we are going to need your broken looking glass today."

Her voice trailed off as she closed her eyes and thought of Jaycee. She had barely furrowed her eyebrows when the book appeared on her lap. Her eyes glisten as she looked down at it. When Jubilee opened the book, it showed Jaycee talking to a royal official. The man looked very sad and seemed to be pleading with Jaycee.

He said, "I heard that you had come back to Galilee from Judaea. Everyone is talking about you and the miracles you have done in Jerusalem.[34] Tell me, are they true?" the man asked.

Jaycee stopped, putting a gentle hand on the man's arm, and nodded. The man continued, "the Galileans are greatly impressed by the reports of signs you performed in Jerusalem. We know you are a teacher who has come from the God King. Rabbi, my son, is very, very ill; my servants have told me that he is dying and that there is no other way. Please, I have come to you to beg you to save him."

The man dropped his head as tears trickled through the dust on his cheeks.

---

34   N.B.C. – 'In Jerusalem… Jesus was not well received.'

'The Galileans were clearly greatly impressed by the reports of signs performed in Jerusalem at the Passover' (cf. 2:23) **p.1035**

N.B.C. cf. – *'The words of v 48 are addressed to the Galileans as a whole,'* p.1035

"And I know," said Jaycee, "that you are an officer in the service of King Herod Antipas and a powerful member of the Jewish Sanhedrin. You sit on the ruling council."[35]

The man looked up into Jaycee's eyes.

After a moment of silence, Jaycee gave him an unexpected answer. "You Galileans come to me only for the excitement of signs and miracles, like a magic show, coming to your towns, to entertain you, but you have no faith."[36]

There was mercy in Jaycee's eyes and righteousness. He showed a little of the same kind of anger He had shown with the cheating merchants in the temple courtyard.

He continued, exclaiming, "You think that I am self-taught. You wonder how I know such things because I was not taught in your Temple;[37] yet you call me rabbi as if I was a Jewish teacher of Israel!"

Jaycee waited for a few moments then seemed to calm down. Then He spoke gently with deep feeling, to the waiting man. He said, "You, who are a teacher of Israel, I tell you the truth, no one can see the kingdom of God unless he is born again of water and spirit.[38]"

His words rang in the man's ears as Jaycee looked at him. The man was visibly shaken by these words because he did not know the meaning of 'water and Spirit.'[39] The watching children could see his surprise as he seemed to think, 'I might not see the kingdom?' All Jews expect this. 'We are his chosen people, and if we follow his laws given to Moses, then we will see God. Won't we?' Blinking, as he tried to

---

35   John 4:46. 'A royal official whose son lay sick in Capernaum.

36   John 4:48' 'Unless you people see miraculous signs and wonders," Jesus told him, "you will never believe."

37   John 7:16 – 'My teaching is not my own. It comes from Him [my Father] who sent me...'

38   John 5:3 – 'The... paralysed' [in spirit are waiting to be saved but their souls are sick – they need to repent and say sorry for their mistakes and hurting others].

39   Meaning: – [water is a symbol of man – red wine is the symbol of God's Holy Spirit.]

74

cope with the pain in his heart, he wondered if he had to change the way he thought about things. He knew, however, that Jaycee was the only chance he had of saving his son.

So he said, "Sir, please, come with me—before my son dies."

He raised his head to look into the eyes of his Saviour.

Jubilee turned to Lydia, her eyes welling up with tears, her bottom lip wobbling as she softly sobbed. Lydia reached up and wiped a tear from her grubby cheek then they both turned her head to see what would take place next. Jaycee felt the man's anguish and the truth of who he was stirring in his heart, bringing the beginning of the nobleman's faith.

Jaycee's voice filled with love and compassion as he spoke his words of power, "You may go. Your son will live."

The man looked astonished at these simple words. He didn't know how to react to the authority in Jaycee's voice. Then the man broke down sobbing with relief. "Thank you, Rabbi," he whispered knowing in his heart that his son would live.

For a moment, he stared at Jaycee hesitating because he knew that he was the true teacher of Gods law. It seemed to the watching children that the man felt he had a vision of his son well and strong with his arms extended for a hug. The man suddenly smiled up at Jaycee with a look of profound relief. He nodded his thanks, too overcome to speak. Up until then, perhaps his belief in being saved had been no more than a kind of magical belief. When faith came to him; it acted rapidly.[40] The nobleman immediately turned around and began to run back to his home and his son. Jubilee closed the cover of the book on her lap and again it disappeared.

Joel spoke first, eagerly asking Lydia, "Does that mean that the boy is going to live here on earth or in the God King's world?"

---

40   N.B.C. page 1035 – *'when faith came it acted rapidly'.*

"I don't know," she replied quietly wiping away her tears. "Perhaps we can find out from the broken looking glass," suggested Jubilee.

Lydia quickly turned to face the little ones in their confusion; in the moment of the passion of the father for his son, she had completely forgotten about her looking glass. It moved in her pocket. Quickly, she pulled back the zip. Reaching, into her pocket, she tried to pull it out quickly, but it became very hot, singing her skin, making her drop it on the ground. She immediately bent down pick it up, with great care. Everyone froze in anticipation, wondering if the glass had received any more damage. They slowly gathered around her, fearful as she opened it. The shining metal of the open case was still warm. Everyone held their breath.

"It looks alright," whispered Lydia.

"Maybe the power of the wonderful thing Jaycee has just done for the nobleman, saved it?" said Jeremy quietly, who understood the power of things. They all sighed with relief.

"We need to ask a question otherwise nothing will come," suggested Sam.

"Why was Jaycee cross with the nobleman?" Jubilee asked.

A picture of a group of Sanhedrin appeared in the half of the mirror. The high priests, elders and wise men were arguing about the miracles Jaycee had been doing. Most of them thought that Jaycee should be stopped. 'Who does He think he is?' They thought. They had not trained Him, and yet the people went to Him instead of going into their Temple, and they were losing the money the people gave them! In the middle of the group of Sanhedrin priests, the children saw the nobleman who came to Jaycee. He looked sad and kept quiet, not joining in the conversations.

"Oh look, there's the father, but why is he not telling the others that he believes in Jaycee?"

"I don't know but have a very strong feeling that these men are going to do Jaycee huge harm one day," said Lydia.

"Oh, o, o no...," Jubilee and Joel both whimpered at her words.

Sam placed his hands on the little one's shoulders saying, "It looks to me as if Jaycee is aware of all these things that are happening.

"The struggle between them seems to be a struggle between good and evil for power," Jeremy suggested.

"You mean they have a political problem?" questioned Lydia.

"What's a poli...ty...tic...", asked Joel.

"Political problem," said Sam helping him.

"It means they want to keep their power in the temple. Jaycee is a problem to them," Jeremy lectured.

"I know why!" exclaimed Joel, his eyes filled with joy and confidence. "It's because the jars told us that Jaycee is God's Son, which means He is powerful and can do things the Jewish leaders can't do?"

Then he gave a double nod of satisfaction at his knowledge.

"You amaze me at times, Joel," said Jeremy. "How do you do it?"

Joel shrugged his shoulders, "I'm just smart, that's all!"

The girls burst out laughing and the atmosphere relaxed.

"Can't those priests save people from dying then?" asked Jubilee, looking solemn.

"I don't think so," replied Sam, shaking his head at his little sister.

"Well then," said Joel, his face lighting up with another bright idea. He pointed to the men in the looking glass. "Maybe they should go and talk to the jars?" This time, they all laughed at his innocence.

Sam, who was now deep thought said, "I reckon that the Jews, elders and the rest of them had better start listening to what Jaycee says and realize who He is!"

"They won't because Jaycee, wasn't taught by them. They're very stubborn, aren't they?" concluded Lydia.

"The second jar told us that Jaycee's dad taught Him to make things with wood when He was a boy," Joel said, nudging Lydia to remember.

"That's right," she said, because he was being taught to work and to provide for himself and perhaps one day his mother, Mary.

They were quiet for a few moments while they each tried to understand who was Jaycee's father. As usual Joel's next question showed how mixed-up he was. "So he has a Spirit father as well?"

"We all do," confirmed Jeremy.

"Does that mean we are like the Transformers then?" he asked, clapping his hands together with glee. "I've always wanted to be one of those. Maybe we are going to transform ourselves into...into—" Joel was interrupted.

"Don't get carried away, Joel. I'm sure we will understand before too long. So, where are we going? Back to Galilee?" Jeremy asked Lydia and Sam.

"Looks like it," Lydia asserted.

"Come on, let's get going. I want to see the man meeting his healthy and happy son."

They felt a breeze building up; the wind was getting stronger by the minute. Then they noticed the land in the distance was getting hazy.

"What's happening over there? The sky is going a funny yellow colour," said Sam, pointing into the distance as he rose up onto his knees to see it properly.

They all stopped to squint and stare, as the palm tree tops slowly disappeared in the clouds of dust. No one spoke for a few moments as they gazed in bewilderment at what was happening.

"I think...it's a sandstorm and it's coming this way," warned Jeremy. "And it looks as if it's going to be a big one."

Sam quickly climbed the fig tree to see further and estimate how much time they had left.

"Quick! Where can we go to protect ourselves?" said Lydia, desperately looking around and holding the children close to her.

Sam picked up his staff and held it firmly to his side. Jeremy picked up Joel and held him over his shoulder. Lydia grabbed Jubilee. Before any of them realized the powerful sandstorm suddenly swept them up into the air, carrying them up and up like feathers, floating in the wind. The sand was so dense that they couldn't see each other as they swirled around and around. Finally, the winds weakened, and they flopped onto a dune covered in rolling bushes of weeds and sitting camels, who were happily munching away as if all this was quite normal.

"And who are you?" asked the first camel, whom Jeremy and Joel had just missed landing on her. She spoke in a smooth, slow judgmental voice while giving them a haughty look.

"But there's sand all over the place!" exclaimed Jeremy in surprise. "And who are you to get haughty with us?" asked Jeremy as he helped Joel to sit up and began brushing him down.

The camel slowly looked them up and down as if there was a bad smell under her nose. Then she just fixed a superior glance on them and waited for an explanation. A second camel's head appeared in the middle of a cloud of dust, looking as if it were floating without a body. This camel had long dark eyelashes, which she fluttered at the first camel.

Joel heard the voice coming through the swirling sand and thought that someone else was near them. Looking up he was surprised, "You're a camel!" he said, his eyes wide with excitement now leaning back on his hands in the warm fine sand.

"This one's smart, isn't he?" said the first camel sarcastically. Closing her eyes in disgust slowly saying, "We are camels of the highest quality, dear," looking now at the second camel who snorted then half closed her eyes in approval of this comment.

MAUREEN – the Haughty Camel

"What are they doing sharing our space?" asked the second camel. Her body began to appear as she realized they were human children that caused her to turn her head away from these lower beings.

Thump. Lydia landed on the sand a few feet away from the second camel, followed by Jubilee with another thump. They both rolled down the bank of the steep sand, ending up behind Joel.

"Oh, that hurt," said Jubilee, trying to brush the sand from her face and hair making her ponytail spraying sand everywhere.

"They can talk!" said Joel, pointing at the camels, his mouth agape.

"Oh no, not more of them," said the first camel. "This is the first time I've seen it raining humans, dear. Something big must be about to happen."

Suddenly, Sam crash-landed on the dune, holding his staff above him which hit both camels on their noses. They yelled, shook their heads rapidly while blinking their watering eyes in stunned dismay.

"It is raining humans. I've heard of raining cats and dogs, but this is just too much for us, dear. I think we need to move away!" the first camel complained to the second. Sam apologized profusely to the camels, which seemed to pacify them.

"I'm sorry, so sorry; I didn't know you were there," Sam said. He put the offending staff down and held his hands together.

"Snivelling helps," commented the second camel.

The first camel, still shaking her head, nodded in agreement as she asked haughtily, "Are there any more of you?"

"No, no," said Sam, "We were 'minding our own business' when the sandstorm came and... and..." Sam shrugged his shoulders and looked towards Jeremy for help.

Lydia had had enough. "You don't have to justify yourself, Sam. We didn't do it on purpose," she explained to the camels.

"Is that so?" drooled the second camel.

"Yes," said Lydia, "Sam has already said sorry."

The look of disdain remained on the camel's faces making Sam feel very small.

"Don't let them belittle you, Sam. We are as good as them. In fact, we're better," Lydia concluded righteously raising her chin in opposition.

"Is that so too?" said the first camel, still looking down her nose at all of them.

"Oh, for goodness sake!" said Jeremy, taking a step between them. "What are your names?" he commanded. Both of the camels their eyes and looked away in disgust as if they didn't care.

"Mine is Jeremy, this is Lydia, this is Joel, this is Sam and—"

"Hello, dear. My name is Maureen," drawled the first camel in a low, smooth voice as Jubilee smiled up at them.

"I am Hazel. What's your name?" drawled the second camel in an even lower, silkier voice to Jubilee.

Outperformed by Hazel, Maureen looked away with a snooty expression.

"I'm Jubilee," she said, smiling up at them. Maureen shot Hazel a glare.

Lydia, exasperated at the competition between these two female animals, said, "For goodness sake—"

Jeremy interrupted her, holding his hands up. "Not now, Lyd... we need to find out where we are and how to get out of here."

The dust had been settling while they had been talking; they could now see three more camels. Lydia quickly realized that Jubilee had the best chance of getting help from these camels. She winked at Jubilee as she moved over to sit down beside her young sister.

She whispered in Jubilee's ear, "Can you ask them to take us to Cana in Galilee where the nobleman lives?"

Jubilee looked into her sister's eyes and nodded, accepting the challenge. "I'll try, but will they know how to get there?"

Maureen raised her nose and eyebrows, snorting sharply through her large bruised nostrils and said, "Know? Know? I know how to solve everyone's problems because I'm so much smarter."

The other camels became interested in the developing action.

"Yes," said Jubilee, winking at Lydia, "I realized that as soon as I saw you."

"You did, dear?" said Maureen with delight, dropping her head to smile at someone who appreciated her.

"Oh, yes, she did. I did, too," volunteered Lydia, who could see that Maureen needed to be superior to everyone else, but Maureen wasn't sure about Lydia— too much competition.

The camel narrowed her eyes into slits as she lowered her head again to re-examine Lydia, deciding she couldn't trust her. Maureen turned her gaze back to Jubilee. Lydia flinched at Maureen's terribly bad breath, which made her gulp and held her breath but resisted putting her hand over her nose.

"Can I help you, dear?" Maureen smoothly turned her attention back to Jubilee, who smiled broadly in return.

"Yes, please. Can you carry us to the road going to Cana where the nobleman lives with his family?"

Maureen's head shot back in disbelief, looking at Jubilee aghast. Raising her head as high as she could, she snorted, "Carry! Carry? I don't do carry!"

Jubilee's face fell as she frantically tried to think up another tactic. Jubilee and Lydia, along with the others, were shocked by Maureen's response.

"Oh dear," said Jeremy, looking at Sam, "Now what do we do?"

Jubilee's eyes welled up with tears.

Maureen, who shocked and saw she had made a big mistake, "But the others do!" she said quickly, lowering her head a little but maintained her position of superiority.

Jubilee blinked at Maureen's sudden change of heart. Jeremy decided to jump in on this offer. He looked at Sam, gesturing for him to stand up quickly.

Jeremy said to the camel, "Great! That would be wonderful. Would you be kind enough to arrange it for us, please?" Jeremy asked, exchanging looks with Sam.

Hazel had been listening to the conversation. "I don't do carry either," she said quickly.

"Yes, you do," said Maureen with sharp authority, raising her head higher than Hazel's.

Hazel smouldered under the gaze but didn't argue any further.

"Just climb onto the other camels' backs while they are sitting down, dear," said Maureen.

She turned to face Jeremy, who held his breath and made sure not to get too close, saying, "You and the young boy will have to ride together."

"Yes! Yes! Of course!" agreed Jeremy, who would have done this anyway.

The children began to climb on the camels. They felt the strong, but soft hairs on their backs; as they settled themselves in the saddles and held on tight to the beaded ropes around the camel's neck.

Sam, speaking almost for the first time as he adjusted his staff by his side, said to his camel, "What about the man who owns you?" He looked at the tent not far from them.

Hazel decided to answer. "Him? Oh, the owner will still be asleep when we get back. He's old, and he needs to sleep a lot, you know. That suits us," she snorted spraying the air with fine spit.

Before another word was said, Maureen led the camels away, her hips slowly and gracefully swinging from side to side with ease, in a superior manner. She carried nothing herself.

"Wow!" said Joel, "This is just brilliant!"

He grinned at Jubilee, who grinned back but didn't feel too sure of the swaying forward and back motion. Jeremy held on to make sure Joel didn't fall off with the unusual rocking movement. He imagined it was like being in the saddles of drunk sailors after a good night out. Slowly, in a line following Maureen, they travelled along a smooth, fresh track for what seemed like hours and hours. They were now tired and began to slump in their saddles as the camels plodded and on and on.

"Look," said Sam suddenly to everyone.

Riding on the second camel behind Maureen, he had seen dust in the distance rising on the road in front of them.

"Maybe it's the nobleman and his men on their donkeys."

The camels quickened their pace to join them. The soft pads of their large feet plodding on the hardened track made them all bounce up and down even more.

"Wow. It's getting busy here; like the roads back home— almost a traffic jam," joked Lydia as she held on to her camel's neck craning her head around to see the boys.

Their tired bodies jerked and swayed on the hard cloth woven saddles as the camels rushed forward to catch up. Then they saw men running towards them. As they came nearer, they could see that they were waving their arms wildly in the air, shouting and leaping. Their actions made clouds of dust, in the hot late morning sun; like a circus of clowns, performing and full of joy.

The shouts that came from the servants became clearer. "The boy lives; he lives! He is saved! It is wonderful! We have never have seen such life in him!" they exclaimed.

The nobleman swung his leg over the donkey's head as he jumped off, grinning as widely as the rest of his group. His servants threw themselves on their knees with combined exhaustion and delight at carrying the wonderful message to the boy's father. All of them spoke and shouted the news at the same time, their head coverings falling off as they ran.

Immediately the father, his face concerned and intrigued, asked, "At what time did this happen?"

Next Page 87

Both cherubs fell over laughing as they rolled around holding their stomachs. "They want to know…. Ha, ha, ha!"

"The new temple… Ha, ha, ha!" Bumper suddenly stopped and took a stern stance in mid-air. "You have met the new Temple!" he said with exasperation and his fists on his hips as he leaned forward to make the point. "That's Jaycee! Don't you know anything at all? He is the living law; The Word, don't you know!"[28]

Each child's face showed confusion thinking, how could Jaycee be the new Temple? He's not made from stone, hollow and cold. Suddenly, there was a large puff of pink smoke, and the cherubs were gone.

"Well, it looks like we have new friends and an awful lot to learn," Jeremy said, letting out a huge sigh, as though he'd been holding his breath for the entire conversation.

"And," said Sam grinning to Jeremy and Lydia, "there has been the second sign!"

"What do you think it was?" asked Lydia.

"It has to be that God's Temple must be kept clean," Sam reasoned.

"Because that's where God lives!" explained Joel, catching on.

"That's what Jaycee was doing; he was cleaning out the evil in the temple!" Jubilee chimed in.

"Because it's sacred," Sam finished with a smile.

"One day, there is going to be a new Temple for everyone," he finished, not feeling too sure about the words he heard himself say.

Back to Page 70

---

28   **John 1:2** – [*The Word*- later called Jesus] '*was with him* [God] *in the beginning*' (when God made the universe).

"The fever left him at lunch time yesterday, at the seventh hour past dawn,"[41] said a servant joyfully.

"Golly," Joel whispered to Jeremy behind him, "Wasn't that the time...?" He turned to look at Jubilee, who nodded at him.

The girls had already realized it. "Shhhh," said Lydia, winking at Joel. "I want to listen."

The nobleman closed his eyes, then sank to the floor to his knees in prayer and thanks. Smiling up at everyone, he said, "That was the exact hour that Jaycee told me my son would live."[42]

All the men stood in amazement as they heard this, giving each other questioning glances and wanting an explanation, but no one spoke. Then their master quickly remounted his donkey. The rest did the same, hurrying off as fast as they could. The camels followed. The donkeys' fast trot made the nobleman and his followers shake up and down furiously. Their heads bobbed about as they held on firmly to their saddles.

The Nobleman's Home

The children asked the camels to wait outside as they crept into the flower-strewn inner courtyard, where they saw the young boy sitting on his father's lap. The nobleman's tears of joy fell on the boy's soft, dark curly hair as he held his son tightly, the boy enjoying his father's arms around him. Lydia gulped, but Jubilee gripped her hand and smiled up at her. Sam and Jeremy exchanged glances of amazement and, just to join in, Joel did, too. Suddenly the boy jumped off his father's lap and ran towards them.

"Hello!" he said, bounding up to them. He seemed to be able to see all of them, even Jeremy, and Lydia. "Can you

---

41 John 4:52. *'The fever left him yesterday at the seventh hour.'*

42 John 4:53. *"Your son will live." So he and all his household believed.'*

come and play with me? I'm much better now, you know." After a short pause, he added, "Would you like to come to my party? We are all going to have lots of fun and also listen to my father tell us how his new faith helped him to believe in Jaycee—He's the Son of God, you know."

The children all nodded. The whole household, including the servants, now believed, through the wonder of their newfound faith, in the man called 'The Word'.

"That must be the Third Sign," said Sam. "Jaycee healed the boy at a distance, just by saying a word. Amazing."

He looked up into the sky as if to see that God had given him a sign.

"Yes," Jubilee agreed. "And that proves who Jaycee is," she finished, also looking up and smiling at the sky.

Chapter 7

THE HEALING OF
THE LAME MAN AND LEVI
THE STUBBORN MULE

At the Pool of Bethesda with Five Colonnades. According to John 5:1-18

WHILE JEREMY WAS TALKING TO the nobleman, the nobleman mentioned that the boy's only chance of a cure had been to take him to the pool of healing at Bethesda in Jerusalem. With the time needed to cover the distance, probably two to three days, his son would surely have died on the way there. Not only that, but everyone believed that the healing only took place when the waters stirred in the grand pool with five colonnades, near the sheep gate.

"Near the sheep gate?" said Joel, who had been listening to their conversation and interrupted them. "He needed to go to a hospital."

The nobleman looked at Joel and frowned; he didn't understand.

Joel grinned, holding his nose. "A sheep gate doesn't sound like a good place to get someone healed, does it? "Can we go there?" said Joel, nodding enthusiastically at Jeremy.

"It's quite a long way—maybe three days' ride," the nobleman argued waving his hand to the side in disagreement.

"But whatever you decide to do," he said, "I'll help where I can."

He found these children very confusing; he'd never met anyone like them before, and they certainly didn't seem to follow any of the laws that he knew. They spoke of, things he'd never heard of, and the boys and girls behaved equally with each other! He wondered from which part of Israel they came. He decided they had shown deep concern for his son, and that was important to him. He smiled saying, "You are very welcome to stay here as long as you like."

"Thank you! That's very kind," said Jeremy, running a hand through his dark hair. "We are trying to find our way home. Perhaps someone in Jerusalem can help us?"

"As you wish, but at least stay the night. Then, in the morning, after you have eaten breakfast, I can give you each a donkey and supplies for your journey," the nobleman insisted hospitably, shaking hands with Jeremy.

"A donkey to ride!" squealed Joel, elbowing Jubilee.

"Brilliant! First a camel ride and now a donkey to ride on my own, it's fun here, isn't it?"

Later, in the quiet of their room, Jubilee went to sit next to Jeremy, frowning up at him questioningly. She asked, "Shouldn't we check with the '*Book of Mirrors*' to see if we should be planning a trip to Jerusalem?"

"I was thinking that," said Sam, exchanging looks with Jeremy as Lydia was sitting with Joel, who lay on the bed, nearly asleep.

"We mustn't get side-tracked into doing what we want to do. It is very important, to us, to find the remaining signs and get home safely," said Lydia.

Jeremy looked at his little family, as they questioned the way they were planning to go. He thought for a moment, then said, "You're right." Joel was so excited. "But, I think it will be interesting to see the healing pool on our way."

Jubilee focused, closed her eyes and bowed her head in prayer, holding out her hands on her lap. The book appeared. She carefully opened it. They all stared at the image of the 'two pools with five covered colonnades located on the eastern side of the city, near the Sheep Gate, just north of the Temple Mount in Jerusalem'.[43]

"Golly, that's a small pool compared to ours in town," said Joel sleepily.

"I think it's for the sheep washing," exclaimed Lydia.

"Ooh, poo, that must be smelly," suggested Joel holding his nose.

"So what are all those poor people doing lying around all over the place and what are they waiting for?" asked Sam trying to change the subject.

"The nobleman told me that they're waiting for an angel to pass over that makes the water ripple. The first person in the pool gets healed. You have to be quick to get in first because no one knows when this is going to happen," said Sam. "Look, there's Jaycee," he pointed out.

"He's talking to that man lying on his mat," said Lydia looking at the man laying crooked and crumpled up the floor as she put her arms around the children as they watched.

"Whatever Jaycee is saying to him, the Pharisees and priests over there don't look happy at all. It's as if they are waiting for Jaycee to do something they don't like. It looks just like a trap." Lydia reasoned, not talking to anyone in particular.[44] Then the picture in the book began to vanish.

---

43   John 5:1-15 [*covered* meaning roof – shade from the sun].

John 5:2 The name Bethesda means "house of mercy or house of grace." 'Recent archaeological discoveries have again confirmed the Biblical account. There were five porches and the fifth one divided the rectangular pool into two separate compartments'- the smaller one by the fifth column for the sheep cleansing.

44   John 5:16. – 'because Jesus (Jaycee) was doing these things on the Sabbath [holy day], the Jews persecuted him'. This was [the beginning of violent opposition to Jesus, centred in Jerusalem, which would eventually explode in a capital charge (**John 11.47-53**) and Jesus's arrest and death.] **Tom Wright, John for Everyone.pt. 1**, p60.

"I would say that that is confirmation that we are still on the right track, wouldn't you two?" observed Jeremy looking at Sam and Jubilee. They nodded in agreement.

"Whatever is going to happen, those priests seemed to be getting ready to cause Jaycee trouble," said Lydia.

The following morning, five donkeys and one mule waited to carry them on their journey. The mule, named Levi, carried the supplies on the traditional yellow, green, and red woven saddlecloth with heavy leather bags of food and water. The nobleman had given each of them new clothes and scarves for their heads to protect them from the strong sun. Joel giggled at Jubilee, and she giggled back at him as he strutted around in circles wearing his new headdress.

Jeremy smiled as he watched them, while they waited for Lydia, who was always last. He felt comforted as he slung the full water-skin of pink water over his shoulder and felt it swing slightly on his hip.

When Lydia arrived, Sam held his stick high above his head and yelled out, "Are we ready for another adventure?"

Lydia raised her eyebrow, then touched her zip pocket. The little looking glass was still there. Jeremy seemed worried, and the babies held hands in sudden apprehension. The nobleman and his son waved goodbye as they set off with Jeremy leading and Sam keeping guard at the rear. They hadn't travelled very far when a large insect flew around Lydia's hair, then landed on Lydia's nose. Instinctively, she swiped at it knocking her scarf over her eyes making her pull hard on the donkey's neck rope to halt him. He leapt up in the air as if he had just had a bite on his rear end by the now angry insect. Lydia and her donkey shot off at great speed while she howled and struggled to get her scarf off her eyes. The panicked donkey shot past Jubilee, and then Joel, then Jeremy, with Sam following close behind her. Great clouds of dust rose like a sandstorm before Sam finally reached over and grabbed her reins. His larger donkey stopped, digging in all four hooves. Sam shot over his donkey's head, followed by Lydia flying over her animal's head. They landed in the dust with Sam still hanging onto the reins of her donkey.

"What happened?" said the distressed donkey to the mule, who trotted up to join them. "You were at the back; you must have seen everything."

"Oh no," said Sam. "Not more talking animals."

"That is quite normal here, don't you know?" said the mule. "Why shouldn't we talk? We've always done it, but you never bothered to learn our language."

"Well," said the mule, "If you think I'm going to travel like this all the way to Bethesda, you've got another think coming."

Everyone looked at the mule. "I have rules based on laws of Moses, don't you know, and I'm not going to change them, so there. I am staying right here."

"You jolly well are going," said Jeremy firmly as he took the mule's reins.

"I'm not YOU," said the mule firmly. "I am Levi."

Sam blinked; Lydia couldn't believe it and the babies began to giggle.

"And I'm Esther," said Lydia's donkey shyly as she went to stand beside Levi. Lydia and Sam were still sitting on the floor rubbing themselves.

They turned to watch and listen to why Jeremy was struggling. "Well, I'm Jeremy, and I'm in charge of this lot. You, Levi, are going to come with us, and that's that."

Jeremy gave a strong, determined yank on Levi's rope. Levi leaned slightly backwards, his four hooves firmly planted in the dust.

Sam struggled up, on his feet, then went to help by pushing Levi's rear end. It made no difference. The mule was adamant. The girls put their hands over their mouths to hide their laughter. Joel looked at the donkey and then at Lydia and began to see the funny side of it all.

"I've never met such a stubborn mule before," said Jeremy.

"I have," said Joel. "Mum says that Dad is very stubborn because he hates having to change his mind on anything. That's right, isn't it, Jubilee?"

She nodded as she lifted the corner of her mouth to hold in another giggle.

LEVI – THE STUBBORN MULE

"The man next door is very stubborn, too," added Sam silence fell over the group. as he straightened up and put his hands on his hips.

"It's no good, Jeremy. He simply won't move." A silence fell over the group.

"What are we going to do?" asked Jubilee.

Esther moved closer to Levi, as she whispered to Lydia, "I have to tell him he's right and that he is wonderful. He's pretending to be strong, but he's frightened. He finds it very difficult to change because he's scared." Then she winked at Lydia and nuzzled her nose back into Levi's neck, saying quietly, "Will you lead the way for me, Levi? I'm scared, and you are so strong."

Levi snorted. She nuzzled him again. Lydia came over to stroke his head, saying quietly, "Let them think they are in charge, Levi, but we know it's you who knows what to do."

Levi snorted again. "Hmm, well, I'm not afraid," he said as he began to walk forward with Esther by his side. She stayed a step back, letting him take the lead.

The boys and the little ones watched in awe. Jeremy turned to Sam. "Whatever did they say to him to get him to change his mind?"

"I don't know, but we can see who's in charge here, can't we?" said Sam.

"Yes," said Joel confidently. "The girls, and—"

"Don't say another word, Joel," said Lydia quickly interrupting him, winking she said, "We need Levi to think he's in charge."

Joel looked puzzled. That evening, they all sat around a small fire Sam had made of palm fronds. Jeremy passed around the water-skin and they each drank as much as they could, enjoying the fresh bread and figs they brought with them. They would need strength for the next day's journey. Levi and Esther stood with the other donkeys, quietly munching on grass and weeds on the roadside.

"Marvellous," said Lydia, "They have the same problems we have with stubborn people back home. I never realized that people behave like that because they were afraid of change."

Jubilee slowly closed her eyes and fell asleep as the dark blue cloak of night, sprinkled with sparkling sequins, slowly covered them like a blanket, bringing peace and contentment as they each fell asleep.

Levi seemed to smile at Esther as they, too, settled down for the night; they discussed that he should warn the children of the problems that would surely come, as they got closer to Jerusalem. The Pharisees and priests held strictly to the rules and laws, from the time of Moses.

He said to Esther, "The Gentiles and Jews are not happy at the moment, you know. I have a feeling that the powerful Jewish priests want to get rid of Jaycee because He's a popular new rabbi, a teacher with new ways. He has very different ideas about changing things around here. No, they're not going to be happy, not happy."

"We don't need to look for trouble, Levi. The priests are as stubborn as you are at times, so be a good mule for me," she replied softly. Levi snorted and said nothing because he knew she was right.

The next day by noon they had arrived in Jerusalem at the 'Sheep Gate', and the pool of medicinal waters. The whole area teemed with sickly people hoping to get a cure for their long-term illnesses. Like people sad inside themselves back home, pretending everything was alright for them, walking down the high street on a rainy day, doing the week's shopping, not realizing how blessed they were. Silently, Levi and the donkeys looked around, wondering where they would wait while Jeremy and Sam took the others into the pool of magical healing.

"Everyone looks sick and unhappy; they seem to have no hope," remarked Jubilee.

Sam patted Levi as he tied him loosely to a palm tree stump, saying, "Take care of the donkeys for me." Esther trotted over to stand beside Levi.

"Good luck," said Levi. "Don't carry anything on the Sabbath. They won't like it. It will be regarded as work if you do. Use your staff as if you need it, and then you'll be able to get into the pool area."

Sam nodded as he walked away, limping slightly, to follow Jeremy.

The children walked silently past the many people begging and calling out for money. As they entered the pool area, they saw a great number of physically challenged people lying around, the blind, lame, and paralyzed.[45] Then they saw a large crowd gathering around Jaycee as he performed many miraculous signs on the sick.[46] They joined the crowd to watch what he was doing. Jaycee caught sight of a lame man. Everyone knew the man had been there for a very long time. His follower John leaned forward to tell Jaycee that he had learned that this man had been waiting for a cure for thirty-eight years.[47]

"Wow, did you hear that?" said Joel. "Thirty-eight years?"

Jubilee could see the man's dish of coins, half full, by his side. "He must have people who regularly give money to help him feed himself," she whispered to Lydia.

"What's Jaycee going to do? Is He going to heal him and make him better?" asked Joel.

---

45   **John 5:3-4** – *'The blind, the lame the paralysed'* [Sick in mind and body.]

46   **John 6:2** – *'A great crowd followed Him because they saw the miraculous signs he had performed'*.

47   **cf. John 5:6** *[He waited without action, to seek the truth – wasting his life].*

Jaycee just seemed to look at him as if thinking. After a moment or two, Jaycee spoke to the man lying on the ground. "Do you want to get well?" He asked.[48]

"That's a funny thing to ask," said Sam. "Of course he must want to get better. He can't like feeling sick all the time."

"Time?" said Joel, who had been thinking how long the man had lain there. "Thirty-eight years is about six times my age!"

Jubilee nudged him. "Shush. I want to hear what's going on."

"It seems that He is trying to get the man to say what his problem is. I mean, why can't he help himself?" asked Lydia.

"That's because he's sick, silly," said Joel.

"Yes, but sick where? In his mind or his body?" replied Lydia.

"I see what you mean," replied Sam. "Perhaps he doesn't want to get better. He isn't even close enough to the water so that he can be the first in the pool."

"Maybe he doesn't want to get to the water first. That would explain why he is still here so that he is looked after by others!" said Jeremy.

"That's not nice," remarked Jubilee.

The children couldn't understand why the man had lain there for long.

"Perhaps he doesn't realise that he's stuck in a life he doesn't like, or maybe he doesn't know how to change it," Jubilee explained.

"That's a bit deep," said Jeremy.

"Well, it must be difficult to have the courage to change things after such a long time," commented Lydia.

Jaycee spoke. "Get up! Pick up your mat and walk." The watching crowd fell silent as they waited in awe and

---

48 **John** 5:6 NIV study notes p.1571. [The man had *not asked* for help, perhaps he would lose easy money begging or maybe he had lost the will to be cured?]

expectation. So the man stood up, picked up his mat and walked, just like that!

"Wow" said Joel, "Jaycee didn't even touch him. How can he be healed?"

"Jaycee only needed to speak a word for him to be better," said Jeremy.

"That's amaz…," began Joel.

"Not now, not now. Let's listen," interrupted Jeremy. "This is interesting."

"Does the man know who Jaycee is? And how can he be healed if he doesn't have any faith?[49] Grandma says it's important to have faith because that's the mobile phone in our heads to talk to God," said Lydia.

"Golly, look how well he walks, even carrying his mat. I am surprised that his legs are not a bit wobbly after lying down for so long," said Sam.

"Now that's a miracle," said Jeremy as he watched in amazement. The man happily walked away, telling everyone excitedly what had just happened.

"Imagine being able to have the power over sickness,"[50] commented Lydia. "Today is the Sabbath— a holy day! Remember what Levi said? The Jewish Pharisees won't like this at all. No, not at all."

Jaycee slipped away into the crowds; John and his friends followed.

"I think it's time to get back to Levi and the others," said Jeremy. "Several people here look shocked. It's against their laws to carry anything on a Sabbath. Remember what Levi said? It's regarded as working!"

---

49 **Mark 5:34** – *'He said…your faith has healed you, go in peace and be freed from your suffering'*

50 **Mark 2:1-12 cf.–** *'When He saw their faith He said to the paralytic "Son, your sins are forgiven."* [Symbolic of turning to God through faith.]

[The prophet Isaiah envisioned some 850 years before 'Jesus/Jaycee' came to earth that he would perform miracles and heal people – **See Matthew 8:17; 12: 18-21; Luke 4: 18-19**]

"That's just plain silly," said Sam.

"I know, I know, but the man is carrying his mat as well as being healed. We don't want to get mixed up in any trouble, do we?"

The children simply couldn't understand the whole thing. They wished they had someone to explain it all to them. The looking glass in Lydia's chest pocket began to jump. "Uh-oh! I think we have to stop."

"But we can't—not here," said Jeremy, "Too many people seem to be looking at us. Let's just get back to Levi and the donkeys and get out of here." A pink flash shot across in front of Levi, making him jolt to a halt. "Now what?" he yelled. "Don't panic! It must be the cherubs."

"Now we have angels!" exclaimed Levi. "Do they talk as well?"

"Yes. And if it is the cherubs, that means that we are in imminent danger," said Jeremy, looking around.

A group of men, who seemed to be priests, were beginning to walk towards them. "Didn't we see all of you with Jaycee in the pool area?"

"We thought you all looked different. You're not from around here, are you?" asked another.

"Err, no," hesitated Sam. Turning to Lydia, he whispered, "How can we tell them we are from another dimension?"

"Arrest them," snapped the man who looked the most important. "You were carrying a stick; I saw you. The law says that's forbidden."

They knew that they were in imminent danger. Jubilee's face had gone white with fear. Sam's stick suddenly lit up as it turned into the sapphire sword, a bright blue beam coming from its tip. Instinctively, he swung it around in the air, covering them in a large pink bubble. The priests blinked. So did the others watching the scene develop.

"Where have they gone?" said one man.

"Did you see them go?" asked another.

"I've gone blind," said another. "I-I can't see. What's happening?"

"That's very simple," said a small voice. "You were blind before, so what's the difference?"

"Thumper!" yelled Joel.

"Hello," said Bumper as he flew past, smacking into Joel's back. Joel looked up from the floor, where he had landed inside the bubble. "Looks like we got here just in time," the cherub said.

"Oh, we are so glad to see you two. How did you know we needed you?" asked Lydia.

"It was in Sam's heart; his love for all of you filled his thoughts, lighting his sword and calling us. Simple!" relied Thumper.

"How could the angry men see us?" asked Lydia.

Thumper shrugged his shoulders. "Well, remember I told you, you are beginning to blend in with the essence of the time warp. You'll blink in and out because your reception still isn't too good. There will be times when you feel intense emotion and, well, then they can see you."

"Oh, for goodness sake," said Jeremy, "All I want is for us to get out of here."

Bumper chipped in to explain as he came to a stop in mid-air. "We can do that for you, but I'm afraid that the animals can't come with you. We don't transport mules and donkeys, because they can find their way home," said Bumper.

Lydia gasped, Jubilee began to cry, and Joel stamped his feet. Jeremy and Sam couldn't believe this; the angry priest were almost on them?

"We need time to say goodbye to them, don't we? They are our friends, and they've brought us all the way here," said Lydia, also standing her ground with Joel.

The cherubs looked at one another. Another quick flash of Sam's sword and time flipped backwards. They were back just leaving the pool area. Instinctively they all began to run back to Levi and the donkeys.

They had just enough time to hug their animal friends telling them, "We have to go, now." Levi and Esther nodded, they understood. "Take care we will make sure to see you all again. You'd better leave now too. Get home as safely as you can." Finished Lydia and Jubilee. Then Lydia grabbed the little ones as they were whisked away in the now floating bubble.

They landed in the branches of an enormous tree, high on a hilltop. It was so big that they couldn't see the ends of it. Jubilee couldn't believe her eyes. The treetop looked like an enormous mansion with many, many rooms. The smaller branches and leaves filled in the spaces between branches, making the floor seem never ending, like a huge field in a woodland.

"A tree house. How wonderful," exclaimed Lydia feeling more peaceful and grateful to be away from the angry priests. She grinned with relief, as she looked around at this place of peace and wonder. Sam and Jeremy were also thrilled as they stood in wonder staring around in disbelief.

"We're just like the Robinson family, stranded on a desert island tree with sky all around us like a huge sea." "You'll be safe here for the night," grinned Thumper. "This is a very special place. It's called the Tree of Life." [51]

"Er, isn't that supposed to be in God's garden?"

"That's right," giggled Bumper. "I don't bump into anything anywhere here. It's just wonderful."

They flew off into the branches high above the children's heads.

For a moment, the children all looked at one another. They were shocked by what happened, and still surprised that Jaycee had healed the lame man, by only saying a few

---

51 **Genesis 2:9 – Meaning: –** [Giving life, **without** death, to those who eat its fruit – (by following Christ.)]

words, and without even touching him. All this in the midst of the stubborn Jews, like Levi, who couldn't—or wouldn't—believe that Jaycee was God's Son, the Messiah.

The looking glass in Lydia's pocket began to shake again. She grinned. "Time to ask questions and find the answers."

"But I'm thirsty," whispered Joel.

"Me, too," said Jubilee.

Jeremy took the water-skin from his shoulder. "Pass it around; let everyone have a drink."

They nodded as they moved closer to Lydia to see what the looking glass would tell them. Words appeared on the glass. Those who have lost sight of what is truly important—more important than the law—justice, mercy and faithfulness,[52] means that— The cracked glass was blank. "Oh, no, we can't see anymore," said Lydia.

"What does that mean?" asked Jubilee.

"It means being fair, kind, and truthful," replied Lydia.

The glass flickered, then it displayed the words, 'Beware of the Blind Guides.'

"Is it talking about people who don't know what they are talking about, who can take us the wrong way?"

"Yup. Exactly," chipped in Sam. "Like some people we know back home, who are determined to make you live the way they think you should; so we walk about feeling miserable all day."

Joel thought about this for a moment. He loves computers, Gameboys, X-boxes and everything like that. "Well, I think God gave each of us a different microchip in our brains that make us all different. Simple," he said slapping his sides with his hands.

Lydia looked at him, "That could be true because you are hopeless at making your bed properly or putting your things away, but you are great at helping mum with the TV

---

52 **Matthew 23:23** cf. *'woe to you teachers of the law'* [those pretending to observe the law].

controls, and, I don't like anyone controlling me either!" Grandad says he followed his dream and became a top man in the Navy. Everyone has the freedom to express themselves and make their way in life.

"Yes, and Grandma told me about that once," said

Sam. "She said something about those who would pick a gnat out of their food, but swallow a camel.[53] She said that means that they don't want to see anyone else's point of view, they just use the law to keep control of things their way."

"You mean like the camel Maureen?" suggest Joel. "I wouldn't want to swallow her, would you?"

They all burst out laughing at the idea, lightening the atmosphere as they began to relaxing. The mirror flickered again; this time they saw half of a book of law.

"And what does that mean?" asked Sam. "Maybe Jaycee is the new law," said Jeremy smiling. They all turned to look at him. Maybe the written Law of Moses was the first part, and Jaycee is the new living law?" he suggested. No one spoke for a few moments; even Joel was quiet.

"Carrying a mat on the Sabbath being against their law seems very silly to me," said Jubilee. "What's more important than the man being healed by Jaycee, even if it is his Holyday? It's pretty obvious to me who we should believe. Don't you think so, Lydia?"

She still wasn't sure, she had to think about all this a little more.

"It also seems they have interpreted their traditional laws all wrong. It's about time they updated them," Jeremy concluded, remembering his studying this at school.

"Well, I suppose I agree," said Lydia remembering a few things she had heard at school. "The miracle we just saw proves that Jaycee is very powerful because He only used a

---

53 **Matthew 24:24.** (A.J. Köstenberger p.96) 'False prophets... who perform great signs and miracles to deceive'.

word. I mean, He didn't even touch the man, but He gave him a brand new life."

A soft calm settled about them as they all considered this. Jubilee, now feeling sleepy, looked up from where she now lay, listening to them all and beginning to worry what was going to happen next.

"I know the answer," said Sam after a few more moments of thought. "They didn't need to jump into the pool of water when it ripples to get better; that's just making excuses not to change things. Jaycee must be the real thing, he's the one who gives new life, through the living water, you know, the right things to think about, to solve problems.[54]"

He turned over and fell asleep covering himself with a thick blanket of leaves. The others did the same. Lydia carefully put the looking glass away, still stunned by her brother's comments. Jubilee closed her eyes, also thinking about Sam's precise words. Shaken.

Jeremy thought he ought to pay more attention when they next looked into Jubilee's Book. He whispered to Sam, "We didn't look in the *'Book of Mirrors'* to see what is going to happen next. We should be ready for tomorrow."

"Hmm. No, we didn't, but we do know that today's miracle was the Fourth Sign proving Jaycee is the Son of the God King. Only three more to go, so maybe tomorrow will bring the Fifth Sign. I wonder where that will be and, more to the point, how will we get there, now that we don't have the donkeys."

Thumper and Bumper sat on a branch high up in the top of the tree as if sitting on the beams of a cathedral, looking down on the children in the pews of a church. Thumper said, "I'm a bit worried about getting them through the City of Self."

---

54 **Meaning:** – [when we live **in/with** Jesus we are swimming around in the guiding love of God.]

"Me, too," said Bumper. "We haven't done this before—and it's a long way back to Galilee from Jerusalem."

Chapter 8

JAYCEE BANISHES FEAR AND THE CATERPILLAR'S SCARLET THREAD

The Forest of Lost Souls and the City of Self

A GENTLE BREEZE BLEW OVER their faces, and awakened them to the scent of sweet young leaves, a little like new mown grass at home. Jeremy and Sam were the first to wake up. They nodded to each other, and then crept to the edge of the branches and peered down below them in wonder. Everything looked far away quite normal, until they realized that the people still looked like tree trunks topped with a few sprigs of green flapping as they moved. Each one hiding inside themselves, reflecting an image showing the way they wanted to look at everyone else. It was all confusing to watch.[55]

Lydia woke up. Blinking and worried, "Where are the cherubs?" she asked, feeling she would be happier if they were watching over them. Someone hiccupped; leaves fluttered down on them.

"Look out!" said a small voice. "You're falling off the bran—"

---

55 **Meaning**: – [They are reflecting out/giving a false face to everyone, by pretending to be better than anyone else. Blind to themselves.]

Bumper landed beside them. "Where am I? Where am I?" He said.

"You tell us! We have no idea," Sam quipped.

"Have you forgotten how to fly?" asked Joel also waking up.

Thumper flew down to join them. "Don't worry about him; he's still in his dreams."

"Oh. Can you live in your dreams as well?" asked Joel.

"You are, aren't you?" said Thumper.

"Me?" Joel replied in confusion.

"Yes, you. You all are," Thumper said again.

Joel considered the possibility of this. He often dreamed in colour, but when he woke up, he didn't know what his dreams had been about though some bits of them did seem real at the time. Bumper could see Joel trying to sort out what he had just said.

Sam also seemed to be considering the possibility that they were all dreaming the same dream. "Is that possible? he asked Bumper, "We're all in the same dream?"

"It's a bit deep to explain now. I'll tell you later," Bumper said.

Joel decided that his tummy was more important right now. "I'm hungry," he said.

"I am, too," agreed Sam, who couldn't make up his mind about whether they were all on the same adventure in a dream.

Jubilee grinned at their usual morning banter thinking, 'Thank goodness that hunger always brings them back to reality. We're in enough trouble as it is, without more difficulties.'

Before she could say anything more, Bumper said, "Today you are going to take a journey and learn all about being hungry—but not just in your stomach." He laughed, patting his small tummy.

"How else can we be hungry then?" asked Sam, who had never thought of being hungry any other way.

Jubilee decided to speak up. "Before we start our next part of this journey, we need to see what the Book of Mirrors will tell us."

Thumper looked at Bumper and frowned. The children moved to sit together in the middle of the tree floor. Jubilee closed her eyes and placed her open hands on her lap as she asked the book come to her. It didn't. Shocked, she looked around. "What's wrong? She asked out loud.

The looking glass in Lydia's pocket began jumping and getting heated, which made her get it out as quickly as she could, but it wouldn't open. "What's going on?" she asked.

"The looking glass answers our questions; the '*Book of Mirrors*' tells you what is recorded," smiled Thumper.

Immediately the glass sprang open; they saw in the half a glass a city full of proud, angry looking people all walking with their noses held high in the air. Some had their noses so high that they couldn't even see where they were going! But something didn't seem right. A sign came into the middle of the page. It read, 'The City of Self.'

"That's odd," said Sam.

Then they looked back at the people who seemed determined to get somewhere. But where? The looking glass now changed to show them what they were about to experience. They saw people getting infuriated with each other, grabbing things they wanted out of envy and jealousy. One man pushed another man roughly to one side.

"Don't be so arrogant!" the pushed man yelled.

"You're the one who's rude!" yelled the first man.

"But you're the one who's always been jealous and envied my house."

The first man burst into a great rage, yelling, "Get out of my way! I'm much more important that you are, and I'll walk over anyone who gets in my way!"

The children watched in silence. Why did everyone seem angry and selfish? They were behaving like spoilt children each determined to go their own way, not caring at all for the needs of anyone except themselves. Their faces showed bitterness, sadness and strain as they rushed around determined to finish the tasks they had given themselves. It was obvious something was seriously wrong.

"What on earth is going on?" quietly as if thinking aloud, Jeremy said. "I can't see where they are all rushing to and from in the broken part. Why are they all so arrogant with each other?"

For what seemed like a few minutes as the children continued to watch the selfish behaviour, Joel asked, "What does arrogant mean?"

"It means that they only think of themselves and their own opinions and their idea of how to live a successful life," said Bumper softly.

"Hmmm," said Lydia. "If this is what I think it is; there will also be all kinds of other selfish things, like immorality, jealousy, hate, rage, drunkenness,

witchcraft, and everything else horrible."[56]

"What's immorality?" asked Joel softly.

"The way people act when they don't have good morals or ways of living with respect for others," whispered Lydia, trying not to miss the action on the glass.

"Oh, oh," said Joel, as he thought about respect.

"I hope we don't have to go through there. It looks awful," whispered Jubilee.

"It is," Thumper sighed. "And, yes, you have to walk through the 'City of Self' where no one cares about anyone but themselves."

"Oh," Joel muttered again, thinking, 'That must be what the word 'respect' means, caring about others.'

---

56 **Galatians 5:18-21** – not under the law –**Meaning:** – [they are trying to please God by only observing the law to receive salvation, which can only be obtained through redemption and the love of Christ.]

"Why do we have to go through the city?" Jeremy asked, curious about the 'City of Self'.

"Because there is no detour around the Forest of Lost Souls, they cover the whole world, that's why Jaycee has come especially for these sad and unhappy people – to save their inner self. He will show them the way out," Thumper said solemnly.

"Do you mean the part that has a force field…" hesitated Lydia, remembering that they saw theirs.

Bumper and Thumper smiled at one another, "Did He allow them to see that?"

"That's amazing if He did," replied Thumper.

The children hadn't heard this. They were still talking about people who acted as though they were 'lost'. As they watched, they each began remember people they knew that were like that back home. Is that why they were so difficult to understand? The little cherubs knew all about their difficult neighbours back home.

"Don't they know they are spiteful and horrible?" Lydia asked, out of curiosity.

"No. Like the many thistles who live in the 'City of Self'," Bumper explained.

"So we can't escape going through this place?" whispered Sam, taking Joel's hand to stop him from pulling up the leaves beneath them who no longer seemed able to cope with this.

"No. The only route goes straight through the middle. Oh—and we can't come with you," Thumper informed the group.

"Why not?" asked Jeremy, suddenly concerned.

"Because each one of us has to walk this journey alone unless you walk with Jaycee in your hearts," the cherubs explained.

A wave of revelation washed over all the children as they realized the task ahead would be much harder than they anticipated.

"But we know Jaycee," exclaimed Sam.

"It's one thing to know who He is, but another thing to live with Him," Bumper explained truthfully.

"Do you mean He's, like, being our best friend all the time, even when we don't know it?" Joel asked still pulling leaves off the floor beneath him with his other hand.

"You've been drinking that pink water again, haven't you?" grinned Bumper, putting his hands on his hips. The children fell quiet as they exchanged glances.

"I am not looking forward to this experience," said Jeremy, sighing and flicking the end of his nose.

"Me neither," said Jubilee, cuddling closer to Lydia. The page in the glass faded, and then it closed.

"But...but...how do we get through them and what is on the other side?" asked Jubilee, her little face full of worry.

"Look in your hearts and you will know how to behave. Remember, these people are like the trees; they can't move out of their habits because their roots are too firmly sunk into what they believe which convinces them they know all the answers. They say 'I don't need God, I can manage,' so they feel safe acting in the only way they know. In a way, they are blind and trapped, but they'd never admit it." Thumper said sadly.

"Can't Jaycee help them?" asked Joel, sauntering back into the conversation.

Thumper smiled. "Yes, He can, but they have to choose to go to Him. It doesn't work the other way around. We have a very safe and fun way for you to continue this journey. Here—hold this, Jeremy." Thumper gave him a fine thread of scarlet silk to hold.

"What is it?" he asked, peering down at the silk thread now in his hands.

"You'll see. And this is your friend, who will help you along the journey," Bumper added.

The children turned to look at who Bumper was introducing to them. Shock stunned them rigid. No one moved as they took in the creature before them. A huge caterpillar had silently crept up behind the cherub. Now he sat high upon his tail, smiling down on Jeremy though it was difficult to read his expression because he didn't seem to have a mouth, just another wrinkle.

"Hello. I'm Bomby Mori," said the caterpillar in a high squeaky voice, "but you can call me Bomby."

"Don't panic," said the silkworm, "I am honoured to be of assistance to you!"

The children's mouths all fell open as they looked up at the strange sight of the big bulbous custard coloured caterpillar. Jeremy gulped.

Bomby ignored this and continued, "I have been asked to give you a silk thread of life to keep you connected to the right path. It's very, very strong, but becomes invisible to the eye when you're down there."

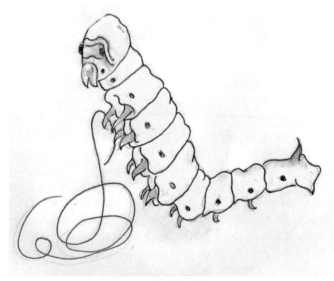

BOMBY MORI
THE GIANT SILKWORM

He nodded towards the edge of the branches and moved towards the children in a squirmy motion. Jeremy gulped again as he stared up at the large floppy creature that seemed to resemble a collapsed blancmange, or a pile of squashed pillows on top of one another. His wrinkled head sat like a pin cushion on the top.

"Oh!" said Jeremy finally.

"Don't panic, I'm honoured to be of assistance to you," said Bomby, still ignoring their surprised faces. "This scarlet silk thread will let you down to the world below [57]—a bit like abseiling," he joked, suddenly showing a huge grin at the children through the fold of his chin.

How does he know about abseiling? Jeremy wondered.

Unperturbed Bomby continued, "It will also keep you on the narrow pathway right through the city. But don't go too far off the path because I can only make it long enough for this journey. If you break it, you are on your own," he said, suddenly serious as the wrinkles on his forehead began to fall over his eyes.

Jeremy was speechless. He'd never expected anything like this, and he was very scared, but he masked it well. He had many thoughts about the near future that worried him; not just about the City of Self, but about all the new people he had met and whether or not he could trust them. Again he decided not to let the others see that he was afraid.

Bomby held out the thread and solemnly bowed his head. Smiling, he cooed, "I usually live on mulberry trees in India, where King Solomon used to buy silk." He ran out of breath and stopped for a moment before taking a deep breath. Then he said, "Of course my ancestors come from China, but these days some of my cousins live in Africa." He had puffed out all of his air again, so he stopped and took another deep breath... "I'm here on holiday to see them,

---

57 **Joshua 2:** 17-18 *'Behold, when we come into the land, you shall tie this scarlet cord in the window through which you let us down'* – [symbolic of being close to God].

114

but I'm happy to take a break to help you." He then held his middle bulge, where his stomach must be, and grinned down at Jeremy, who still didn't speak. So he continued, "I know I look frightening, but you should see me when I change into a moth. I will be so beautiful," he said as he lifted his tiny eyes, to look above him in wonder. "I'll be all white with soft, feathery wings." He seemed to think for a while and then said, "A bit like you will be when you get to heaven." He nodded his head so much in confirmation of this that he nearly wobbled over. Jeremy had to jump up to hold him upright until he stopped quivering.

"Are you alright?" Jeremy quickly asked.

"Oh, thank you, dear boy," Bomby said kindly.

Jeremy felt Bomby's soft skin, warm and smooth like his grandmother's soft leather gloves. Surprise made him smile as he stepped back; the caterpillar wasn't slimy as he had expected.

Bomby looked at Joel, chuckling with glee. "You can close your mouth now. I won't bite you. I'm a vegetarian, so I only eat leaves."

Joel had been thinking about him turning into a moth. He stood beside Jeremy and looked up at the magnificent creature, gulped back his fear, and said, "But…. I'm not a bug! Or a caterpillar or an insect!" he exclaimed, worried that something awful might happen to him down there.

Bomby looked surprised. The folds of his forehead skin again fell over one another. He looked down at the small boy. Then he slowly bent his soft, floppy pale yellow body down, bringing his face level with Joel to slowly examining the little boy. Joel stood very still but slipped his hand into Sam's hand.

"Aren't you? Well, you look like an insect to me!"

Sam burst into laughter at the creature's sense of humour as he pulled Joel closer, ruffling his hair.

This idea had never entered Joel's mind before, but he decided that he wasn't the odd one. "I'm not the alien here—you are!" he said adamantly clenching his small fists.

"That's funny," said Bomby, smiling, "Each of us thinks of himself as normal. I suppose we just come from different worlds, that's all."

Giggling and laughter echoed behind the children. Sam, Lydia, Jubilee, and Joel all swivelled around. Several other huge, grinning, custard-coloured caterpillars sat there on their tails, waiting to hand them their threads of life.

"Don't worry, we aren't aliens either," said the smallest one, who looked like a girl caterpillar. She smiled coyly and flapped her eyelashes. "We are the same as Bomby, and we have also worked with royalty in our time."

Thumper and Bumper managed to fly around them without crashing into anything. The cherubs firmly tied the silk cords around the children's waists.

"Right then. Off you go!" said Bomby, pushing Jeremy off the high branch of the tree.

"Wha-a-a-a-a-a—!" yelled Jeremy.

Then Bomby pushed Sam. "Wha-a-a-a-a—!" yelled Sam.

By then Lydia knew what to expect from Bomby. Angry, she stood with both feet apart and both fists up. "Don't you dare push me or Jubilee or Joel!" Jubilee was visibly shaking at the thought of being pushed over the edge.

Bomby had been enjoying himself, but the look on Lydia's face made him stop. All of his feet trampled on each other as he came to a grinding halt. "They are quite safe. Honestly! My silk is the strongest!" He gave it a firm tug to justify himself.

Lydia kept her fists up, arguing fiercely, "I don't care. Don't push!"

Then she heard her brothers' voices. "Yeah, this is brilliant! Just like abseiling. Wheee!"

They all heard their whoops of joy echoing from below them. Joel got very excited and decided he wanted to join

116

them. He got ready, shifting his weight nervously from one foot to the other, then jumped off on his own.

Jubilee squealed, and Lydia grew white as paper. They both felt sick, terrified at their little brother falling to…. Thumper and Bumper came to stand by the girls.

"He's alright," they said together. "Really!" They gave the girls a few moments to gather their thoughts and understand that Joel was going to be alright.

"Would you like us to go down with you?" said Thumper gently. "It only takes a little faith."

"Yes, please," said Jubilee quickly. She turned to look at Lydia, smiling and putting on a brave face. "Come on, big sister, I'll hold your hand as well."

Bumper said, "And we'll make sure you go down really slowly?"

Lydia nodded. Carefully, and closing their eyes, they stepped off the treetop and floated, their silken cords dangling above them. Lydia began to smile, and soon they were laughing, but they kept holding hands.

The City of Self [58]

Jeremy and Sam waited for them as they gently landed on a narrow path. Thumper and Bumper had vanished, so they were on their own now. It was up to them. ——————

"That was just brilliant!" said Joel, jumping up and down as he ran to meet his brothers. He sped down the hill tumbling playfully into Sam's arms.

"Can we do it again?" he asked, his large grey eyes beaming up at his brother, who laughed.

"No!" said Lydia firmly, shaking her head.

"Well," Sam started, trying to motivate them to move. "We might as well get on with our journey."

---

58 2 Timothy 3: 1-2 'But understand this that in, the last days, there will come times of difficulty. For people will be lovers of self, lovers of money, proud, arrogant, abusive, disobedient to their parents, ungrateful, unholy'.

A man came bounding up to them. "And who are you? I haven't seen you before! You don't belong here!" he exclaimed, taking a good look at them.

They turned in surprise to look straight at the man, who appeared from nowhere.

"We're...only passing through," said Sam, smiling in greeting.

"Just so long as you are. Don't think you can take anything of mine as you—pass through. Off you go," he instructed, moving them on rudely.

A crowd gathered to look at the children inquisitively. One woman with her nose in the air haughtily asked, "Where do you dreadful people come from?" She didn't wait for an answer.

Another person pushed through the crowd, saying, "They're peasants and not worth talking to."

"You don't know anything about us!" snapped Lydia in defence, frowning. "And we are much politer than you are!"

Jeremy took the lead. "Don't bother with them. Just walk away." He furrowed his eyebrows, pushing Lydia and the kids on, wanting to keep them safe. They headed towards the city centre followed by a growing mob of angry people.

"How can they be afraid of us?" whispered Jubilee.

"Let's just stick together and stay on this path. Remember, we mustn't stray off it, no matter what happens!" said Sam, holding his staff firmly in his right hand.

Ahead of them, all the people were arguing, each of them adamant that they were correct. They disputed over boundaries, money, possessions, and each other. No one smiled. The sky looked like a massive, mouldy duvet, filled with clouds of tears.

"Have you noticed that there are no flowers?" whispered Jubilee to Lydia.

"No trees either," said Sam, gazing into the distance. "Everywhere looks grey and hopeless."

"Where are the birds?" asked Lydia, searching the sky.

"Remember, this is the 'City of Self'. No one here notices anything beautiful; they are only interested in their busy lives," said Jeremy.

"How sad," said Jubilee, absorbing it all very quickly? "They all seem too busy fighting over things that will rot and turn to dust." [59]

Another group of men headed their way, looking rough and scary as if they might rob them. Jeremy knew they meant business. He quickly scanned their surroundings, looking for somewhere safe.

"Look, there's an old church building! Let's run over there and take cover, and then we can rest and decide what to do next," said Sam. They tried to look as though they were strolling down the stone path. Jeremy took the lead, Lydia held hands with the two little ones, and Sam watched from behind. As they got closer to the church door, they couldn't help quickening their pace. They wanted to get inside where they would be safe; they couldn't help beginning to run.

A booming voice said, "No one can enter unless they have the Holy Spirit with them!"

The children all stared at one another.

"Did you hear that?" asked Joel.

They all nodded. "Did the door say that Holy Ghost is in here?" asked Jubilee.

"I think so. But... well, he would be, wouldn't he!" replied Jeremy.

"How do you know that?" asked Sam, doing a double take.

"Because we couldn't get in here unless he were with us— the door said so," Jubilee pointed out cleverly.

"Golly, perhaps this church has another ghost, and it's haunted," hoped Joel, looking around in the hope of seeing one. Then he shivered.

59　**Hebrews 1:11** *'They [things of earth] will perish, but you will remain; [these things] will wear out like a garment'.*

Jubilee gasped now, out of breath from running. "Don't be silly. We are still safe with the silk cord around us!"

"The door talks!" added Sam.

"I can't cope with all this," said Lydia.

"The door talks!" added Sam.

Jubilee quickly held her hand. They heard a deep rumbling laugh. A face began to appear in the old wooden door. They were shocked and completely surprised. As they watched, the door creaked as it started to open. Without any hesitation, Lydia rushed in with Jubilee. Jeremy swiftly picked up Joel, who was still looking at the door, and swept with him hanging sideways into the church. Sam came in last; his staff held high. The door slammed shut just managing to stop the crowd as they rushed down the path towards them.

"I haven't heard such innocence in a long time," said the huge face with a broad smile in the wooden door.

"Oh no, now the door is talking to us," said Jeremy in exasperation. He struggled to recover from safely locating his family inside the church; his hands now on his hips and Joel safe on a pew bench.

The eyebrows of the face on door rose high in surprise. Then he smiled down at Jeremy.

"Don't worry, I won't let anyone enter. I'm sorry that I was so slow in opening the door, but you see, I don't often have the chance to receive guests." His voice trailed away, his face dropped in sadness as he looked at the floor. Then his face began to fade away.

"It's okay. When God closes a door, somewhere he opens a window—no pun intended," said Sam, walking forward to touch the door handle, grinning. The face immediately came back, "No one has shown me any affection for years and years and…," tears began to appear in the wood of his face.

THE SAD CHURCH DOOR

Sam was surprised and tried to comfort him by listening to his sadness. "Doesn't anyone come here to pray?" he asked, looking around warily.

The door's face lit up a little. "Yes, I have three elderly women who come here sometimes. They take it in turn to bring in a few flowers from their secret gardens, but they are too old and frail to clean and repair anything." His face returned to looking at the floor.

"We'll pray for you," said Sam, placing the palm of his hand on the rim of the beautifully engraved door panel.

"Will you? How wonderful. Prayer is very powerful, you know. My friend, the Holy Ghost will take your prayers to Jaycee's Father," he spoke convincingly.

"Will he?" asked Joel in surprise.

"Yes, that's one of his many duties, you see. I know that Sam's staff is extraordinary, it was made from a branch of my friend's tree in the forest, cedar wood isn't it. How do you think it works? How does anything else work, for that matter?" He smiled at them and whispered, "Thank you for coming here."

Then his face disappeared. Jeremy gulped back his sadness for him as he stared at the door. Sam smiled, and Lydia looked at Jubilee, who seemed to understand things like this. Sam sank to sit the floor. He looked up to the ceiling of the church and admired the stained glass, which showed 'Jesus ministering to his disciples.' "That's beautiful," he said, pursing his lips. "But it seems that the people here can't see its beauty. That's a shame."

Jeremy became confident. "I think we'll be safe here until morning, and then we'll leave before the early sunlight comes." Turning, he strolled down the aisle of the church, running a finger along the dusty pews. He started to think of for how long the building had been neglected, but then again, this is the City of Self, he reminded himself.

"Where are we going to find any food?" asked Sam, looking bewildered.

Jeremy didn't answer; he just took the water-skin from his shoulder and passed it around.

"What's the plan for tomorrow then? Where are we headed?" asked Lydia as the little ones cuddled up to her as they sat on a dry and cracked bench, exhausted after having to run to the church, for safety.

"Bumper told us we would find a way through with our hearts," Jubilee said, putting a hand to her heart.

"That means being kind to everyone we meet, then," said Sam, crossing his arms. "However difficult they are."

Everybody appears so different to the people we see back home; different fears, insecurities, worries, and sadness in their lives," said Jubilee, resting her chin in the palm of her hand. She did that a lot, sitting in a daydreaming position. "So we'll just have to be tolerant and patient. As Grandma says, 'love covers everything'."

Joel grinned. He liked Jubilee. She was always so calm and collected; he looked across at her endearingly. "Humph. That's easier said than done," remarked Jeremy, worried about leading his family through this maze.

Somehow the room began to fill with light as if the sun were shining through the dusty windows.

"I feel a bit better now," said Joel as he took a drink from the water-skin, then passed it around to the others. After they had drunk, they wandered around the inside of this forgotten house of God.

"It's like a home without a soul," said Sam quietly as he examined each empty alcove and corner. The bench seats looked old and weary used only for spider webs in the corners. The stone walls were damp as if they had been crying for a long time.

Jeremy murmured from the back of the church, "I think we should pray for this church. Don't you!"

They nodded to one another; then the others walked quietly over to a bench near the front.

Jubilee said, "I don't think anyone has prayed in this church for a long time. Maybe our prayers would breathe new life into this place of God and this city."

Joel didn't know how this was going to work. If God didn't answer their prayers, why should he listen now? So he asked Jubilee, "What difference will it make if we pray for this church?"

She replied, "Because thoughts are things. Things that God can use to change something." "Things?" said Joel.

"Yes," said Jubilee. "They are spiritual things we create by our thoughts. The Good things – 'prayers',[60] God can use to bring about something kind for someone else. See?"

"And what about the bad thoughts?"

"That is the problem," said Sam joining in.

Jeremy nodded in agreement. "Those thoughts are used by Satan, the 'Prince of Darkness'."

Lydia was listening. She hadn't heard of this before. Her boyfriend back home hadn't told her of this. She was intrigued, so she asked, "How does that affect us?"

"Simple," said Jubilee looking at the expression on her face, slowly realizing that she was beginning to understand. "We speak how we think. So, if we believe correctly, we will act properly. You see!" No answer came from Lydia. All she could think of was, 'thoughts are things' that can be used in heaven, and 'bad thoughts…'. She didn't want to think about that.

"Come on, we'll all sit here, in the front row," said Jeremy. They each closed their eyes and dropped their heads in silence.

Jubilee said, "I think we should also pray and ask for protection on our journey?"

Jeremy nodded in agreement and then led the prayers, saying, "Let us pray for the church first."

The watching door could not believe what he was hearing. Tears began to swell in his woody eyes as he watched the children in disbelief. He never thought that this was ever going to happen in his church. But no one was looking at him.

---

60   **Revelation 4 & 5** the *24 elders who represent the entire church* [of the world] (**Acts 15:6, I Chronicles 24**) are…

Revelation 5:8 *holding a harp and golden bowls full of incense, which are the prayers of the saints* – Us – our prayers are spiritual *things* used in heaven!

"The people of this city seem so sad inside themselves. Please help them to come to this Church and feel your loving presence. We ask that this lovely church be filled with joy and happiness for those who live around. May they find joy and laughter in new friendships," they prayed.

"May they come and to clean, repair and bring Your life back into this place," Sam concluded.

"And please take care of us as we learn many things walking through this forgotten place of yours," said Jubilee. They all said "Amen."

They settled and slept in the vestry where grey gowns hung in tatters. Jeremy made sure the door to the small room was closed and locked. Early the next morning, before the light of day, they quietly prepared to leave the safety of the church.

As they closed the front door, it felt warmer and somehow looked happier. The wood looked alive now than when they entered; with a fresh honey colour. As the children stood before the old front door, the face came back. Smiling broadly, he said, "You have broken a long held curse on me. I am the last elder of this church. You have released me to welcome anyone who comes here to talk to God. Your prayers are already beginning to work. Thank you!"

The children stood in silence before the shinier door, amazed at the feeling that was now coming from the once tired and cold church building. They travelled quietly down the narrow path away from the church, saving their energy for the hills they could see in the distance. As they walked past sad, neglected houses, the people coming out of their homes noticed them. The children smiled and carefully waved as if to say, 'we don't want to take anything from you, we'd like to be friendly.'

They remembered their grandmother telling them that no one knew another person's pain or what others had suffered. So they always had to be kind, even when it was very difficult. "Remember," she would remind all of them at different times. "We are not responsible for what other people do to us, but we are responsible, for how we react to them."

They walked along the dry, dusty path through the city; everywhere seemed to resemble the results of a war bombed city. Destruction and rubble lay in all directions, similar to the pictures of the Second World War that they had seen when they went to visit Granddad.

Joel quietly walked with his brothers and sisters through the devastation and desolation. He thought that these people needed someone to explain to them how to find the right path for their lives. They needed to drink lots of living water.

They found the following days hard going. They consistently tried to be patient and kind, to understand why the people were so sad and afraid. So many people were angry, hurtful, suspicious and spiteful, like the thistles in the forest, but the children didn't shout back in anger; Lydia made sure of that.

One time, Granddad had told them that God made everyone with a different sim card inside their heads. We each behave, differently because we don't all think the same way.

As Joel said, in his innocence, "If they have Jaycee inside them, then they will be able to understand each other's programs much better. That would give everyone peace, wouldn't it?"

The days seemed to stretch into weeks. They became weary, tired, and anxious. When would all of this be coming to an end? With the living water in Jeremy's water-skin, they never seemed to be hungry, which surprised them.

Lydia, wiping the sweat from her brow, she tended to Jubilee and Joel. "I'm beginning to get blisters on my feet! How much longer will we have to travel on this road?" Jubilee complained.

"I don't know," Jeremy replied honestly, giving Jubilee a sympathetic yet understanding look as if to say, some things in life are inevitable.

"This place is just terrible; it can't be right," complained, Lydia. She was fed up with this. Then the looking glass in her pocket began to wriggle.

"Uh-oh! What's happening? Oh, my glass wants me to open it." She pulled it out of her pocket and pried open the case.

They all came to stand near her. A picture of Sam's staff materialized. It said, "Hold it high and point to the sky."

Sam immediately obeyed. He stood a metre away with his feet apart, the staff turned into the sapphire that he held high above his head, pointing towards the sky. Their surroundings grew hazy; the scene before their eyes slowly changed from desolation to a lovely town filled with trees and colourful flowers. Many different kinds of birds sang happily, as they flew and played from tree to tree.

"Golly, what's happening?" asked Jubilee, anticipation rising in her voice.

"I'm not sure," said Lydia, looking down at Jubilee. "Is this real? Am I dreaming?"

Jubilee smiled and gave her a quick pinch to check. "No, not dreaming," she replied, with her big hazel eyes beaming, her relaxed face began to smile with wonder.

Lydia looked down at the glass. Amazement filled her, and she immediately understood. "This is how we see the world; the desolation here is what the sad and fearful people see because they are blind to how things can be," she said aloud.

"You mean this is all a mirage?" asked Sam, a little unsettled.

"It's the way they see it. We all have a choice how to see the world. It's not all bad?"

"Yes," said Joel. "Like when we're afraid to go to the dentist, but when we get there it isn't as bad as we had expected. You get a sticker and a sugar-free lollipop! Remember when I had to go, and I was sure that—"

"We get the message, Joel, and you are quite right," Jeremy interrupted, smiling at him.

The beautiful day slowly disappeared, leaving them back under the dull grey skies of the 'City of Self'.

"Oh, it didn't last," said Jubilee, frowning as she looked around at the returning grey, cold and dusty desolation resembling a cement quarry.

"No, but we don't have to be afraid anymore," Lydia said, bending down to hug Jubilee, who had wrapped her arms around Lydia's waist as she cried.

"What a sad place." In silence, they looked around.

"Over there—look!" said Jeremy. "A little bit of it is still here."

They all followed Jeremy's pointing finger and saw a house that still had part of its roof on in one corner.

"There's a garden with trees in it. That's amazing. Let's climb over this broken fence and spend the night there," said Joel with glee and hope.

"No. We have to stay on this path," said Jeremy, stopping him.

"It's so much nicer over there. I'm tired and fed up," said Joel, beginning to cry and stamp his feet.

Lydia had tears in her eyes as well, and Sam looked exhausted. "What do you think?" she said.

Sam shrugged his shoulders. He looked towards the green patch and thought he could see fruit hanging on the branches. Then he looked back at the little ones. "It's only just over the fence; we could easily come back," said Sam, looking at the small distance between the places.

Jeremy nodded. "Okay, but just for the night."

Joel ran and climbed over the fence. Jubilee followed him, but before Lydia could get her foot over, they heard a terrible screeching noise. "What's that?" she yelled, looking around desperately for it. "It sounds like the skidding tires of a racing car."

Jeremy jumped up, yelling at the top of his voice, "The cord! The cord! It's about to snap! We mustn't break it. We are being tempted. It's not real—come back, Joel, Jubilee. NOW!"

Joel stood stock still, trying to gather his thoughts.

"Quick, Joel, NOW!" yelled Lydia.

"Come back NOW!" Sam joined in desperately afraid or them.

Jubilee reached for her brother's hand to pull her back. Joel turned and began running back to the fence where Jubilee waited for him with her arms outstretched. She just managed to grab his hand, but it started to slip out of hers as the house and garden disappeared. Sam and Jeremy held onto her legs as she reached further over the fence. Joel began to sink. Lydia started to scream at him to hold on as they all held onto Jubilee in a terrible struggle to bring him back over the fence. His head and arms became visible. Then, slowly, the rest of him bounced back over the fence. They all fell onto the hard earthen floor, exhausted and shocked.

"Wow, that was close," said Jeremy wiping his brow as they all gasped for air.

Distressed at what nearly happened they stared at each other in disbelief. Over the fence, desolation had returned, but where they were now sitting—had become a beautiful garden with the birds playing, darting in and out of the many coloured trees and flowers!

"What's happening now?" marvelled Joel. "This is amazing." They all began to laugh with relief.

"Is this another dream?" asked Lydia.

"No, it's real," said Jubilee, "It's all over. We aren't looking in a mirror anymore, like these people, who are only a dull reflection of what they could be." Joel breathed in the clean air, contemplating whether or not it was real.

"Well, if it is, don't you think we ought to ask Jaycee to help them?" Jubilee chimed in, once again resting her chin in thought.

"Now that's a brilliant idea," said Jeremy, grinning at Lydia.

"Out of the mouths of children," Lydia agreed, smiling back at her older brother.

Sam joined them, taking Jubilee's hand and saying, "Come on, we'll do it now."

They moved to sit in a circle on the green grass. The daisies smiled up at them as they closed their eyes to pray to Jaycee, God's son, for the people in the 'City of Self'.

After a few minutes, Joel whispered to Jubilee, "Do you think He heard us?"

Jubilee grinned and nodded. "Oh, I'm sure he did— because we believe in Him and have faith, don't we?" She giggled and poked Joel in the tummy.

Jeremy suddenly jumped up to look into the distance. So did Sam. "What's that over there?" he asked Sam as they held themselves up.

"It looks like a blue lake or sea," he replied, trying to think where they might be.

"It can't be, can it?" said Jeremy.

"Funny, though, it looks to me like the Sea of Tiberius, known earlier as the Sea of Galilee. I saw a picture of it once at school, just like this," Sam said, recollecting the image.

In a flash, the cords pull tight, spinning them up through the air. They heard giggling and laughing.

"They made it, they made it," said familiar voices.

"What's happeninggggggggg?" yelled Lydia terrified at this unexpected happening.

"We're spinning, round and round…. Like at the fair on the spinning swings…." Joel squealed.

"This is fu-un-un-un-un-unnnn," squealed Joel again as Thumper and Bumper joined them flying, round and round as if on the swings at a fair. They all burst out laughing, except Lydia.

Chapter 9

THE MANNA BREAD AND GREGORY THE LOCUST

'The years the locusts have eaten[61] *– will be restored.'*

SLOWLY THE SPINNING STOPPED, GIVING them the chance to look around.

"We're hanging from a tree, and I think it's a cedar tree," said Jeremy. They dangled from their scarlet threads, looking down to the grass below.

"And how do we get down from here?" yelled Sam, grabbing for his stick, which floated above his head, following him everywhere. He pushed it firmly back into his belt.

"Patience, patience," said Lydia, who was wondering the same thing, but didn't want to alarm the others.

Jeremy glanced around at the countryside, trying to sort out where they are now. The springtime sky was a bright, ice blue colour, which reminded him of his grandmother's aquamarine ring. The emerald spring green grass looked like a magnificent carpet, spread out and ready for something special to happen. On the opposite side of the lake, a large crowd of people walked up the mountainside. The distant crowds reminded him of ants following one another, but too far away for Jeremy to make out what was going on.

---

61 **Joel** 2:25 *'I will repay for the years the locusts have eaten – the great locust and the young locust...my great army.'*

132

He could only see tiny spots of white and grey robes as the people slowly moved up the hillside.

The children, intrigued by trying to see what was happening, didn't realize that their threads were slowly stretching. Lydia noticed it first. "We're going down!" she called out.

Hanging on to her thread, Jubilee swung sideways to see how much further they had to go to reach the ground. "Have you noticed how this thread doesn't seem to hurt us tied around our waists?" she pondered, feeling the strong silken fibres with her fingertips.

"Hmm," murmured Lydia, more interested in getting down than the boys, who were still looking around them.

"It's a bit like feeling safe without knowing why," Jubilee added in passing.

Gradually, they all landed safely. Without thinking, they each stood staring across the water, watching the people slowly move up the hillside.

Suddenly there was an enormous cracking sound. The ground shook like an earthquake; leaves fell from the tall tree above them. The rumbling and then splitting sound sliced through the air. They gasped in awe, staring up at the trunk of the tree. It split completely in two, opening up like a huge book. Their eyes bulged as they tried to take in the amazing sight. Both sides of the trunk were now two mirrors, each showing a different scene.

Joel opened his mouth to say, "It's amaz…." He couldn't get the words out, so he gulped instead.

"What's happening, Jeremy?" whispered Jubilee.

"I don't know," he replied, for once looking worried. "What do we do now?" asked Sam.

"Wait quietly," said Lydia, trying to come up with a plan of action.

A voice came from the left mirror. "This is the story of the past coming into the future. One thousand five hundred years before Jaycee came, the people of Israel had been first saved from slavery by God's man Moses, in the great exodus. Then they wandered around and around in the desert for years and years. They were soon bored and ver-r-r-y hungry. They were not happy. So God sent them food like bread from his kingdom in the skies—for years and years—despite this miracle, they were still not happy!"

The voice boomed and echoed around them, making Lydia quiver.

"On the right, you can see eight hundred years ago, when another man of God, called Elisha, was leading the people. There were one hundred prophets then, men of God, similar to priests, who were also hungry, not just for food for their bodies, but for food for their minds and souls as well. God fed them with another kind of bread. They still did not understand." The voice paused.

Suddenly, it started again. "Today you will see what is about to happen for the third time. It will be the dawn of a new understanding when men begin to see the truth. First you have to go back in time to see the beginning." It finished, seeming to take a breath. Jubilee searched for the source of the voice, baffled by how she couldn't pinpoint it.

As they stood amazed by the two mirrors in the great tree, they heard an ear-piercing sound. The split wood crunched back together. It was so piercing that they immediately placed their hands over their ears. The sounds shook the air; the tree groaned like an earthquake trying to go back together. It almost sounded as if the earth were in great pain as the two huge mirrors struggled to fold back together, yet nothing was broken.

The children stood in shock, still staring up at the great tree.

"And how on earth are we going to go back in time?" asked Jeremy in a small disbelieving voice.

No one answered him. They heard a most peculiar sound behind them, a sound like rushing winds or trains on fire. Smoke and sand billowed everywhere.

"Helicopters!" squealed Joel, his face lighting up.

"Oh no, what now?" Said Sam.

Jubilee clapped her hands over her closed eyes; she didn't want to see what was coming; her knees began to tremble in the most adorable way.

Joel swung around with delight, wanting to see what their next adventure was going to be, but even he didn't expect to see what he saw. Huge locusts, as big as horses, landed in a row before them with saddles on their backs. The great creatures waited as the clouds of dust settled.

Jubilee and Lydia both screamed. The boys jumped up; Sam raised his stick to defend them.

GREGORY – THE LEADER OF THE LOCUSTS OF GOD'S ARMY

"Don't do that, old boy!" said the largest brown and yellow locust in a thick drawl. "We have come to show you that the years the locusts have eaten up will be restored." [62]

---

62 **Meaning:** – ['the years' man has wasted in his life by selfish living, "I don't need God – I can manage?" not trusting in the message of Jaycee.]

The children were too shocked and stunned to move. They stood stiff, silent and unmoving. They didn't understand a word the giant insect was saying.

"What...what do you mean?" asked Jeremy forcing himself to listen.

"How can years be eaten?" asked Joel, folding his arms and furrowing his eyebrows.

"Hello, little one," said the smiling locust. "How is time eaten? It's eaten when it's not put to the best use. Wasted, like being ignored. A bit like you ignoring your mother when she tells you to stop playing games on your computer and to study your homework instead," he nodded to Joel, as he finished.

Joel's mouth dropped open in surprise, and his eyes widened. "How do you know about...?" he asked curiously.

"Simple, we work for the Holy God King, and the time has come to change all that," the locust said cheerfully.

Still no one else spoke or moved. They were completely stunned. A smaller locust hopped forward to stand nearby.

Her antenna wiggled, and she winked at Joel. He blinked. "Did that one just wink, at me?" he whispered to Jubilee from the side of his mouth.

"My name is Solitary," she purred. "I'm a tree cricket. You can call me Sally." She turned to look up at the much larger locust, saying calmly, "Don't frighten them. They've probably never seen anything like us before." Turning back to face the children, she said, "We are travellers in time. His name is Gregarius, but we call him Gregory. We don't hurt or ignore those who know Jaycee. One of his angels has told us to take you back to the beginning so that you may understand what is about to happen next."

"You mean back one thousand five hundred years?" asked Sam.

"Yes, exactly—to the beginning of the time of the tribe of Israel," they said in unison, exchanging proud grins with each other.

Still the children didn't know what to do or to say. Lydia blinked, trying to work out what was about to happen. How on earth could they trust such creatures? She had never liked flying bugs, but perhaps she should have faith. Sam came to stand beside Jeremy. They looked up at the large, horsey looking insects. Sam lowered his stick, which had not lit up at all, possibly a sign that it was not needed.

SALLY – THE LADY LOCUST WHO LIVED IN A TREE

"Don't be afraid of us. We have come to help you. We are the only ones allowed to fly back through time, because we were there in the beginning," Sally spoke, sounding very wise.

Then all the locusts turned to look at Joel. They bowed their heads to him.

"You have a very honoured name little man," said Gregory. "Because in the original '*Book of Mirrors*', kept safe in the Hall of Writings, you can read all about us." At this, the locusts nodded to each other in agreement.

"We are sorry for what happened, so we all want to help to put things right again, don't we?" said Sally as she turned around to look at her friends.

"Will it be scary? Going back, I mean," Jubilee asked.

"No, because we are the army of the God King, and His angels will protect us from our enemies.[63] And then we will be filled with joy and laughter, so we won't be afraid anymore,"[64] Sally replied.

Gregory joined in, "We will even be given fresh rain to enjoy, sparkling water from above to remind us that

He is looking after us when difficult times come. [65]Then things will begin to be reversed at last." He took a breath, musing.

Sally became annoyed. "Did you have to tell them about the rain?" she groaned, slapping a smooth claw over her forehead in annoyance.

"Yes," whispered Gregory, a glimmer of hope in his eyes. "Because Apollyon will be defeated, at last."

"Shhhh! Don't let the children know about the evil angel of the bottomless pit! That really will frighten them." She stopped him, pushing in front and slapping a claw over his mouth.

A moment or two of silence passed between the locusts and the children. Then Jeremy thought he should step

---

63 Joel 2 11; '*The Lord thunders at the head of his army... mighty are those who obey his command*'.

64 Joel 1:16 '*Joy and gladness from the house of our God*'.

65 Luke 6:21 'blessed are you who weep now, for you will laugh'

forward first, to show the others not to be afraid. He looked to Sam, who joined him, tucking his stick into his belt; Lydia was still weighing up the situation. This whirlwind they were riding had introduced them to simply amazing creatures. In her wildest dreams, this just would not be happening—but it was! Was this all a dream? Could they all be sharing the same dream? No. Of course not. That was silly.

Jubilee, always sensitive to Lydia's fears, tugged at her skirt. "It'll be alright, Lyd. I'm sure that Thumper and Bumper will be keeping their eyes on us all the time. Sam's stick hasn't turned into a sword, and your looking glass isn't jumping, so this must be part of what we have to do to find the next sign, the Fifth Sign. Then there will be only two more to go. Come on, we will ride on the smaller locusts. Have faith."

Golly, she is wise for her age. Lydia looked down at her young sister. "I love you, Jubilee; you're so kind and thoughtful," she said, bending down to place a kiss on Jubilee's cheek.

"Come on, you two, we're all waiting for you," yelled Jeremy.

"Men!" said Lydia in exasperation, "They always want us to hurry up!" She shared the joke with Jubilee, who, for the life of her, could not understand Lydia's meaning.

Sam laughed as he pulled on his locust's neck rein, making the creature leap high into the air. Sam's head jerked backwards as if in a convertible sports car. "HiHo, here we go!" he yelled as the sound of flapping wings filled the air.

"I want to ride that big one!" yelled Joel, his mouth agape with wonder. "Not on your own, you don't," said Lydia as she grabbed his collar. "You, young man, will ride with me—and no arguments." The large brown locust kneeled to allow them to mount.

"Well, can I sit in front of you then?" Joel pleaded raising an eyebrow.

"If you like!" Lydia hugged him into place as she slipped her arms around his waist and held on to the locust's rein.

A shy, green lady locust kneeled to let Jubilee climb into her seat. As soon as Jubilee held the reins, the creature took flight with huge leaps of high speed.

"Don't let go of your reins," yelled Gregory to the group behind him as he took the lead. "Whatever happens, they will keep you safe on their backs." The children immediately threw their hands over the reins in obedience.

Sam's locust flew over in a large circle. "Yippee!" he screamed with delight as if he were on a ride at a fair. Jeremy followed him. "Men," said Lydia again under her breath again, "they always go too far."

"Why can't they just sit in their seats and behave themselves?" Jubilee giggled again.

The locusts all began to sing as they flew higher and higher.

> Then, after doing all those things, I will pour out my
> Spirit upon all people.
> Your sons and daughters will prophesy.
> Your old men will dream dreams,
> And your young men will see visions.
> In those days, I will pour out my Spirit
> Even on servants—men and women alike. [66]

The day aged into the night. The stars grew larger, letting streams of light slice through the thick blue veil that covered the earth below them. The moon shone brightly and split into two, and then three, then four and... the day came back, over and over again. Each time the darkness came, they began to fall asleep, and their grips on the reins would ease.

"Faster, faster! We must go faster," yelled Gregory, "They are being affected by the darkness. We must get them into

---

66   Joel 2:28-29, NLT 'I will pour out my Spirit on all people.'

the final light. Everyone, close up, close up— we mustn't lose them. The rest of you, fly below us, just in case we need to catch them."

"I'm getting scared. Is it Apollyon's scouts?" Sally yelled back, her face reflecting her anxiety about maybe having to fight.

"Could be. That devil never lets up, does he?" Gregory joked, trying to lighten the conversation.

"Let's fly towards the moon. It gets brighter the nearer we get to it; maybe it will keep the children awake," shouted Sally.

"Brilliant idea! Okay, everyone, head for the moon," Gregory instructed.

"What? What's happening" asked Joel as the brilliant white rays lit his face as they all began to wake up in the new light, which helped them to hold onto the reins of the locusts. The time flashed by like a train in the dark, with the lights in its windows flashing past at great speed.

They awoke again, to find themselves sitting in another desert. The many people nearby didn't bother to look at the children; they were too busy collecting a crop of some sort.

"Where on earth are we now?" exclaimed Lydia

"That's the point," said Jeremy. "I'm not sure where we are on the earth, but it's must be another time or dimension."

"What are they gathering to put in their baskets?" asked Sam, brushing sand off his lap.

"Looks like cream-coloured honeycomb blobs to me," said Lydia, becoming used to finding herself in funny places. She shook the sand out of her hair, ruffling her lank brown locks.

"How did we get here?" asked Jeremy, rubbing his head. He sounded, and felt very confused. "The last thing I remember was riding on a large locust?"

Jubilee smiled. "I can't see Maureen anywhere." She had struck up an unusual friendship with Maureen the camel, she remembered.

"Thank goodness for that!" said Lydia. "She was a handful, wasn't she?"

"That's right. She doesn't 'do' carry," replied Jubilee, which made them all laugh.

The people around them were still bent low, pulling the cream 'stuff' off the tamarind bushes. The spindly plants had small but very stunning pink flowers; the tiny petals fell off as the people searched the bushes, pulling their branches from side to side.

"I've got it!" said Jeremy. "They are collecting manna[67] to eat. Yes, it's in the *'Book of Mirrors'*, that they ——————

had to receive it every day so that they would have enough to eat." He watched the people intently.

"How odd," said Joel, not understanding it entirely, kicking the dirt flippantly with his foot.

"And I'm hungry," said Sam.

"You're always hungry. If the day ever came when you weren't, I'd be anxious about you," said Lydia giving him a cock-eyed look.

"What's the matter, Lydia?" asked Sam, swinging an arm around her neck. She didn't look impressed.

"Well, we didn't get the chance to look into the *'Book of Mirrors'* before we left to see what was going to happen. I have just remembered something! Jaycee said that He was the 'Bread of life',"[68] she said, looking very genuinely concerned.

---

67   **Exodus 16:31** – *"it was white like coriander seed and tasted like wafers with honey."* **Meaning**: – [The people of Israel called this wafer bread 'manna' that God had sent down because they were hungry. Jesus called himself the "true bread of life – in the spiritual sense – **NIV** study notes p.110.]

Deuteronomy 8:16 – He gave you manna to eat in the desert... to humble and test you.

John 6:49 – Your forefathers ate the manna in the desert – yet they died; **Revelation 2:17** 'I will give you some of the hidden manna – the spiritual bread.

68   **John 6:48** – "JC – *Bread of life.*"

"That is symbolic, isn't it?" said, Sam. "Didn't it also say somewhere, that even though they ate this manna bread, they died?" asked Sam.

"But only their bodies died, not necessarily their souls," said Jubilee quietly. "It seems that we are here to learn that we all have a choice."

Joel bounded over to her and pulled her up for a piggy-back ride, then nearly toppled over. "I've decided I'm not hungry anymore," said Joel looking concerned.

"Well, I'm hungry," said Sam, who jumped up to join the others gathering the manna.

"Wait, wait!" yelled Lydia. But Sam didn't wait.

She and Joel watched him enjoying eating the bread from the bushes. Slowly, Jubilee put Joel down. He stood still for a moment, then began to run towards Sam.

Chapter 10

APOLLYON'S SCOUTS IN THE BATTLE OF THE LOCUSTS

The feeding of the 100 prophets[69]

THUMPER AND BUMPER FLEW STRAIGHT past them as they sat watching Sam. He didn't die. He just grinned and grinned as he swallowed down the delicious bread.

"Come on, you lot, this stuff tastes great! It's just like the honey wafers Mum likes to eat when she watches TV after supper," Sam managed to say around all the food in his mouth.

"You mean the ones Dad buys her for a treat?" said Joel, who now had a look of hope on his face.

A blurred pink streak flew in circles around them. Thumper managed not to hit anything, and Bumper only bounced once because he landed up in a tamarind Bush, which he managed to hang onto like an anchor.

"Aren't you hungry?" Thumper asked the watching, children.

"I'm so glad to see you two," said Lydia. "I'm not sure about all this. Firstly, we are attached by a silken cord; then we are pushed off a very, very huge, high tree. After that,

---

69   **2 Kings 4:42** NIV study notes.p.519. The people looked [to] Elisha as the true representative of their covenant [contract/agreement with] God.

we see misery everywhere and then we are dangling from a merry-go-round swing chair, similar to ones in the fair at our village back home. This adventure is followed by a ride on a friendly Locust with a horse saddle; to travel back through history! My mind is still going round and round," she complained about, with a little exaggeration. "Now I'm too afraid to eat this new kind of bread because I might die!"

Jeremy and Jubilee burst out laughing at her ramblings and bewilderment but nodded in agreement as Lydia took a deep breath, her shoulders falling in a gesture of hopelessness. Joel sat there grinning at her as he remembered their adventures with glee. Then he cut in.

"Yes," he nodded. "It's all been just amazing…"

"So what's going to happen now?" Lydia managed to continue, interrupting Joel casually before he said anything more.

Bumper came to join them. "Are you going to tell them or shall I?" he asked Thumper, who nodded. "You won't die, silly, this bread has come from our God King in the skies. It doesn't kill you—that's the point. It saves your body to live on; that's much better, isn't it?"

"The bread you are here to learn about is the bread for your soul. It's a different kind of food because it feeds your mind, which feeds your inner self," they said nodding enthusiastically at the children.

The children looked confused.

Jeremy pondered this information. "You mean there's more than one kind of bread? This bread is for our bodies – and there's another kind of bread for our souls?

The cherubs grinned and then nodded.

"Oh goody," said Joel, rubbing his tummy. "I'm hungry."

He immediately jumped up and ran to join Sam, who held out a big lump of manna for him.

"Well," said Thumper. "At least he's got half of the message."

They sighed; of course it took much effort to explain some things to Joel who was still so young. Jeremy, Lydia, and Jubilee stood up; the cherubs flew by their sides as they walked over to gather the manna with everyone else. The cherubs didn't eat any bread, but they flew about in circles like small airplanes ducking and diving as if fighting off enemy planes in battle.

"I'm suspicious of those two," whispered Lydia to Jeremy.

"Oh. Why?" he asked, curiously looking up at them enjoying themselves in the blue skies above their heads. He needed to take notice of Lydia's suspicions, just in case he was missing something. He knew his priority was to protect everyone.

"We've been brought here for a reason, remember? And we heard them saying that we were beginning to learn. Well, we know now that we learn through experiences, so what does all this mean?" she finished, looking Jeremy straight in the eye.

"You always were one for trying to work things out and make sense of everything, thank goodness," he nodded standing quietly for a moment as he watched the others enjoying the bread.

"So, we won't die while we are trying to eat this stuff, so how will we die?"

"And that's my point," Lydia exclaimed, holding out the palms of her hands as if in an open prayer.

"I don't know, but everything here seems to mean something else. I wonder, does this manna bread do things to us?" Jeremy asked, with an investigative face. "Or for us?" he pondered softly.

"Or change us?" Lydia added as they began to bounce ideas off one another.

"Now that's another point," replied Jeremy as he held up a piece and examined it more closely.

"I don't know, but Jaycee has sent us here to learn, so perhaps we should do just that, and stop worrying," Lydia said sensibly.

Thumper and Bumper had been listening to them talking. "Well, at last they are beginning to understand some of the stories," said Thumper.

"Yes," replied Bumper. "Now they have to know about the young prophets. How they need to have special food for their spirits. The real them inside their bodies that are their energy force of life itself."

"That's true. And they need to learn the reason why they have to live in these earthly bodies. Is it to learn the truth of what's it all about?" Thumper said, nudging Bumper in mid-flight.

"And only Jaycee can tell them the answer to that."

Joel had collected a pile of manna bread in the long robe that the nobleman had given him.

"Look, I've saved some for later!" he said, excitedly, pleased with himself.

Thumper flew over. "You can't do that," he said, looking apologetic.

"Why not?" asked Joel frowning who thought it was a good idea. "I want to save it for later."

"Because it won't last. It goes bad," Bumper explained, putting a hand on his shoulder as he fluttered by his side in the air.

"Goes bad?" asked Joel looking down at his gathered fresh bread in confusion.

"Yes, it has to be eaten now while it's fresh in your minds, or it will drift away and Appol—" Thumper thundered over, interrupting Bumper.

"Don't!" snapped Thumper. "We aren't allowed to tell them yet." He groaned, giving Bumper a light tap on the nose and rolling his eyes.

"Uh-oh," said Lydia, widening her eyes. "What did I tell you, Jeremy? What is going to happen now?"

147

Then they heard a low humming sound getting closer as if a giant bumble bee was closing in on their discussions. They looked up and saw a large locust with a golden crown on his head, flying overhead, resembling an enemy plane scouting before a battle commenced. Their conversation halted.

"Oh no! They're here already," whispered Thumper to Bumper.

"We've got to get the children away from here, as quickly as possible!" yelled Bumper back to Thumper.

"What's the matter?" asked Lydia frowning. Shading her eyes from the bright sun with her hand all she could see was a small black spot with a glint of gold on the top.

"What's going on?" asked Jeremy, as he followed her gaze.

Sam came over to join them with Joel by his side. They followed their gaze up into the skies above them. Suddenly his staff in his belt lit up. Pulling it out of his belt a brilliant blue streak shot across the sky. Instinctively he stood firm, feet apart and ready for action.

They heard a rushing wind and the sound of a crackling forest fire. Now looking to the left, they saw a dark grey smoke cloud filled with flames rising from a great fire, as if from a mountain volcano. The cloud left the valley from behind the distant blue mountain as it moved menacingly across the sky towards them. Then another cloud appeared to the right, but this cloud was white, filled with flashing white and sapphire rays of light. It was closing rapidly.

Then they saw their locusts swooping down towards them, and heard Gregory's voice, "You must get mounted up, quickly. NOW! We don't have much time.

They discovered us too soon, much too soon." He sounded worried as everyone jumped to work.

Lydia grabbed Joel, pulling him to her side.

Jeremy swung himself into the air as he mounted Gregory's flying saddle. The second great brown locust simply grabbed Sam and swung him into the air, managing to catch him in the saddle as they swept high into the sky, moving towards the dark cloud on the left.

Sally and her lady friend swept down to Lydia, Joel, and Jubilee. "Quick, quick! Oh, we had hoped that you would have more time here," she sadly said as she hurried them along.

"What's happening?" yelled Lydia as she landed in the saddle, extremely anxious and worried.

"It's Apollyon's scouts. They found us," gasped Sally, her breath catching in her throat. "Hold on— tightly. We might just have enough time." They set off to the right, away from the advancing locusts, who looked as though they were all wearing golden crowns.

"Who are they?"[70] shouted Jubilee across to Sally as they flew beside her.

"They are spiritual beings who follow Satan's orders. They always try to exert an evil influence on whatever humans do."[71] Sally's voice wobbled, and she looked as if she might cry, but she held it together for the sake of the children.

A lone Apollyon locust, who must have been a scout, stopped to stare at them.

"They look horrible! I...do not...like...them," whispered Jubilee, running her free hand through her hair and pressing her lips into a thin line to stop any tears; she wanted to look brave.

---

70   **Revelation 9:3** *'And out of the smoke locusts came down upon the earth and were given power like that of scorpions of the earth'.* v4 [For those who did not have the seal of God].

Revelation 9:11 NIV Study Bible notes.p.1895. – they had a king over them the angel of the Abyss, whose name in... Greek was Apollyon. [Personification of destruction]

71   **Revelation 9:20; Deuteronomy 4:28** – *'you will worship man-made gods of wood and stone...* (money, home, car, etc.,) *'Which cannot see or hear or eat or smell'* **Meaning:** – [to give too much time to this is meaningless, but time with God is precious.

AN APOLLYON SCOUT OF SATAN

"Look at their long hair; are they females?" asked Lydia.

"Not with those ugly mugs, huge cat's teeth, and fangs" Joel added with a squeal that faded as they flew away.

"And why are they wearing breast-plates?" asked Lydia. "There's hundreds of them. They look as though they are going into battle. Who is the enemy? Not us surely? Why do they have golden crowns on their heads?"

Then both girls screamed as they saw the grey cloud of demon locusts about to swallow the boys. Joel burst out crying and sobbing, "Jeremy! Sam! Oh noooo...," he said, gasping in between each wail.

Sally dived low over the desert. Her friend carrying Jubilee followed. They flew straight into a cave hidden from general view, high up on the side of a large grey mountain. The cave looked as if his mouth was opened – in readiness for their arrival. The locusts landed gasping for breath after the desperate flight and speed they had needed to escape. The children collapsed, lying on the necks of the locusts as they clung to their mounts, sobbing and shaking in disbelief.

Lydia's looking glass began to shake and jump in her pocket. As the girls tumbled to the floor in distress, the friendly locusts lowered their heads in sympathy. They watched as Lydia opened the small, broken looking glass. She wiped the tears from her eyes as Joel held onto her skirt and leg for comfort.

One word came across the screen. "Jaycee" it read in big capital letters.

"Jaycee. That's it. We must pray and ask for His help," Jubilee cried, desperately searching for an answer. "Will He hear us? He's so far away," Lydia worried.

"He can hear us where ever we are," said Jubilee beginning to smile.

They held hands in a circle as the locusts knelt down to join them.

Jeremy stood up in his saddle and shouted, at the locusts to attract their attention. Then Sam raised himself up in his saddle, swinging his sword in a large circle. They heard sizzling and screeching as the blue beam sliced through the evil Scouts of Apollyon. Gregory swooped down to the left as Sam's locust flew down to the right, copying Spitfires flying in a World War II dogfight. As if putting on a show for the crowds, they came together at the bottom of the circle, then drove straight up through the burning, falling golden crowns. Apollyon's beasts snarled, hissed and growled with hate. Clouds filled with bits of wings, legs, bent breastplates and crowns fell from the sky. Several of Apollyon's vicious locusts made a last attempt to attack Gregory. They swarmed in from all directions, leaving no way out. Jeremy held on, ducking his head as the creatures ferociously bit at Gregory.

In their cave, the girls and Joel continued to hold hands, praying, as if they knew they must not break their circle of communication with Jaycee. The locusts with them watched in peace. They knew that the scouts of the devil could not hurt these children because they knew Jaycee, but this didn't mean that the children were not afraid.

In the air, the evil scouts fought relentlessly. And the boys fought back. No way, were they going to let go, not when the locusts of the God King's army showed such courage.

Jeremy suddenly heard Gregory groan in pain. Then he faltered in flight and began to fall sideways.

"Sam! Sam...," yelled Jeremy.

Sam had seen what had happened. One of Gregory's great legs hung by a thread of flesh, however, his mighty wings kept beating. Gregory turned back to the fight, his limb swinging uselessly beneath him.

The sight of Gregory's injury enraged Sam. He shouted,

"Jaycee, we need you. Help! Please help us. We don't want to die, and Gregory desperately needs your help" he cried with desperation and pressure clear in his voice.

Blue lightning flashed across the sky. Lydia and Jubilee felt the pain in Sam's heart as he shouted for help. They fell to their knees feeling his despair and anguish in the pale light of their safety in the cave.

Joel was scared and began to sob. Sally looked up— and smiled. "They will be alright. Your faith has reached Jaycee; He heard you," she said calmly.

At that very moment, the evil scouts turned away. The boys and their locusts shakily flopped down to the sandy ground below exhausted and devastated by the evil; they had witnessed. Sam turned to see Jeremy kneeling by Gregory's side. Tears streamed down his face. He heard Jeremy saying quietly to Gregory,

"You fought so hard for us." Gratefully, he extended his hand to the locust to touch him on his forehead as they gazed at one another for a few moments of shared companionship between a boy and creature of this world. Gregory tried to smile up at Jeremy managing only to slightly nod his great head. He felt comforted by the loving touch of this young boy who behaved like a man.

Sam quietly joined them. He knelt down and placed his hand on Jeremy's shoulder in sympathy. He waited when he saw Jeremy trying to put gently, Gregory's huge broken leg back in place. Streams of tears of desperation and hopelessness at the situation ran down his cheeks. The locust would surely die without this magnificent leaping leg. Sam's heart filled with pain as he saw their dying friend lying hopelessly in the soft sand. He tried to swallow the aching lump of sadness in his throat as his eyes stared at this tragic scene.

Their tears fell in silence. Then Sam placed his hand on Jeremy's shoulder to comfort him. Instantly, a blue beam shot from his sword; the three of them glowed like white fire, but only for a split moment. Their force fields began to fill the surrounding air with startling brilliant waves of light as power surged through the three of them.[72] Gregory jerked. They heard a swishing sound. Gregory's leg, which Jeremy still held, was drawn back to Gregory's body. He healed in an instant.[73]

---

72 **Matthew 18:20** cf. *'For where two or three come together in my name, there I am with them.'*

73 **Romans 15:30** *'by* [Jaycee] *our Lord...and the love of the Spirit, to join me in my struggle by praying to God for* [those we love].

Shocked, the boys stared down at Gregory's hip and leg, now back in place. "Love heals everything."[74] The words echoed around them in the cool breeze that stayed with them.

In the cave, the children's hands fell apart. They stared at each other—then instinctively ran towards the entrance, to look out for the boys. They could see them jumping up and down, laughing, in the distance as Gregory stood up.

"Well, that's nice," Lydia started to say. Then she snapped, "Here we were, worried sick about them and they are messing about!"

"I wish I had been messing about with them," said Joel with a sad voice. "I could have bashed those wicked locusts as they flew past. I could, you know," he said with a sad nod. Then he paused, as if thinking, "But why did they attack us in the first place?" Joel, always inquisitive needed to know this.

"Because they didn't want us to find out the truth—the truth we have been brought here to find," said Jubilee, sounding mature and looking at Joel.

"There must be a great battle coming in the future with this lot. This battle is just the beginning," Joel speculated.

"Well, thank goodness that is over," said Thumper. "Now the children can get on with visiting the one hundred prophets and finding out about the bread of life."

"It's time for us to join them again," said Sally with a smile, glad to see the boys laughing.

The two gentle green locusts landed quietly beside the boys.

"What happened?" asked Lydia still feeling angry, yet pleased. They hugged each other crying with relief.

"I'm very, very thirsty," said Joel.

"Me, too," said the girls together.

---

74   **Romans 12:9-19** *'Love must be sincere...'*

Sam put his staff back under his belt with a smile. Jeremy looked up and nudged Sam playfully, grinning. "I knew that sword of yours would come in handy at some time," he said.

Gregory danced and hopped around as he tried out his leg.

"What's the matter with him?" asked Jubilee.

"We've just had a dreadful time in the cave, and he's jumping for joy!" said Lydia, annoyed.

The boys burst out laughing. Soon the girls couldn't help grinning. Sally and her friend flapped their wings, making a soft breeze and cooling them all down in the heat of the day. The boys explained with joy and fervour what had happened. As they finished, they turned to look at Gregory.

"Well, no wonder he is jumping for joy," said Lydia, now feeling a little ashamed of her anger. She added, "You were very brave to fight so hard. Thank you," she said quietly. Suddenly exhausted, she dropped her eyes to the floor.

Gregory spoke gently. "I'm afraid it's time to mount up again, we must finish our journey." No one moved.

"But I'm thirsty," said Joel. In case anyone was listening, he added, "And hungry." "We all are," agreed Sam.

Jeremy stood up, took the water-skin from his back, and passed it to Joel.

"You first, little one," he said to a bewildered Joel. After Joel had drunk his fill, Jubilee took a turn.

Gregory said again, "We must go; time is running out."

Jubilee spluttered as she tried to drink.

"What do you mean?" she asked, taking several more gulps of water, which seemed to be a darker pink in colour. "We aren't going to start disappearing again, are we?"

"Not another mirage!" said Lydia with concern.

"No," said Gregory, "But we do have to fly through time again. This next flight will take us back through time to when one hundred prophets were in for an amazing surprise."

"Really? Prophets? Aren't they supposed to know everything?" said Sam.

"Well, that depends on how much faith they have. You see, we all need to be fed with food for our spirits as well as for our stomachs," Gregory said, stretching out his healed leg with pleasure.

"So now we are talking about the other kind of manna, er, bread?" said Jubilee.

"That's right, the kind of bread that keeps your soul alive—forever!" Gregory said excitedly.

Joel shook his head. He didn't understand that at all. And now he not only felt hungry, he felt fatigued as well.

Jubilee noticed this and asked, pleading, "Can't we rest for a while—and recover a bit?"

"We can, but we need to get a good start. We don't need those evil Scouts of Apollyon to decide to come back. It's best if we leave this time span," Gregory said, convincing everyone that it truly was best.

Joel looked up, eyes wide, ready to rush off. "Okay. I don't feel hungry or tired anymore. I want to go away from here. Let's go!"

Smiling tiredly, they all nodded in agreement. "It isn't too far to go this time," said Gregory, "Only three hundred years through time to a town called Bethel, near Dan in the northern kingdom."

Once again they flew high into the sky as the evening sun slowly disappeared behind the dark purple mountains. They lost the light of the sun, and the sky became black. Once again, as the darkness came, the children began to fall asleep. The locusts quickened their speed to get them through the spinning days and nights until time became one. Lydia, struggling to keep her eyes open, tightened her grip on Sally's collar. Jubilee rode with Sam, who also fought to stay awake as he held on to her. He tried to wave regularly to Lydia to help her stay awake. Just as they felt they could stay awake no longer, the moon seemed to grow larger and larger and brighter and brighter. As the locusts flew close to the moon, its soft blue light was enough to keep them awake—and safe as they travelled through time.

Finally, the days and nights stopped flashing and spinning. The brilliant orange sun rose slowly and triumphantly, looking huge as it swallowed the dim light of the moon. The locusts instinctively knew that the day of feeding the young priests with wisdom through truth had come. This wisdom symbolized by, 'the first ripe corn, the best; along with some ears of new corn'.[75] ———————————————

Sally called to Gregory, "The northern kingdom is below us now in the timespan we need. We only need to find the house of Elisha, the well-known and respected prophet. He isn't one of the evil King Jeroboam's men. He's a real prophet."

"I know," said Gregory as he flew alongside her. "It's not far now to Bethel, only twelve miles north of Jerusalem and the town of Dan is close by in the far north—near Mount Hermon."[76]

"Thank goodness," said Sally. "I'm getting tired. Look down there; at the signs of famine; the people here are suffering, so sad. They're the ones who think they don't need God in their lives, they would rather have an easier life and keep their boss and neighbour happy."[77] Gregory agreed, squinting into the distance.

"They don't know they are blind. Now we have to concentrate on finding Elisha's servant boy, Gehazi because we can follow him to find the one hundred young student prophets who are being misled by the evil king and his priests."

---

75   **2 Kings 4:42 Meaning:** [that they were to be given the true (spiritual food/teaching) of God. New corn meaning new wisdom.]

76   **1 Kings 12:29** NIV Study Bible notes – p.487.

77   **1 Kings 12:30 cf.** 'And this thing became a sin.' Which violated the second commandment (**Exodus 20:4-6**) 'You shall not make for yourself an idol' **Meaning:** – [something that becomes more important than God – a person, hobby, money, possessions etc...]

The children awoke to the smell of sweet smelling smoke. They also heard the sound of many people talking as they walked up the mountainside, in the hill country of Ephraim, ruled by the selfish and evil King Jeroboam.[78]

"Did they say they had come from Ephraim?" asked Jubilee.

"I think so," said Jeremy.

"At least we know where we are," Jeremy advised.

"Ooh, it smells like a roast lamb to me," said Joel, growing quite tearful as he thought of home. "When we have Sunday roast lamb lunch at home with Mum and Dad."

"Don't forget the mint sauce as well," added Sam licking his lips as he remembered.

No one else spoke. By now they were all standing, fascinated as they watched people arriving on the high hill where they had awakened. The locusts had gone. The children were on their own.

"Golly, look over there," said Lydia, as she pointed at a tall pillar that held two shining objects. "What is it?"

After a few moments of staring hard in the bright morning light, the children distinctly saw two golden calf statues.

"What is going on?" asked Jubilee.

"They are sacrificing meat on their altars, that's what," said Jeremy.

"It's not dinner time, and I missed my corn flakes and popcorn with milk and sugar for breakfast as well," said Joel, looking at Jubilee for her encouragement. She stretched out a hand and their fingertips brushed.

"Shush, Joel, not now. Something is very wrong here."

---

78 **1 Kings 12:25** (Jeroboam fortified Schechem in the hill country of Ephraim and lived there)

They all looked back at the growing crowds. A group came towards them. They heard the man who was leading them say,

"It's good of King Jeroboam to build these altars. It's so much closer for us to pray here, rather than having to walk twelve miles down to Jerusalem. My old donkey can't carry me that far anymore."

A woman, who seemed to be his wife, shook her head in sadness, saying, "This used to be the place the wicked pagans worshipped idols made of wood or gold. The earth here is full of their evil ways; their hearts have gone bad. Our God King wouldn't like it at all—no, not at all."

"Be quiet, woman. You don't know what you are saying. How can the earth be bad?" the man replied.

"Because it has been filled with the spilt blood of evil, that's why! All I know is that we are not doing things the way the God King told Moses we should do them. These changes have broken the promise our own wise man and prophet Elijah gave us." She looked sad as she walked slowly behind the man, saying, "Most of our God-fearing Levite priests have gone south to Judah,"[79] she continued.

"I told you to be quiet, woman. We need to worship the two golden calves to get strength and fertility," the man concluded.

The woman muttered under her breath, "I don't need any more fertility!"

They moved away.

"Does this mean they are doing witchcraft?" asked Joel.

Lydia frowned, speaking cautiously, "I have a horrible feeling we are not in a good place."

They looked around to see more of the king's priests coming, their fine clothes and jewellery obviously worn for show. Their pompous parade of heavily laden animals

---

79 **2 Chronicles 11:13-17** 'Jeroboam and his sons rejected [our] priests of [God].

caused the earth to tremble; like the Zulu warriors Grandma had seen as a child in Africa did. The ground continued to grumble and moan, beneath their feet.

Joel nudged Jubilee, whispering, "The priest's snobby[80] faces make them look like Maureen, don't they?"

Jubilee suddenly grinned and looked at Lydia. "Do you think its light enough for us to look in the Book of Mirrors to make sure we don't go the wrong way from here?"

"Yes, yes, we must do that," Lydia confirmed, brushing herself off.

They moved away from the hilltop and the altars burning their sacrifices. In the cover of a small group of trees, they sat down. Jubilee closed her eyes and asked for the Book of Mirrors. Nothing happened.

"What's the matter, Jubilee?" asked Sam.

"I don't know, but I get a strong feeling the Book doesn't like it here," she said, looking around while she spoke, but not looking at Sam.

"Now what do we do?" asked Lydia.

"Follow our hearts! That's all we can do. We know Jaycee is with us in spirit, so we can't go too wrong," Jubilee said, full of hope.

At that moment, a young boy came rushing towards them with a sack on his back. Worry filled his face as he talked to himself, "Hurry, hurry, I must hurry."

Jubilee stepped in front of him, acting like a grownup lady. "Excuse me, but where are you going?"

The young boy, who looked the same age as Sam, was startled.

"Going? Going? Where else but to see our wise prophet Elisha?" he said, looking nervous and scared of her. When Jubilee didn't answer him, he looked even more anxious. Clearly aware of his important job, he said, "The young

---

80 **Proverbs 6:16-19** Six things the Lord hates, first – Haughty eyes.

prophets must get this bread. It's special, and they are very hungry."

Lydia, pleased that they had found a guide, jumped in, "I think that's where we have to go, too. Can we follow you, please?"

He thought for a moment as he looked at the five children who seemed to be lost.

"Alright, but you must keep up with me. I cannot be late. They are waiting for me." He turned and hurried off.

Jeremy took Joel's hand. Lydia held Jubilee's hand, and Sam gripped his amazing cedar staff in readiness for any danger.

"Is your bag heavy?" asked Joel, skipping alongside the boy.

The boy smiled down at Joel; he seemed surprised.

"No, not very. I suppose it might be because it contains wonderful healing powers for our priest Elisha to give his students. They do need it because they are going blind." [81] The boy spoke humbly, and Joel decided he would make a good friend.

"I didn't know that bread was medicine. Did you, Jubilee?" said Joel. The boy frowned at Joel, thinking that these children were very odd indeed. "So what makes it special?" persisted Joel

"It's made from the first seeds of the barley crop; it is the best," Jubilee explained, rolling her eyes at Joel.

Lydia wondered if they were going to use the bread to make a paste, to put on the eyes of the students. But that didn't seem right. Jaycee could heal without even touching

---

81   **2 Kings 4: 42 cf.** NIV [A man came from Baal Shalishah, (15 Roman miles north of Demopolis) an apostate (false teaching) area – defected from Jesus (Jaycee) bringing twenty loaves of barley bread baked from the *first ripe grain*, [first teaching of God] with some heads of *new grain* [new teaching]. *"Give it to the people to eat,"* [consume- take in] *Elisha said.* Because Elisha was a true man of God.

people, so this bread the boy was carrying must have magical powers.

She whispered to Sam, "I think we had better take care of this boy. He does seem to be on a special errand." Sam nodded and straightened his back to raise himself slightly taller than the boy, hoping he looked like a warrior. "Would you like me to carry the bag for you?" he asked. When the boy looked tired and doubtful, as if he wondered if would be safe, Sam suggested, "I'll walk in front of you so that you can see me all the time."

The girls came to stand with them. Feeling hospitable, Jubilee said, "We won't take any, we promise. You can have a drink of our special water and then you won't feel hungry or thirsty anymore."

Joel added, "Yes, It's called living water. God's son made it."

"And," said Jeremy confidently, "Our water-skin is always full, no matter how much we drink."

The boy stared at Jeremy, who paused and asked, "What's your name?"

"I am Gehazi, a servant of the prophet Elisha," he replied, not smiling too much.

"Golly," whispered Joel. "We thought we were looking for a man. This boy is the one Gregory told Sally about when we were flying here."

"You have heard of me?" Gehazi asked, stunned.

"Yes, we were told by the locust—" Joel started, preparing to rattle on.

"Not now, Joel. There's a good boy," said Lydia, smiling. Keeping her distance, so as not to frighten the boy, she introduced them all.

"No need to delay Gehazi. He's in a hurry." She smiled at the boy, saying, "My name's Lydia. My brother here is Jeremy—short for Jeremiah and this is Sam—short for Samuel. My sister's name is Jubilee, meaning celebration, and you've heard us calling our young brother Joel."

162

Gehazi stopped. Took in what she had just told him, and smiled looking at the children differently. He turned to Sam and said,

"You have the name of a great prophet. You can carry my bag of bread."

Sam took the bag and gripping it tightly, he carefully placed the strap over his left shoulder.

Gehazi talked to them as they walked along.

"The problem here is that in the northern kingdom, where the young Prophets[82] are studying, people no longer follow the teaching of God's chosen teachers. The evil Apostate King, who doesn't believe in the God King, and his gang of priests want to mislead these young prophets."

Gehazi said all that without seeming to run out of breath.

"But, but...," said Joel, putting his hand up to get attention. "What does apot— apstit—" Joel stuttered and stopped.

"Apostate," said Sam smiling down at him.

"Yes. What does that mean?" Joel continued, looking inquisitively at Gehazi's concerned face and his big, brown eyes.

"It means that they are false teachers of God's word. King Jeroboam wants to combine his political interest in making people worship his way with evil practices. He wants to control the people through fear. The priests make up teachings of their own."[83] They are making the prophets go blind to the truth."

Gehazi, finally finished, looked back at Jubilee. She knew what was coming next. She looked sideways at

Joel.

"Dad says we have teachers like that at our school, doesn't he, Jubilee?" Joel said, relating the two situations.

---

82   **Zondervan** – p.542. *'He ordered them to be distributed to the young prophets*

83   **1 Kings 13:19** – NIV cf. Study notes. 'false prophecy comes from one's own imagination' **(Jeremiah 23:16; Ezekiel 13:2,7)**

"What I don't understand," said Jeremy, "is why they don't listen to their wise men. They could tell the king what the best thing to do is. Is it because they want to please the king? If they keep quiet, perhaps, he might give them more money or a better position in the church?" He continued, talking out loud and trying to get it straight in his head. "It sounds like men wanting to please their boss," he finished. ————

"And isn't that rather dangerous?" said Lydia.

"It certainly is! So the God King is sending me to give this bread to Elisha—so that they can begin to think clearly again and find the truth," Gehazi confirmed.

"So, to find the truth, we have to listen to the correct teachers, the ones who love the God King," concluded Jeremy with a nod of his head. "And the truth is the food or bread for our souls."

Jubilee smiled at her older brother, who always seemed to be so wise. They were beginning to understand. It seemed that the young prophets had healthy bodies, but their minds and souls were sick.[84]

Sam added, "They just need the right diet, right Lyd, fresh fruit with some new grain and vegetables, not burgers and bread all the time?"[85]

She frowned looking at Sam. "You mean not get fat on the wrong food for their minds or their bodies!" "Exactly!" he laughed.

Lydia rolled her eyes.

Gehazi wondered what a diet was, and why the children thought it was funny.

---

84 NIV Study Bible. p.519 – [The solution was that the *young* priests (in spiritual understanding however *old* they were in body) needed to look to Elisha as a representative of God, rather than the false 'gods' of the 2 calves of the apostate [unbelieving] king and his priests].

85 **Lev 23:20** – *first fruits with some new grain.* **Meaning:** – [new understanding – Portions for God.]

"And Gehazi is making sure that the young prophets won't go hungry for the right information, ever again," said Jubilee skipping in front of them leading the way.

Lydia chose a place for them to rest for the night. Jeremy passed around the skin of living water, as they watched the deep orange sun send pink rays and golden beams across the sky, lighting the thinly stretched clouds like tired eyelids. The sun slowly went to sleep behind the falling purple curtain of night.

Gehazi sat next to Jeremy and answered his question of 'will there be enough bread for the young prophets?' He whispered in reply, "Don't worry. Elisha told me, 'they will eat and have some left over'."[86] Jeremy nodded, feeling humbled by this young boy's incredible wisdom.

Dawn came with a sudden sound of whirring blades filling the early morning sky above them. Blinking they each turned to see where the noise was coming from as they forced themselves to remember where they were. The dust sprang in whirlwinds around them. Instinctively, they closed their eyes for protection and placed their hands over their heads.

"What now?" screamed Lydia as she grabbed at Jubilee and Joel. "This is just getting too much!"

---

86 **2 Kings 4:43** – [The bread was multiplied at the word of the Lord through Elisha].

165

Chapter 11

Jaycee (Jesus) in
THE LIVING MIRRORS
OF TIME AND NEPH THE
FRIENDLY NEPHILIM GIANT

Psalm 25:16-17 The Lonely lost and hurting [87]

Mark 16.16 NIV 'Whoever believes and is baptized will [save their souls] but whoever does not believe will be condemned'.

AN ENORMOUS WHITE CLOUD WAS descending from the skies, getting closer and closer as they watched. The next thing they knew, they were floating in the cloud. Lydia, with her gift of compassion for the safety of her brothers and sister, yelled, "Quick, hold hands! It looks as though we are starting to fall through the sky, like skydivers. Jubilee! Joel! Are you listening?"

Sam yelled back," Skydivers go down, we are falling up, aren't we?" Sam circled his arms around in a back-ward circle motion to try and understand his theory. "Get together," insisted Lydia. Scrambling about and reaching for their hands. "Come on, come over here. I don't care which

---

87   **Psalm 25:16-17 "(NCV) New Century Version** *"Turn to me and have mercy on me, because I am lonely and hurting. My troubles have grown larger; free me from my problems.".*

way we are going. Joel, stop messing about. Come over here and hold my hand."

Jubilee called back, "We'd better pray to Jaycee. We need his help." A look of despair flashed across her face. With their eyes wide open, they each thought of Jaycee. Help, Jaycee, we don't' know what's happening. Joel scrunched up his face as he prayed.

Lydia screeched at the top of her voice. "Joel, will you do as I say?" she screamed in confusion, her voice filled with fear and panic.

The wind flattened her hair on her shoulders as they gathered speed going up and up. The others reached out, grabbing handfuls of air as they struggled to swim towards her. Jeremy and Sam were doing the crawl, Jubilee tried doing the breaststroke, and Joel just floated around in all directions, flapping his arms and hands. Then the wind slowed down. Now they floated gently together and at last, managed to hold hands—all except Joel.

"Joel," yelled Lydia again harshly, her eyebrows furrowed. "Come over here and do as you are told!"

"But it's fun," he giggled, "I like sitting on a cloud."

"Don't be silly!" yelled Sam and Jeremy together. "You might float away and then what would you do?" Sam persisted, deciding to back Lydia up.

Jubilee bumped down beside him. "He's sitting on something; I can feel it, too." She fiddled with the cloud fluff below her.

Joel frowned, feeling around to find, on what she was sitting. "You are higher up than me!"

They both looked down to see on what they were sitting.

"It's a staircase," said Sam in amazement as he joined them. "Like an escalator in the big shop back home. We are still going up." He brushed away the cloud fluff to find the pattern of the stairs.

Someone laughed saying, "Jeans, shoes, and sports equipment!"

"Tea and coffee shop on the top floor," said someone else.

"Thumper, Bumper," said Jubilee with relief. "Thank goodness you two are here—but why are you here now? What's happened?"

"What a silly question!" said Thumper. "We live here, don't we?"

Again they flew around in circles like a Spitfire plane, flipping over and over before dive-rolling towards the children, who were now all sitting on different steps of the moving stairway.

"Now where are we going?" Lydia asked in exasperation as she brushed her hair back behind her ears.

"Oh, that's simple," replied Thumper, nudging his companion. "You tell them, Bumper."

"To the Maze of Mirrors, that's where we are going," Bumper said happily. He couldn't hold it in any longer.

"Where?" asked Sam, trying to make sense of their present predicament as the whirling wind died away.

"I can't cope with all this," said Lydia, shaking her head. "I just can't cope. If we aren't in a sandstorm, riding on locusts, talking to jars of water, listening to haughty camels talk or having to deal with a stubborn mule…"

Jeremy put his hand on her shoulder from the step above her.

"Don't worry sis', I'm sure it'll all workout— somehow!" He took her hand and smiled reassuringly. "Jaycee wants us to come here, so it's got to be good. His parable stories in the '*Book of Mirrors*' are all interesting, and they teach us so much. We just need to think about what the story is saying, that's all."

"We need to find out the truth so that we don't go wrong," said Sam, giving Lydia a reassuring pat on her back.

Jubilee nodded. "We have to come here to learn all about the seven signs that prove who Jaycee is."

"I still want to know if he hears my prayers, don't I," said Joel.

Lydia felt foolish. She knew they were right, and she knew she had to stop being afraid. Jaycee had promised that he would always be with them, even if they couldn't see him because he never breaks a promise.

Joel held her other hand. "I still want to know if this is a dream. If it is, are we all having the same one?" he said, astounded at the idea.

"I'd like to know that as well," said Sam. "I mean, how can I defend and protect you all, if I don't know where I am?" he added sweetly.

"Which dimension are we in now?" questioned Lydia, touching the clouds around them.

No one spoke. Not even Joel, who looked from one to the other to find out the answer. The cherubs stopped flying around and began hovering in mid-air, right in front of them.

"Will you tell them or shall I?" asked Thumper of Bumper.

Bumper coughed, cleared his throat, and started to speak to Jeremy. Then he decided to whisper to Thumper first, "Do you think I'll be able to get to my next grade of two and three quarters if I do this correctly?"

"Not until we finish this assignment, no!" Thumper exclaimed.

Bumper frowned, twisted his chubby fingers together, crossed his feet, fluffed up his wings as if they were wet as he began to blush a bright red.

"Oh, for goodness sake, spit it out!" said Lydia in exasperation.

Bumper coughed twice, raising his eyebrow. "Yes and halfway."

"Halfway what?" asked Jeremy and Sam together.

"Yes, you are all having the same dream, and you are halfway between," the cherubs replied in unison raising their shoulders as if the answer was obvious.

"How can anyone be halfway to nowhere?" commented Jubilee, grinning at her brothers.

169

"Oh, that's easy. A lot of people are halfway, but they don't know it—and that's a big problem, you know," said Thumper with an air of authority.

Bumper nodded his head in strong affirmation. "People on earth in the third dimension don't believe in the possibility of living in heaven where Jaycee lives with the God King. Many of them don't even want to think about it. They are halfway from there to here." Then he added confidently, "That's why you are going to meet someone else who is halfway. He's the keeper of the outpost, because the escalator was stopped once when the rules were broken, and God brought a flood to clean the earth."

No one spoke as they tried to take in what they had learned. Bumper felt brave enough to continue. "You are being taken from the fourth dimension into the fifth dimension, but you can't go through the main gate, you have to go through the little gate in the cloud wall instead. That's where you will meet your guide to the Mirrors of Time." The cherubs were bursting with excitement.

Lydia had been rubbing her eyes, longing for it all to be a dream. Now she flipped. "I can't cope with all this.

Who broke the rules and why did the escalator get stuck here?" [88]

"Oh dear, I was afraid she'd ask that," said Bumper to Thumper. "It's too complicated to tell her, isn't it?"

Thumper turned to her and, still withholding secrets, said, "You'll find out soon enough."

They could no longer see the land beneath them. Silence filled their thoughts as they struggled to cope with what

---

88   **Ezekiel 32:27** speaks of "the fallen mighty of the uncircumcised, [unclean] which are gone down to the grave with their weapons of war"; *"Dictionary of deities and demons in the Bible", pp. 72–4.*

J. C. Greenfield mentions that "it has been proposed that the tale of the Nephilim, alluded to in **Genesis 6** is based on some of the negative aspects of the Apkallu tradition". The Apkallu in Sumerian mythology were seven legendary culture heroes from before the Flood, of human descent, but possessing extraordinary wisdom from the gods.

seemed to be their next adventure. Joel suddenly had a brilliant idea. "Well, if this is all a dream, why don't we just wake ourselves up?" he suggested, shrugging his shoulders and holding his hands up in question.

Jeremy smiled at his young brother, who seemed to see everything so simply. "We can't do that," he said, "because we are now halfway. Which side would we wake up in?"

Joel sighed and shrugged his shoulders again.

"We prayed to Jaycee, so we must have faith that he heard us. and he'll answer us in his time—not ours!" said Jubilee.

They all exchanged hopeful looks. Just then, the stairs stopped moving.

"Uh-oh, now what?" said Sam, holding onto his stick, ready for action. As the clouds cleared, they saw that the stairs were so wide they seemed to go on forever into the distance.

"Golly," said Joel, marvelling. Amused by the thought, he asked, "Do they go all around the world?"

"Looks like it," said Jeremy as they tried to take in the possibility of such a thing. "I never thought of anything like this, did you, Sam?"

Sam shook his head, furrowed his eyebrow, and pouted his bottom lip. They both shook their heads in disbelief. The girl's eyes widened at the great possibility. Slowly the soft clouds cleared away, revealing a large white gate with a golden crest of arms on a shield. The crest smiled down at them. Then frowned, as if judging them, then smiled again. Silently, the great gate slowly changed into the entrance to a rainbow tunnel, leading high into the sky. A man of great size and strength[89] stood there, grinning down at them. Around his neck hung a very large golden clock, which looked like a pocket watch in shape, but it was far too big to put in a

---

89   Numbers 13:31-33

pocket. In his right hand, he held a sword of truth.[90] Slowly the children stood up from their step, lifting their heads to stare up at him. Sam thought he must be about ten foot tall. He stood very straight and wore a pale grey robe. His skin was a pale brown, the colour of honey, under the fair hair that shone like gold. His face was strong and handsome, but his eyes seemed to be quite sad as if he secretly regretted something. Then they saw his huge, cream-colored wings open up on his back; just like the wings of Grandma's turtle doves in her garden.

"So," he said, "I have to open the great door of the Mirrors of Time for you. I wonder why?" he continued in a low and inquisitive voice as he tilted his massive head to one side. They waited. Then they heard a loud clunk. "That's it," said the giant. "We are now connected to the main engine. We have clearance. Come along, follow me!" he said as he floated past them.

Joel made a move to step off the stairs, but the angel man said, "Wait, wait. The link has not yet made. Don't break the chain of time or you'll spin back to below and we don't want that now, do we?"

He winked at Jubilee. She shyly grinned up at him as she searched for Sam's hand. The staircase disappeared. They floated in all directions around the entrance to the tunnel. "Don't try so hard," said the giant man. "You simply have to have faith in following Jaycee's wishes and go with the flow. Watch, I'll show you." —He swished away so quickly that they didn't see which way he went.

The opening into the rainbow tunnel was small but once inside everywhere looked huge, which surprised them as

---

90 **Symbolic meaning:** – [of the words of Jesus].
Numbers calls the Nehilim, the sons of Anak, or descendants of the Anakim (Annunnaki). They were also known in ancient times as the Rephaim, Emim, Zazummim, and Anakim, all very tall (from 7-12 foot) or "giant" people in those days. The biblical Goliath was a Rephaim, and giant in Hebrew is repha. Scores of giant red-haired mummies were discovered in a cave near Lovelock in Nevada.

they looked around in wonder. They continued to float about, looking at the astonishing range of deep colours all around them. They didn't feel afraid, just bewildered at being inside a rainbow. Silence. They looked at each other and waited. "Oh dear, sorry about that," said the giant, as his face appeared above them in mid-air. His voice reverberated. "I forgot to tell you where we are going. This clock doesn't travel very well, and if–I'm not careful it can lose a fraction of a second or two of—time, and that's nasty, yes, that's very nasty. This time all of you hold onto my hand — that'll do the trick. Here we go, up to the Mirrors of Time."

Like passing through time with the locusts, the shades of colours they had never seen before flashed before their eyes. This time, there was no darkness, no journey close to the moon, just warmth and beauty sparking all around them as they drifted into a deep sleep.

When they opened their eyes, they stood before a narrow wooden door in a huge wall. The giant stood beside them. Pointing towards the narrow door, he boomed, "This is the door we have to pass through."

"I thought it would be bigger than that," said Joel.

"Me, too," said Sam, sighing and searching for a way out. "It's hardly a door to a garden of mirrors, more like the door to Alice in Wonderland."

The great man laughed. "That's because it's the eye of the needle to the home of the God King. Only those who know Jaycee can get through this doorway," he said, winking at Lydia. This time, she listened attentively.

"You can't get through that little doorway," said Joel adamantly. "You are just too big."

NEPH – THE SAD BUT FRIENDLY GIANT NEPHILIM

At this, the giant threw back his head and roared with laughter – then he simply floated straight through the wall, he didn't bother with the doorway.

"Wow," said Jeremy, giving him credit. "That is amazing."

One by one, Jeremy led them through the narrow passage into a great garden, where huge, brilliant flowers floated about freely, with no roots. Each flower sang its joyful song as it passed by. Birds and butterflies danced from one blossom to another.

Lydia, who looked peaceful, spoke for the first time in a long while. "This I like. This scenario I can cope with."

They stopped beside a shoal of brightly coloured fish that reminded her of the ones in Grandma's fish pond in France. They also swam around freely, in and out of the flowers along with the many amazing birds of startling colours. Everything seemed to be migrating towards the sun in the centre of the bright blue sky. Lydia held Jubilee's hand gently as they silently admired the wondrous scene of the free floating fish with large chiffon tails that swayed gently behind them. Then the fish came to swim around the heads of the children, to examine their laughing faces.

"They are playing with us aren't they, Lyd?" said Jubilee, seeming unsure.

Somehow the giant knew what the boys were thinking. He suddenly appeared beside them. Jeremy and Sam turned to look at him. Sam, feeling brave, as he clutched his staff asked the first question. His voice was shaking. "Who are you and where do you come from?"

"Why are you so big?" asked Joel, who decided to join his older brothers.

The giant looked sadly at the boys and said, "I am a child of the Nephilim; we are the called Elieoud.[91] We are

---

91   1 **Book of Enoch 20:2, 25 and Jubilees.** The Greek, Aramaic, and main Ge'ez manuscripts obtained in the 19th century and held in the British Museum and Vatican Library, connect the origin of the Nephil-

considered a separate race from the Nephilim, but we share their fate.[92]" He looked away.

Lydia and Jubilee had heard what was being said. Lydia asked, "Did your parents do something bad?

"Who are the Nephilim?" asked Jeremy, folding his arms.

"Good questions. My father was a fallen angel, a Nephilim. They were known as watchers. My mother was a daughter of the earth-men. Samyaza, an angel of high rank, led a rebel gang of angels who went to earth and fell in love with the beautiful daughters of humanity. Their children were all born as giants." He looked down to his feet. His face fell into a very sad expression. Ashamed, he said, "I am known as Neph."

He peeked up at the children, hoping for encouragement. Jubilee's heart hurt as she saw the look on Neph's face. Instinctively she moved towards him to take his hand and comfort him. "Oh, you have six fingers!" she marvelled.

"Yes, and six toes as well," he replied, extending his hands out in front of them all.

"How odd!" said Lydia, looking down.

Joel studied his feet with amazement, then asked, "How do you get shoes big enough to get all your toes in?" He crouched down to get a closer look. The giant grinned.

"You people call us sons of God. Others call us angels[93] and others say we are the heroes of old men of renown, but, in God's eyes, we are all sinners. [94]

---

im with the fallen angels, and in particular with the egrégoroi (watchers).

92   NBC p.65 – 'The Nephilim are the ancient superman supposed to be the offspring of these spirit-human unions. Some Nephilim were in Canaan when Israel invaded (**Numbers 13:33**).

93   **Job 1:6**; perhaps **Psalms – 29:1** – mighty ones. **Jude 6-7**. Jewish lit. **Jude 6:1** – angels.

94   In the **Book of Jubilees** [sometimes called the Lesser Genesis, is an ancient Jewish religious work of 50 chapters, 2nd century BC, known as the book of division] also states that God granted ten percent of the disembodied spirits of the Nephilim to remain after the flood. [Others

So you see, I'm halfway from here to there." He looked sad as he shrugged his shoulders.

"You mean you're halfway between knowing the God King and not knowing him at all, like a lot of people on Earth where we come from," said Joel, looking pleased with himself.

Jeremy and Sam laughed.

"Exactly. A lot of people down there are walking around blind, to the truth, just because they are stubborn.

"Like Levi, the mule," Sam explained, leaning on his staff.

"It wasn't your fault that your parents did something wrong, was it?" Lydia replied, feeling sympathetic towards Neph.

"No, but we are now under man's corrupt ideas, and we will have to meet judgement. That's why you have come to see the truth for yourselves, in the Mirrors of Time. I have been given the honour of being the holder of the key. It is so sweet to meet you all; it's been such a long time since I had visitors," he replied sitting down with his face now level with theirs. He grinned.

Suddenly they all felt pleased that they were here and had met each other. "I still don't understand," pleaded Sam, feeling insecure. "Why us?"

"Well, did you pray to be able to understand all these things?" Neph asked, resting his head on his fist and his elbow on his knee.

They looked at each other in silence, remembering the night of the storm and the strong blue-white light that flashed across their room. "You... you mean, Jaycee heard us?" Lydia asked in complete surprise.

"Of course, He must have heard you, because He always hear us when we pray to Him," Jubilee reminded her.

---

do not agree with this, though commonly mentioned in ancient mythologies – Allusions also in **Wisdom of Solomon 14:6**, (Proverbs and Ecclesiastes) and in the nondeuterocanonical **3 Maccabees 2:4**]

Again silence fell as they thought about this. "We've met him — well, almost," said Joel, gleaming. "He looked at us."

They hadn't noticed that the birds, flowers, butterflies, and fish had all moved away. Neph looked up to the single star in the sky that hung above them. Sam's staff immediately lit up and its bright blue beam of light connected with the star. Instinctively he held his staff high above his head. At that very moment, the '*Book of Mirrors*' appeared in Jubilee's hands in front of her. Lydia's zip pocket unzipped, and the looking glass jumped out to sit in the palm of her hand. The water-skin sack on Jeremy's shoulder swung, round in front of him — empty! Then they all disappeared, even Sam's staff!

The star above them had become huge looking like a solid cloud of dense snow, each flake as large as dinner plates glistening and sparkling as it slowly descended. "Wow!" exclaimed Joel. "A spaceship. I told you we were aliens, and nobody believed me!" he said, putting his hands on his hips and nodding indignantly.

Neph laughed out loud as he slapped his thigh. "This is no spaceship, little man. This light can only be entered into by those who are pure in heart —and that's you, children! We are at 'The Mirrors of Time'. You come first little man," said Neph picking up Joel and passing him into the cloud, "because you are the most innocent."

Lydia gasped as Joel disappeared. "I don't like it when my family keep disappearing. No! I don't like it!"

"Would you like to go next then?" asked Neph, who was about to pick up Jubilee next, but he hesitated.

Lydia didn't know what to do.

"We'll be alright," said Jubilee to her big sister putting her hand on her arm. "Honestly!" She walked over to Neph and raised her arms in readiness to be lifted.

"Why don't we just float in?" asked Sam.

"Because you can't. You have to have someone to show you the way. That's me. I'm your guide on this adventure."

Neph completed putting Lydia, Sam and Jeremy into the cloud; then he followed them.

The air was pure and fresh as if they were breathing in crystal cool mountain air as tiny flakes of sparkling snow floated all around them. Breathing deeply, they walked down a magnificent corridor filled with enormous double-sided mirrors framed in ornate gold. They obediently followed Neph as he showed them the way.

"Now let me see... This one? No. A bit further along. Yes, here we are. The Gospel of St John. He's the one follower, disciple, who understood the spiritual side of Jaycee. Interesting, isn't it?" he pondered aloud as the children listened carefully.

No one spoke because their mouths hung open in awe. "Err, which mirror do we look in?" Jubilee asked quietly, not afraid to ask for help when she needed it.

"Gather around and I'll show you," Neph instructed, relaxing a little and seeming to enjoy their company. Neph had a soft side to him; that was rarely seen. They stood before the first great mirror. Neph bowed his head and muttered a few words, which Jeremy thought were Greek. Slowly an image appeared. Again, they saw the manna bread they had eaten with the people of Israel over eighteen hundred years before, to the time they had journeyed with the giant locusts. They stared in wonder at the vivid scene and remembered that they had been afraid to eat it. This bread filled their stomachs when they were so hungry in the desert. The picture faded.

In the second mirror, they saw Jaycee. He smiled; the words above him said, "The Bread of life – the one who comes."

Neph spoke quietly, "Now the word bread means Jaycee because he is the food for the mind to save man's soul. Without this, men will die when the time comes."

JESUS CHRIST (JAYCEE)
("Prince of Peace" by Akiane – age 8.
www.Art-SoulWorks.com)

180

Then Jaycee spoke from the mirror. "I am the bread of life. I am the bread that came. I am the living bread [knowledge]; this is my flesh, which I will give." [95]

As they heard him speak a deep peace flared in their hearts.

They felt calm, despite the bewildering things they had been through and the unbelievable surroundings they shared. For a few moments, they became aware that time was standing still. Then Jaycee took the freshly baked bread from the table, broke it up and passed it to the disciples. They watched Jaycee. The picture seemed so real.

"I don't understand," whispered Joel.

"That's the problem", said Neph smiling. "[96] A lot of other people don't understand either. We can take in knowledge for our minds as well as food for our tummies, can't we? Like you take in learning at school," Neph explained, looking expectantly at Jeremy.

"I see," said Jeremy. "You mean the word 'bread' means knowing Jaycee and his Father, the God King. It's symbolic."

Neph smiled and nodded his head. He looked pleased. The mirror faded and disappeared. They turned to follow Neph, who was moving further down the corridor. Sam grinned down at Joel, who was obviously thinking about all this. Joel whispered up to him, "So, are we spirits now? Because I can still feel my body, can't you?"

Sam didn't get a chance to answer. "Follow me," said Neph. "You wanted to know the truth about the Son of God, didn't you? So I'm going to show you something special—a current moment in time." He clapped his large

---

95 **John 6:33-51.** (v 35 *Then Jesus declared, "I am the bread of life. He who comes to me will never go hungry, and he who believes in me will never be thirsty*.) **Meaning:** – ['flesh' – he gave his body to die on the cross so that we could follow him, when we die, to go into the next world of spirit.]

96 **Meaning:** – [They think the word 'food' means only to take it in through our mouths. But the original meaning in Greek meant 'to take in, to consume, breathe in to ourselves].

hands together making a loud smacking noise. Slowly they followed him further down the long corridor, walking past the floating mirrors, one after another. Sam noticed that they all seemed to be recording the words of Jaycee. Neph smiled, he knew that the children were beginning to tune into the most important reason for them to be there. Finally, they came to a mirror that looked at them, as if it was expecting their arrival. They all stood before the great mirror. Slowly the cloud in the glass began to clear. They saw Jaycee as they had seen him at the temple when he cleared out the moneylenders. ─────────────────

Joel couldn't contain himself. He blurted out, "Hello. You helped us when we were being attacked by the locusts, didn't you?"

The moment was so real that the others joined in. "Yes," said Jeremy suddenly smiling. "We were very scared, and Gregory's leg was so badly hurt, it was awesome when your light came through Sam's staff and completely healed him."

"Yes," joined in Lydia and Jubilee, speaking almost in unison. "We prayed so hard in the cave, we just knew you would hear us."

Sam smiled at them all, joking, "Ahem. You are talking to a mirror!"

"Not quite," said Jaycee. They turned to look at him in complete surprise. It was all so real. "You came to find the truth, didn't you?" he said, his voice serious but soft. "You prayed to me on the night of the storm, when the lightning came. You wanted to know if I am the Son of God?"

"Um, yes," whispered Joel, who had forgotten that night when they were all so scared.

Jaycee stepped forward in the huge mirror. The warmth of His smile brought such love. They simply knew He was their best friend. "I tell you the truth. No one can enter the kingdom of God unless he is born again".[97] His words warmed the hearts of the children.

Joel immediately spoke up. "How can anyone be born again? That's silly!"

"Joel!" snapped Lydia, tapping him on the back. "Be quiet!"

Jaycee grinned at Joel's remark. Then He said, "I tell you the truth, no-one can enter the kingdom of God unless he is born of water[98] and the spirit.[99] Flesh gives birth to flesh, but the Spirit gives life to the spirit." [100]

"You children do not understand these things,"[101] Neph thought sadly.

Then before anyone could ask another question, Jaycee stepped out of the mirror, looked at Joel, and, laughing, said, "This is amazing!" Joel was so stunned by what he heard, he almost fell backwards. Lydia caught him.

Then Jaycee looked at the giant and said, "Hello, Neph. Watch over them for me."

The giant was so astonished that Jaycee knew his name. With laughter on his face, Jaycee said kindly, "You can all close your mouths now. I will always be with you, and," tilting his head to one side he said, "I always hear your prayers, but sometimes you pray for the wrong things, things that will hurt you. I will do whatever you ask in my name so that [I – the Son of God] may bring glory to my

---

97 **John 3:3** *Born again* ['The Greek may also mean "born from above"].

98 **John v.5** [Born of Water here refers to being made pure in mind/ spirit – that is no longer relying on material things/money to bring us love and salvation. It won't!

99 **Meaning:** – [of *living water* – and the spiritual knowledge of who Jaycee is] **John 3:5** Jesus said, *"no-one can enter the kingdom of God unless he is born of water and the spirit"*, [that is – in body **and** mind.]

100 **John 3:8** *"The wind blows wherever it pleases. The Holy Spirit works as he pleases in his renewal of the human heart".*

101 **John v.10-11** *"I tell you the truth, we speak of things we know, [because we were witnesses]and we testify to what we have seen, but still you do not accept our testimony."*

Father. You may ask me for anything in my name, and I will do it."[102]

He smiled as he turned to walk away giving them a gentle wave. He disappeared before their eyes. They seemed to stand in silence for a long while watching the mirror where he had been, even Neph was speechless.

"That was just brilliant," said Jeremy softly. Lydia couldn't speak. Jubilee was still smiling, and Sam was too mesmerized to do anything.

Joel was in disbelief. "He DID hear my prayers," he whispered.

The mirror didn't come back. The clock around Neph's neck clanged loudly. "Times up, we have to go!" he exclaimed taking Joel and Jubilee's hands, they began to float through the thick white sparkling clouds, back into the rainbow tunnel.

"This rainbow tunnel is beautiful," said Jubilee, looking up at Neph with admiration. "What does it mean?"

"Yes," said Sam. "It seems as if it stands for something really important."

"It does," said Neph with his head to one side and a huge grin on his face. "It means that when God makes a promise, he keeps it.[103] He asked me to watch over you, which means I belong to him too. I never knew that," Neph said with an enormous feeling of pride and gratefulness inside himself.

"Does that mean you are no longer halfway?" asked Sam, piecing the puzzle together.

Neph's face bore an expression of absolute wonder. Full of thoughts, he couldn't speak, yet he had a new feeling of belonging after so very long. He began to skip. They all joined in jumping towards the small opening through which

---

102 **John 14:13-14**

103 **Genesis 9:12-16** NIV – God said, "*This is a sign of the covenant [agreement] between me and you...I have set my rainbow in the clouds... the sign... between me and you and all living creatures of every kind*". NBC 'a pledge of God's goodwill', p.67

they had come. "He knows me," Neph kept saying. "He knows me".

The children laughed with him. "He knows us, too," said Joel, hugging Lydia. Jubilee couldn't stop smiling up at Jeremy, who smiled back at her, and Sam threw his head back laughing loudly placing his hands on his hips as he stood with his feet apart. Finally, they found themselves standing on the top step of the stairs.

Before Neph could close the gate behind them, Jubilee reached up to take his hand saying, "You aren't going to leave us, are you?"

He smiled down at her, then, as if on an impulse, he bent down picked her up above his dangling clock and cradled her in his huge arms as if she was a baby. "I'll always be with you from now on because you have all become one of us," he reassured her. Lydia was the hard one to convince. She gazed at him with the same worried look.

Joel pulled at his robe, to draw his attention. "Does that mean you are now our guardian angel—whatever happens?" he asked, hoping he had someone to whom he could contact.

Again Neph laughed, and then he murmured, "I will be able to watch over you and report back on how you are living your lives."

Quietly he looked deeply into each of their eyes. Holding Jubilee on one arm, he put his other hand down to hug Lydia to his side. She looked up at him questioningly with a lump in her throat; she whispered back, "I like the idea of you being our guardian angel, Neph. I'm going to miss you." Her green eyes were wide with fear at losing touch with him. He had become a dear friend. She hoped that they would meet again.

Neph smiled as his eyes began to glisten. To his amazement, a tear began to run slowly down his cheek. "I... I... haven't cried with joy in my heart for a long, long time. I... feel wonderful. The huge man that stood before Lydia was stunned. He saw true love for him in her heart. He realized that she loved him for himself.

Jubilee reached up and wiped away the tears now streaming down his face. The other children gathered around him as he held tightly onto the little ones in his arms. Slowly he bent to put Jubilee and Joel down. They all hugged him as they said goodbye.

The gate began to open. Gently he pushed them towards the stairs that would carry them back to finish their journey. He watched as they turned back to look up at him. Then he slowly closed the gate. His clock chimed; the ticking became louder as if they were running out of time there. The stairs began to move, going down as the clouds surrounded him as he disappeared from their sight. The spaceship cloud with the living mirrors above them away like a contented whisper in the sunset.

Chapter 12

THE RIVER OF LIFE AND THE LAKES OF CHOICE

THEY RODE ON THE MOVING stairs in silence, each one of them remembering the meeting with Jaycee in the Mirrors of Time, and how much he loved them all. The next thing they heard was an excited Thumper and Bumper, greeting them while darting around their heads, saying, "You can now play with us in the waters of life!" [104]

"Now what is going to happen?" said Lydia, still sad at not having Neph to talk to, as a friend.

Pointing behind them, Joel yelled, "Look, look!"

They swivelled around to see a wide, gleaming silver river running between large Cedar trees that were growing on the river banks. The serene waters glided elegantly below them and in the distance, they could see the white tops of the waves rolling down the stream, just where they were heading. As they approached they could see brightly coloured birds, all darting in and out of the trees, singing and whistling to one another as if they were very excited about something.

Worried, Sam yelled out, "We are going to drown! Lyd, hold onto the young ones!"

---

104 **Jeremiah 2:13** – Jesus (Jaycee) said, "Me, the spring of living water".

"I'm not a baby anymore," yelled Joel looking forward to splashing in the clean waters below them.

"Me, neither," added Jubilee with excitement. They both spoke without taking their eyes off the approaching rolling waves of water.

Lydia gulped. "We don't… have … time… to…"

Sam said, "I wish I had my staff." He reached his hand up, waiting for it to appear, but… nothing happened.

"I wish I had my looking glass," replied Lydia.

"And I wish I had my '*Book of Mirrors*' so that we could know what was about to happen," said Jubilee., "But… there's…no time."

"You will, you will," laughed Thumper as he flew back out of the water, flicking Jubilee's hair in fun as he deliberately flew too close to her.

He hadn't noticed Bumper coming from the other direction and flew straight into him. He hadn't been looking where he was going either. In momentary shock, they fell through the sky with their wings opened wide, like two starling birds which had flown into a glass window back home. In horror, the children watched as the two cherubs fell, lifeless into the water… and disappeared.

Watching for a sign from them, Jubilee cried out, "Oh no, they'll drown!"

Sam thought, I thought they were cherubs, not fish. To their absolute surprise, both cherubs flew straight back out of the water and high into the blue sky above them.

"Whoopee! It's so good to be off duty and back home again," said Thumper to Bumper as they darted back to be with the children who were much nearer the river. Then the children heard baby voices gurgling as they blew bubbles, which rose above the water as it rushed towards them.

"What's going on?" Jeremy managed to ask just before a wave engulfed him. "Wow, this isn't water, is it?" asked Jeremy in surprise as he tried to hold it in the palm of his hand.

LIVING WATER BABIES

Joel, who had disappeared beneath the water, instinctively held his nose as his eyes and cheeks bulged in a desperate effort to hold his breath. Lydia managed to grab Joel's arm as he swept past her. Jubilee clung onto Sam, who was a strong swimmer. They heard the swimming babies giggling as they blew bubbles without seeming to notice anything unusual at all.

Joel couldn't hold on to his nose any longer. He simply had to gulp. So he did. He blinked. Lydia saw this. She started to call out to him, and as she opened her mouth, she also looked surprised.

Effortlessly, Jeremy and Sam joined them. "This isn't like the water we know, is it?" said Sam.

"No. It's like fresh mountain air," said Sam. "My lungs feel amazing—"

"—Grandma," Jubilee completed the phrase, giving Joel a sarcastic look as he floated about with the water babies.

"What's that noise?" asked Lydia.

Jeremy raised himself as high as he could out of the water.

"Uh-oh... I think we're going to go over a waterfall," he said, looking back to see everyone and check they were alright.

"A what?" screamed Lydia with sudden fear?

Each of them tried to look towards the smooth water ahead of them, which just seemed to disappear. No one spoke as they floated closer and closer, in the warm, smooth, crystal clear white water. Then immediately in front of them, the water rose up into the shape of a head. It smiled down at them.

"Don't be afraid; I am with you. I am the living water that feeds the earth with knowledge and truth." As the head spoke, he became flesh and stood on the surface of the water. Jubilee recognized him first. Sam couldn't believe his eyes. Jeremy and Lydia felt a wonderful peace. As usual, Joel was the first to speak.

"Jaycee!" he yelled as they all fell over the edge into a massive lake of still waters beneath them.

They surfaced, now gasping for air, as if by instinct, but then realized they didn't need to. They stopped thrashing their arms and legs about to stay afloat because were floating naturally. On the banks of the pool, they saw all kinds of animals drinking the water. Others walked and lay down together. In the middle of the bank, Jaycee stood beside a young lamb.

Instinctively, the children began to swim and paddle towards him. Jaycee smiled and put up his hand to stop them.

"The time for you is not yet. You have three more signs to see, and the next one is the beginning of understanding." Then He smiled, waved, and disappeared.

They stood in silence in the shallow water. They so wanted to speak to him and ask so many more questions about the bread. As they walked slowly from the lake towards the bank, they realized that their clothes were still dry. Thumper and Bumper came to sit with them as they tried to understand the scene before them.

"What did He mean, that our time is not yet?" Joel asked, his inquisitive mind active as usual.

Thumper coughed, cleared his throat, folded his wings, puffed up his small chest and said, "He knows each one of us. He knew when we were born when we were young—like all of you—and he knows when our time will come for us to join him."[105]

The children sat in silence for a moment. Then Jubilee said, "I always felt, somehow, that He has always been near us." She didn't wait for a response.

"Maybe that's why you are the Keeper of the Book of Mirrors," suggested Lydia.

Jeremy nodded, and Sam smiled at her, saying, "You were always more tuned in than we were."

"I was, too!" Joel jumped into the conversation. This statement made the others laugh and this seemed to make them more settled.

"You think we are all aliens," laughed Jeremy nudging him with his elbow.

"Where is this place?" asked Sam, wondering if he would be needed to protect them from what was coming next though he knew Jeremy always took the lead.

---

105 **John 21:18-19 cf.** "*I tell you the truth, when you were younger you dressed yourself and went where you wanted; but when you are old you will stretch out your hands and someone else will dress you and lead you where you do not want to go.*' Jaycee said this to Peter. [Indicating he knew how Peter would die – as He knows all of us.]

191

The cherubs stood still in mid-air as they looked at each other. "I suppose we can tell them now, can't we?" asked Bumper. Thumper nodded. "You can tell them this time."

Bumper grinned at having this privilege. So he puffed up his chest, coughed to cleared his throat, and held his hands together in front of him.

"This is where the sparks of spiritual life come from before they are born on earth,"[106] he said.

No one spoke.

So Thumper continued, "Uh-hum. Yes, these spirits are the souls that will live in the earthly babies. They will grow as they live in bodies of flesh for a special time arranged by Father God. Their time on earth is watched by their angels. When they are born, they will begin to learn things of the spirit; important things, like loving others apart from themselves, even when it is very, very hard at times. They learn to have compassion for others in pain, patience with others who are difficult to be with, and so on. You know, invisible things you can't touch or see on earth."

The children all looked amazed. Shocked, Thumper whispered to Bumper, "I thought they understood that they are made in the image of our Father God, who made them?"

The cherubs looked back at the children, who all looked at one another as if they each hoped that one of them understood.

"Image of God?" asked Joel in his innocence. He looked down at his body, perplexed. "How can we be like him? We don't know how he looks. So how can we know we look like him?"

"Oh goody, goody," said Bumper. "They want to know. Can I tell them the next bit?" Thumper nodded reluctantly.

Bumper stood firm in mid-air, puffed up his chest, fluttered his wings, and said, "You don't look physically like

---

106 **Romans 8:28-29 cf.** *'For those God foreknew he also predestined to be conformed to the likeness of his son'*.

192

him. It's your spirit in you that is learning how to be like him. See?" He did a quick flight, around the children who all looked so very confused. The children did not react. They were silent. So Thumper cleared his throat and flew over to stand beside Bumper.

"Hmm-hum. The human race, or tribe, of humanity, has to learn, as one body, from their mistakes. That helps them to learn about spiritual things, ready for when they pass into the kingdom. You know, inside you when something is right or wrong…" He waited for some reaction. None came.

So Bumper tried to help. "Oh for goodness sake! Being down on earth is called 'the valley of the shadow of death.' You have been living in the shadows; here we live in the light. Simple really," he explained, wiping the curls off his forehead and back in place. Then he folded his arms and waited a reaction.

Sam spoke first. "You mean like my uncle told us. It's a jungle on Earth, the survival of the fittest, it's either eat or be eaten if you want to succeed and get anywhere."

"He sounds like a hard man. He must have been very unhappy?"

"I don't know?" said Sam beginning to think about this. "Come to think of it, he did look unhappy most of the time."

"Where is he hoping to go when his time comes? Probably not up here that's for sure," said Thumper.

"Yes," said Bumper. "He is in for a big, big shock if he's not careful. Those evil locusts don't care who they bite."

"So," said Jeremy, "what happens if people decide not to bother about God?"

The cherubs looked at each other and frowned. They didn't answer.

"Yes," exclaimed Joel, folding his arms and furrowing his brow. "Like the man next door to my friend back home; he's not nice at all. He's grumpy. He says he thinks Mum and Dad are silly religious people, and they don't know what they are talking about!"

"Hmm, well, we can pray for them," said Jubilee quietly.

Sam decided to change the subject because the cherubs didn't answer them.

"So," said Sam, who had been looking at the pool of water that the babies were still playing in. "Is this the only pool with this kind of water?" he asked.

The cherubs exchanged anxious looks. "Oh dear, I was hoping they wouldn't ask that."

"That's where the black holes come in," whispered Bumper.

Sam frowned.

After a few moments, Thumper said quietly, "There is another lake—the black lake. It feeds on the smaller holes. It's named because there is no light in it. Waves of darkness overcome those who are very selfish. They always get pulled in and swallowed —if they don't change," Thumper said sadly.

"How horrible!" said Jubilee.

"Yes," said Bumper. "The mud, around the edges of the black holes on earth, is very tempting, it's sticky and sweet, like dark, thick syrup. If you eat too much of it, you become ill. The problem is that it is invisible. So if you make a step towards temptation before you know it, it begins to stick to your feet and then you think you want more. It's so easy to get sucked in and drown in the emptiness of the sticky black lake."

"The Black hole in our minds has small lights which hover around it as if in space, tempting our strength, to see if we can cheat its power. If our minds don't turn back to the light, they shrink, get lost and disappear... forever." Bumper looked sorry to be the one who broke this news to them.

"You shouldn't have told them all that. Be quiet, Bumper," snapped Thumper. "They aren't ready for that yet."

Bumper's wings sagged as he looked down to his feet. He sighed. "Oh dear, I've got it wrong again."

Jubilee felt sorry for him. "I know what you mean. When I start eating milk chocolate drops, I can't stop; they're so delicious. So I must keep control of myself. Is that what you are saying?"

Bumper looked up with a smile and nodded, but he kept his lips tightly closed while glancing towards Thumper.

"So do you mean we are all chosen before we are born, to have this chance to decide how to live and maybe end up… here, where the light is?" Jeremy concluded.

The cherubs leapt up into the air, flipping over and over with delight, making feathers from their wings float all around them as they rolled down the bank and fell back into the water again.

"They've got it! They've got it." Bumper squealed, rolling around.

"Phew, it was hard work, though, wasn't it?" said Thumper as he shook himself tidy.

Sam said solemnly, "That sounds bad, like a black hole beyond our galaxy of which the scientists talk. No-one knows where black holes lead to, do they?" he asked, thinking of the future and back home.

"We haven't studied that yet," said Thumper. "That is Level 7, and we are only at Level 2 5/8. We do know about the pools of life."

"Yes," said Bumper, thinking deeply. "People down there in the third dimension call it the spring of eternal life, where you can live forever."

"That is where you are going next. Jaycee will give you the answer to the question, 'What's it all about?'" Thumper added.

Joel had heard this before, so he said, "Our auntie back home is always saying that, isn't she, Lydia?"

Lydia gave Joel a sideways look. She blinked, confused. "Which auntie?"

"You know, the lady across the road who likes me to call her auntie!" Joel said, holding his hands out.

"Oh, her!" she said, understanding.

Lydia was wondering where all of this knowledge was going to lead them. And how they were going to find the fifth sign.

"Did you hear what I was thinking?" She flashed a quick look at them both.

"Yes, we talk with our minds, not with our voices. That's how we communicate. Didn't you know that, either? Tsk, tsk, they still don't know very much, do they?" said Thumper as he and Bumper flew away into the clear blue sky and disappeared before their very eyes.

"I want one last swim before we go anywhere!

Please, Jeremy, please?" begged Joel.

"I wish I had my looking glass so that we could ask it what is going to happen next," said Lydia.

"I wish I had my staff—or, should I say, Sword of Truth?" smiled Sam.

"I miss my book," said Jubilee quietly.

"For some reason we don't have our water-skin anymore," frowned Jeremy.

"What about me?" cried Joel with his hands on his hips? "I haven't got anything!"

"Oh, then go and have your last swim and we'll join you," said Lydia.

After a few minutes swimming beneath the surface, they saw shells, fish, snails and luminous plants. The creatures nodded to them; they must have been a curiosity to everything they passed, even the plants? Finally, they swam into a slightly darker water where things seemed to begin to be more 'normal'. It brought back memories of being at the seaside with their parents. They surfaced into bright sunshine on a beach made of pebbles and stones. To their amazement, they saw an entirely different scene before them. "Where are we now?" asked Lydia.

They walked through the shallow waters towards the dry beach.

"My clothes are wet," said Joel in surprise, looking down at his dripping clothes.

"Mine, too," said the others. "What's going on? Where are we?"

"I feel different," said Jubilee.

"Me, too," said Lydia.

"And me," said the boys.

"What's happening to us? I feel good; somehow I'm not so scared anymore," said Lydia as she stepped out of the water.

"I'm all wet," insisted Joel, holding out his hands to Lydia as if asking her for a solution.

"Don't worry. It's a lovely day; you'll soon be dry," Lydia assured him, smiling.

They stood on the sand in a solitary place and gazed at the hundreds of people walking and excitedly talking as they began to make their way up the hill. They heard the people saying that when Jaycee arrived and saw the large crowd still mourning the death of John the Baptist, he would have compassion on them and heal their sick.[107]

"Are we going to see Jaycee again? Is he going to do some more miracles?" asked Joel with excitement. "That's not why we'd like to see him again, is it?" asked Jubilee with a slight frown.

"That's right, Jubilee," said Lydia.

"Quite right," agreed Jeremy. "Remember, he is God's son. How wonderful that we might see him in person, let alone learn what he will teach us." Jeremy reminded everyone but looked at Sam.

---

107 **Matthew 14:13-21. cf.** NBC p.923. Solitary place near Beth-saida...outside the territory of [the feared] King Herod Antipas. Many people wanted to force Jesus [Jaycee] to be their king; perhaps because of his miraculous powers. The people saw Jesus [Jaycee] as the greatest prophet. This meal of feeding the 5,000 (men) [15,000 with women and children] satisfied everyone. This mirrors the coming last supper, for the people would also eat the heavenly bread [meaning: take in spiritual knowledge of God's kingdom] through the words of Jesus [Jaycee].

"Come over here," said Sam encouragingly, with happiness in his voice, smiling his funny, crooked smile. "We'll stay here for a little while so that we can dry out.

With this strong sun coming it shouldn't take too long."

Chapter 13

THE STONE WITH SEVEN EYES

The Fifth Sign – John 6: 1-14 'The feeding of the five thousand.'

"I THINK THIS IS THE Sea of Galilee," said Jeremy, looking to the horizon. "This is going to be the Fifth Sign."

"What is?" asked Joel, kicking the sand and stones.

"It's still a mystery to me," said Lydia. "I mean, exactly who and what is Jaycee? He keeps turning up in the most amazing places and before we know it, he disappears again. Puff, just like that." She clicked her fingers in the air.

"Isn't he supposed to be the Son of the God King?" asked Joel, musing.

"I know that," said Lydia, "I just can't understand what that means; that's all," Lydia said, feeling a bit down. Silently they each nodded.

"This is where Jaycee said we had to come to find the answer," Jeremy said, looking around to see if he had arrived already.

A sudden flash of light passed Sam's hip; his staff sword hit the sand at his side.

"Hey, look! My sword. It's back, and…it's different. It feels real and heavy." He held it in his hands, feeling the new weight.

Lydia's zip pocket jumped. She instinctively slapped her hand to her chest and felt the looking glass beneath her fingers. Unzipping her pocket, she quickly pulled it out and opened it. "Look, look! It's unbroken. The mirror is whole—I can see the whole picture. How wonderful! No more guessing when we try to find out answers," she said, holding it up as everyone turned to see.

Jeremy was about to speak when he felt something swing on his shoulder.

"My water-skin. It's back! Look!" He swung the water-skin around to examine it. To his amazement, it had turned into a golden glass bottle full of rose coloured liquid. He stared at it, not knowing what it meant.

"It looks like our gifts have come back to us," Jeremy suggested, staring intently at each item.

"All except me!" said Joel. "I haven't got anything. Nothing, just nothing." He started to kick the sand and stones beneath his small feet. His bottom lip pushed out as his top lip tucked inside, his mouth in an attempt to hide his disappointment. The others didn't know what to say.

Jubilee was quiet. She sat down, feeling sad because the book hadn't yet come back to her. She looked at her hands, hopefully. Immediately the '*Book of Mirrors*' appeared. Startled, she flinched, but she was so thrilled that she instinctively pulled it to her chest. It glowed white and floated through her fingers, coming to a stop between them in the air. They stared at it, in wonder. The book showed a scene in three dimensions; people who seemed to be acting out an event, while they watched as if they were looking down on a play, in a circular theatre.

"What's happening?" asked Jubilee quietly, not wishing to disturb this wonderful scene before them.

"The Book has become a living thing," whispered Sam. He felt excited that everything was coming together.

They saw a man in a white robe sitting at a table writing in a large book. And as he wrote the play, he became real before their very eyes.

"This is brilliant," whispered Sam. "A floating five-dimensional picture, which seems to include the blending of the two realms of life. The whole world, with a living shadow of both the physical and the spiritual, together in one presentation. A combined existence. How can The Book of Mirrors receive these images? They don't have satellites here, do they?" Sam received no reply, so he said, "Whatever it is, it needs to be tuned properly. Seeing both worlds at the same time is making me feel dizzy".

"Why do all the people want to listen to Jaycee?" asked Joel, who was more interested in why the people were all coming here.

"Because they have already seen the miracles Jaycee has done. Don't you remember? The healing of the boy who was dying, and all of the sick people waiting for healing, by the pool. It's as though Jaycee has become a superstar to them. They want to see more signs and these signs are leading them to see Jaycee," Sam explained, sitting comfortably next to Joel who was absentmindedly uprooting weak grass from the sand.

The book disappeared, flying back into Jubilee's heart. Joel, lay down on the sand feeling fed up. "What's happening to the sky?" he asked.

They all looked up at the clouds, which were beginning to collect in a cluster above the foothills of the Golan Heights. Other people didn't seem to notice the change in the colour of the sky as it blended to a soft, aquamarine blue.

"It reminds me of the living water we swam in!" Jubilee exclaimed.

"That felt like breathing in the mountain air, remember? We could breathe as we swam," Jeremy pointed out.

The purity of the sky struck Sam. "The sky is full of diamonds," he whispered, thinking back to when he was very little and his mum told him the snow in the sky was made of diamonds.

"And isn't it easy to breathe!" commented Jeremy.

"Look at those clouds. They're like a gallery of seats for the angels in heaven, arranged for a special event," Jubilee described. "Almost like a stadium or a coliseum." She looked like she was daydreaming as she gazed up at the sky.

"Will Neph be there?" asked Joel, who had forgotten momentarily about the circular scene.

"Maybe. He said he would be watching over us. Is it just me or can you see hundreds of angels in the clouds? They look as if they are getting ready to sit in front row of the dress circle in a theatre," Lydia said, standing up and shielding her eyes from the sunlight to get a better look. "Dad said he and Mum sat high up in the local theatre, they told us the level is called 'The gods'. Do you remember, Jeremy?"

Jeremy nodded and Joel frowned because he couldn't imagine it. "It looks as if this is happening up there, doesn't it?" Sam said, giving Joel a friendly push, placing his hand on his head as he gently stroked it.

"Angels don't need to sit on seats," said Jeremy, "They just…float about, don't they?"

Jubilee, who was still sitting, answered as she pulled her knees to her chest while she stared intently at the sky above them. "I'm just wondering what all the excitement was for," as her small warm hand absent-mindedly picked up pieces of driftwood on the beach. "The crowd is so big; there must be thousands of people here!"

"Something amazing must be about to happen, Lyd," said Sam, speaking with awe at the gathering sight before them.

"This is as big as a football crowd back home, I think, Jeremy?" Lydia answered as she took Jubilee's hand stopping her from picking the flotsam in the sand.

Jubilee giggled saying, "Jaycee is like a superstar in Hollywood."

Lydia, being practical, wondered where the five of them would sit. They had better start looking, she decided. Sam, though still interested in the present moment, remembered another Jewish celebration about to happen.

Thinking ahead, he asked, "Jeremy, do you think this has anything to do with the Passover meal coming up next week?"

Jeremy thought about it and shook his head. "I don't think so. I do know that their great hero, Moses, gathered all God's chosen people together and led them out of their slavery. He was like the Mafia boss of their time; the Egyptian Pharaoh was very stubborn and acted really cruelly. He didn't want to lose his cheap workforce. It would cause him many problems not to have his army of slaves. On top of all that, he feared them because they had grown to be a nation to reckon with, over the years. God told Pharaoh that, if he didn't let the Israelites go, he'd bring curses on his Nation." Jeremy took a breath, happy with how he recited what he had learned at Bible school back home,

"And did he?" asked Jubilee.

"Yes. The sea turned to blood at one point. Can you imagine that?" Jeremy exclaimed, shivering at the thought of it.

"That's horrible!" said Lydia.

"Then there were millions of frogs everywhere," continued Jeremy, "Then biting gnats and big black flies. I hate those! All their animals got very sick. Everyone had boils, which is nasty, and then the hailstones came, followed by locusts." Jeremy listed the plagues, running through one after another.

"Not our locusts?" Joel said, turning around attentively.

"No. The evil ones, with crowns on their heads were let loose. Remember those?" Sam said, in answer to Joel's question.

"I do," said Joel, frowning as he remembered their dear locust friend Gregory who nearly lost his leg.

"It all ended up with darkness, no light, and finally the first-born child in every family died," Jeremy concluded solemnly, thinking of all the heartbroken families of the period.

"That's all terrible. So what did they do, after it was all over?" asked Lydia and Jubilee.

"God told Moses that the Jews should mark their front door posts with lamb's blood;[108] so that God's spirit would 'pass over' [109] their houses and spare them from that plague," Jeremy explained.

"No wonder they have a special meal to thank God and celebrate being saved," Lydia said, scratching her forehead.

Sam fell silent as he thought about everything that had happened to them and the celebration meal they still had each year to remember what the God King had done for them. Then he said, gratefully, "I wonder if what is about to happen is connected to the 'Passover'."

Lydia had listened intently to their conversation. "Whatever is going on, I don't think there is going to be food—not for this huge crowd. Just imagine how much bread is needed for this many people to eat; at least the sun would cook the dough, so that it was flat and crispy."

Sam looked disappointed. Lydia grinned at him. "You're always hungry, Sam. I'm pretty sure they are here to see what Jaycee is going to say and do."

Lydia stood up and wandered over to a tree with figs on it. She picked a couple, gave one to Sam then and sat down alone, deep in thought, trying to understand everything that was happening.

"More miracles?" Sam suggested, continuing his conversation with Jeremy.

"Probably. He must have healed hundreds and hundreds of people by now. Just think—if we were back home right now, people all over the world would be watching this on their televisions, laptops, and tablets," Jeremy said.

---

108 **Meaning**: – [The blood of 'the Lamb' (Jaycee) being used to mark them as God's children is symbolic of protecting them from death] (Blood being the symbol for life-giving power).

109 **John 6:4** *'The Jewish Passover Feast was near.'*

"And Game Boys," chipped in Joel.

Jeremy laughed playfully at Joel, who didn't understand.

"That won't please the high priests here, will it?" Jubilee added.

"No, and they can't shut down the internet search engines to keep it all quiet, can they?" said Sam with a huge smile.

"No, they can't," giggled Jubilee. "Remember that Levi warned us about the high priest wanting to keep control of the people and the things they are taught."

They both laughed at the thought of their friend, Levi, the stubborn mule, being there with them. Then they remembered that they had witnessed the priests getting angry when they saw Jaycee heal the blind man by the pool of water.

Lydia turned around to look back at them. "What are you talking about?" she asked, her voice serious.

"We were just talking about food," laughed Jeremy. "Sam is starving as well, but we won't find a supermarket here or even a snack bar."

Then Lydia noticed Jaycee, who was not too far in front of them. "Come on, there's a good place just over there by that rock. We'll have a good place to see and hear him!" she commanded with anticipation.

Jaycee turned to a man walking with him. They heard Jaycee ask, "Philip, where shall we buy bread for these people to eat?" [110]

"That's a funny question to ask one of his followers," said Sam.

"Why do you say that?" Jubilee asked.

"Because he must know that there is nowhere to buy bread this far from town. Also no shop would have enough for this many people," said Sam, looking around and hoping that he was wrong.

---

110 **John 6:1-15'** v6 *'He asked this only to test him, for he already had in mind what he was going to do.'*

Lydia used her practical approach to the conversation. "Jaycee must be joking with him. For one thing, he must know that Philip once lived here, so Philip knows there is nowhere here to buy bread. For another thing, even if there was somewhere, none of them has enough money to pay for bread for thousands of people."

"That's true. So what is Jaycee talking about, and what's he going to do about it?" Jeremy wondered, trying to listen hard.

Philip answered Jaycee, sounding worried, "Eight months' wages would not buy enough bread for each one to have just one bite." [111]

As they watched, Jaycee held out his hands and, smiling, told his followers to go to the people and see if anyone had any food with them. After a few minutes, Andrew, who was Simon Peter's brother and another follower of Jaycee, shouted back. "Here is a boy with five small barley loaves and two small fish, but these won't go very far among so many people." [112]

Bewilderment and anxiety grew in the crowd.

Lydia whispered, "That's pretty obvious! Isn't barley bread the cheapest bread that can be bought? Only the poor people eat it."

"Hmm," said Sam, "I remember that it tastes delicious, fresh from the oven, but a bit dry later on in the day."

"True," said Lydia, "but its real bread with nothing good taken out of it, unlike the bread in the supermarkets at home!"

"I don't care," said Joel, rubbing his tummy. "I'm so hungry; I'll eat anything."

---

111 **John 6:7 Meaning:** – [no money can buy this.]

112 **John 6:9 Symbolic meaning:** – [a little spiritual food/ knowledge can multiply when given to others.]

"Oh dear. What's Jaycee going to do?" whispered Jubilee, worried as she watched him. Part of her wanted to help, but she knew that Jaycee was all-powerful; she trusted in him.

"Probably the same thing he did at the wedding when they had no wine. Remember? The master of the ceremony said it was the best wine he had tasted," said Sam, putting his hands on his stomach to stop his tummy rumbling.

They watched Andrew take the basket of food from the boy to Jaycee. Joel gulped and Jeremy grinned at them both. It was obvious to him that Jaycee was about to do something amazing.

Jubilee also remembered the wedding in Galilee. The water jugs had told them they were going to be used, for something very special. She nudged Joel and said, "Do you remember the water jugs and how funny they were?"

Joel nodded. "They said that we were made, in the image of God, didn't they?"

At that moment Jaycee stood up, opened his arms wide and told everyone to sit down because they were going to eat. The children sat down as they watched the many thousands of men, women, and children do the same. There was a murmur of excitement, like a wave of spring water tumbling over smooth rocks as it trickled over the hillside.[113]

"How many people do you think are here?" Lydia asked Jeremy.

"Hmm. I think there are supposed to be about five thousand men, but with women and children, there must be nearer fifteen thousand altogether," Jeremy calculated.

"How on earth can all these people hear what he is saying? I can't see any microphones or loudspeakers anywhere, can you?"

Sam put his hand on her shoulder. "He doesn't need huge flat screens everywhere or loudspeakers, because they will

---

113 **Meaning:** – [God can multiply our work for him many times over.]

all hear him spiritually, in their minds, and that will help them to understand him."

Joel responded, "Oh, you mean like tel..epa..thy?" he said, nudging Jubilee, who giggled at his attempt, to get the word right.

"I guess so, something like that," Jeremy answered.

"So, when we talk and pray to him in our minds, he can also hear us?" asked Jubilee.

"Of course," Sam said, looking at her. "Why not?" "Golly, that's cool, isn't it?" said Joel.

Jaycee raised his hands. The crowd fell silent. The five loaves and the two fish lay before him in the basket, he prayed to his Father God and gave him thanks.[114]

The watching people had all gone very quiet, filled with awe and expectation, as if they somehow knew that this was the beginning of a momentous occasion. Jaycee broke the bread and gave it to his followers to pass to the waiting people. One by one the groups began to eat and they all seemed to be enjoying the meal.

"What's happening? I can't quite see. There won't be any left for us!" said Sam and Joel together.

"It's going to be fine. I don't know how, I just know," said Jubilee.

The children felt so hungry. They simply couldn't take their eyes off Jaycee's hands as he continued to pass out pieces of bread, which smelled as if their mum had just baked it for a picnic.

---

114 **John 6:11** NBCp.1038. The verb John used here is the same as the Synoptic use in the narrative of the Lord's Supper. John stresses that all the people were satisfied v.12 he did the same with the fish. Jews regarded bread as a gift of God. 'The twelve baskets of fragments were intended as a symbolic way to refer to God's provision for the tribes of Israel' (all God's children). John links it with the people's reference to *the Prophet*, an allusion to the prediction of **Deuteronomy 18:15**. The fish became a secret sign written in the sand for Christians to recognise one another.

"I feel as if we are at an amazing picnic for everyone who wants to have Jaycee as their very best friend," said Jubilee with a wide grin.

"My mouth is watering," said Sam.

"Me, too," agreed Jubilee and Lydia together.

"Jeremy," said Joel looking up at him, "how long is it going to take to feed everyone here?"

"I don't know, but with all the followers of Jaycee, who already know and love him, helping him, it shouldn't take too long." He immediately doubted himself when he saw the crowds grow in number.

They turned their attention to look at the quickly moving lines of helpers, laughing and talking to each other as they served the groups of smiling families and friends.

"This is the biggest picnic I have ever seen or been to," said Jeremy, "Even bigger than at school when we have a sports day."

Without noticing how it happened or how long it took, they saw that the hillside had filled with people eating the biggest feast they had ever seen. A natural celebration filled with joy and simple acceptance of what was happening filled the air.

Jubilee gasped; she felt something. She looked at Lydia. "Quick, all of us hold hands." The boys knew not to argue.

Then they heard Neph's soft whisper, "This is the miracle of the multiplication of the loaves."

"A miracle?" Jubilee gasped as if in disbelief.

"Yes, that's it," said Lydia. "It has to be. How else can all this be explained?"

For a few moments, they stared at each other in shock and disbelief at the magnitude of what had just happened. They knew instinctively that this was true. How else can all these people be fed like this?

Thousands of people have enjoyed a meal with them. In disbelief at what they had witnessed, Sam commented, "A real meal and… I didn't see any catering vans coming here?

Any delivery camels stacked up with food gifts like Oxfam? All we saw was Jaycee take the five small round loaves of bread and the two fish from the boy over there."

"Yes," observed Jeremy, "and then Jaycee looked up to heaven and he prayed to his father and asked him to bless the food."

"What does it all mean?" asked Joel quietly trying to find an answer in his mind.

"It means," said Jubilee, "that the bread story is now complete!" A grin stretched across her face from ear to ear. "Yes," said Jubilee. "The manna was food for our stomachs, the barley bread Gehazi carried to the one hundred young prophets was for their minds to get the correct teaching. Today has been for us to share what has happened. Our words to others can multiply, over and over again. Amazing. This proves who Jaycee is in spirit."[115]

At this very moment, they heard and felt the wind swirling around them in circles like tiny tornados as they danced between the families and groups of people, who discussed the miracle of the multiplication of the food, which they had all just eaten. They began to understand the double meaning of what had just happened. The God King can provide for everyone, body and soul.

Joel flopped back on the grass not understanding what had happened, so he and patted his stomach, saying, "Wow, that was great. I feel full."

Lydia and Jubilee laughed, saying, "That'll be the day when you are full!"

Jeremy lay back lazily in the late afternoon sun, closing his eyes in complete satisfaction. Joel wiped the crumbs

---

115 **Deuteronomy 18:15** [**Meaning** – Messianic expectation. [Jewish belief is that a new king will come to save them – but for them it's not Jaycee (Jesus) He is simply the prophet of prophets.] For Christians He is the Messiah of provision and fulfilment – the 'bread' [food for the mind and soul] gives a continual supply of information for eternal life].

from his mouth with the back of his hand. He watched the friends of Jesus telling everyone to pick up any leftover food and put it in the twelve empty baskets.

"Look. What are they doing that for?" he asked.

"The food mustn't be wasted. It can be given to others," said Lydia.

"Why?" Joel asked, intrigued.

"Because… I don't know why. Perhaps it can help others who don't have much! Or don't know much." Lydia wondered at her words.

"Only having a little faith," said Sam, calmly and wisely. "When we listen to Jaycee teach us things we didn't know; we can pass the leftover crumbs of information on to others. Those who weren't here, so that they can get more faith to understand more as well."

Jeremy nodded looking as his warrior brother, thinking, 'My brother is getting wise as he grows up'. Then thoughts came to him of where they should spend the night.

He turned to Lydia, "Where do you think we should head for to spend the night safely?"

Together they looked down towards the beach.

"It's much quieter down there. Only a few people are settling down, with camp fires being prepared." Sam turned to them "I agree, let's head back down to the beach for the night."

They each turned their gaze towards the beach they had walked on earlier; it brought back memories of their last adventure.

"Hmm, good idea. Not so many people there either. Most people are returning to their homes with bags full of leftovers, perhaps for their neighbours."

As the sun sank lower and lower in the sky, the older children walked happily down towards the beach. Joel and Jubilee skipped and laughed, waving their arms about to steady themselves, but Joel fell over as he misjudged a rock in the middle of the path. He immediately jumped up wanting to catch up with Jubilee who was going to reach the beach before him. Together they found a good place, not far away from a group of palm trees where the sand dune was shaped like a huge shell.

"This is it," yelled Joel. "I found the best place. Over here, come on. Over here," he yelled again, waving his arms around furiously.

"Shish," said Lydia, "People over there are beginning to settle down for the night."

He flopped down on the beach as the girls joined him and chose their places for the night. Sam and Jeremy began to look for wood and bracken to start a fire. Sam always kept two flint stones with him. He had learned in the boy scouts how to do this, so had Jeremy. Sam enjoyed making a fire, while Jeremy surveyed the scene, making sure they would be safe.

Joel sat sulking as his small chubby hands sadly grabbed at the sand, which stuck on his fingers. He crossly slapped his hands together, shaking off the rough grains sitting back to watched the others. Something moved beneath his hand. Startled he jumped, wondering what creature he had touched. He couldn't see anything, except a funny looking brown sandy coloured stone, with... seven eyes? Slowly, he carefully picked it up. It was smooth and... looked perfect, like a jewel someone had lost a long time ago. He rubbed it between his small grubby hands, turning it over as he examined it.

Lydia noticed he had a stone in his small hand.

"What is it Joel?" she asked, as the others continued to examine their special gifts that had changed and now looked brand new.

"I don't know. But it's mine, and you can't have it," he said putting it behind his back.

"Don't be silly, Joel," said Lydia. "We won't take your stone from you." Laughing she said, "We each have been given a gift that is special to us. Perhaps...this is yours. Come on, come and show us".

Reluctantly, He moved over to join the others, who had stopped what they were doing to look at what he had found on the beach. Slowly, he brought his hand out from behind him. Lydia became thrilled at the beauty of the intriguing, glistening, many colours in the brown stone with seven crescents that looked like eyes. [116]

"Wow! Look at that," said the others together.

"That's beautiful," said Jubilee quietly, wanting to touch it.

"I wonder why it has seven eyes? What do they mean? Can I touch it, Joel?"

"No! You can't. It's mine," he retorted, clutching it tighter with anger as he swung his hand behind his back. It disappeared. "Oh, what happened?" he asked, looking back at his empty hand. He felt dreadfully disappointed. For a few moments, no one spoke. Then, when Joel had calmed down, the stone appeared back on the floor with all the other stones. Joel bent over to pick it up again, but before he could, the stone rose a few inches from the floor. Joel gasped and froze. As he stared at it, it began to float slowly up and moved to within a few inches of his nose. They all blinked in disbelief.

"It's examining you, Joel," grinned Jeremy. Jubilee giggled at the sight.

Then it immediately shot to within a few inches of Jeremy's nose.

"Now it's examining you," grinned Lydia.

---

116 **John 1:29 cf.** This stone is the Lamb of God. This verse says, *"And I saw in the midst of the throne and of the four living creatures and in the midst of the elders a Lamb standing as having just been slain, having seven horns and seven eyes, which are the seven Spirits of God."* The Lamb (Jesus) has seven eyes. Therefore, the stone with -seven eyes in Zechariah 3 is the Lamb with seven eyes in Revelation 5. Hence, this stone is Christ. **Meaning:** – [of seven eyes – Jaycee (Jesus Christ) can see all and know all.]

The stone then shot over to Sam and waited. Nothing happened. Finally, it placed itself between the girls, who instinctively held hands, wondering what it would do. Joel slowly moved towards it. The stone turned and then, as if it had made a decision, went back to sit in Joel's upturned hand.

Joel grinned. "It's chosen me. Thank you," he whispered, touching it gently with his finger. "I don't think it wants anyone else to touch *him*." "It," said Jeremy, correcting him.

The stone glowed but stayed in Joel's hand. "To me, it's real and living because it has the power to think, so there," Joel said. Then he suddenly jumped up. The stone in his hand was getting very hot!

"Oh, oh, it's hot, hot! It's burning me." Joel screamed, juggling the stone from hand to hand.

"What made that happen?" asked Lydia.

Sam said, "I was thinking something about having faith!"

THE STONE OF SEVEN EYES

"What is faith?" asked Joel.

"Believing that something is true in your heart, even when you can't see it…like the wind," said Jeremy.

At this, the stone came to a sudden halt and started changing colour, shining with all the colours of the rainbow, one after the other.

"It's got stuck. Can't it decide which colour it wants to be?" said Joel

"Maybe you should choose a colour for it?" suggested Sam.

"I… like lilac the same as the stone in mum's ring." Immediately the stone changed its colour to a pale lilac that glinted with specks of gold in the late evening sun. "Wow," exclaimed Joel, shocked at the quick change. "That's brilliant!" The stone shot straight into his trouser pocket, and there it stayed.

The fire the older boys had made now flickered and glowed in the growing darkness as they lay on the shore of the Lake of Galilee. Joel couldn't stop grinning and holding his pocket, to keep his stone safe.

Jeremy grinned at him as he turned to speak to Sam.

"I'm happy to take the first watch."

"Fine" said Sam. "I'll take the second watch."

Most of the people had gone home by now; just one or two families seem to have the same idea to spend the night there. With a pile of wood to feed the fire through the night, they settled down.

"What an exciting day!" said Jubilee as she snuggled up to Lydia, who stroked her hair into place as she relaxed ready to fall asleep.

Joel let his head fall onto Jeremy's lap where he closed his eyes with a smile.

"They've had a busy day. What about Joel? He certainly seems to have found something special with that stone and its seven eyes?" said Lydia.

"Joel's stone could be another ancient stone of wisdom, not of history, but perhaps this time, of things to come," Sam suggested wisely. "What do you think?" he asked looking at Jeremy and Lydia.

"It could be. If it is," said Jeremy smiling, "we now have five gifts to help us finish our journey, and there's only two more signs to go."

Chapter 14

THE NIGHT OF THE STORM –
AND THE LAUGHING DEMONS

*JOHN 6:16-21 – Jaycee walks on water! In a terrify-
ing storm at sea in the middle of the night, Peace can
come.* [117]

EARLIER THAT EVENING, JAYCEE'S TWELVE
followers had gone by boat across the Sea of Galilee to
Capernaum. It would be quieter there, they could rest away
from the many thousands of people who now knew about
Jaycee and his miracles. They couldn't find Jaycee in the
crowds. They waited for a while and then decided to head
off across the lake. Maybe he wanted to be alone.

The still night was calm: the stars shone brightly in a
clear sky. Everywhere seemed peaceful, at least for a while.
Without any warning, strong winds suddenly blew up, and
the waters changed from calm to turbulent in a moment.
The men woke up from their slumbers, shocked and filled
with disbelief at the sudden violent change in their world.
They leapt to regain control of their small fishing vessel,
from the powerful anger of the invisible winds, who fought
amongst themselves, as do wrestling warriors in battle. The
cold raging spray of the waves stung the faces of the twelve

117 **Meaning:** – [In our darkest time, in a sea of rage, in fear and in
hopelessness – Jaycee can save us.]

217

followers of Jaycee in their wake, scattering them carelessly like falling blood red petals full of hope. They were thrown cruelly across the deck, blown as easily as grains of sand drifting through the desert of life.

The men staggered like children, suddenly drunk with disbelief, their bodies and faces being slapped from side to side by the violent cold waters making the men gasp for air. The winds growled and howled in battle, making the waters rise and fall in pain and agony as if tongues of hate licked in lust at their souls in torment. What was happening? So suddenly and without warning a violent argument had begun between the two giants of wind and water. The twelves men's minds screamed with despair in disbelief that they could so suddenly be in peril on the sea. They struggled to clasp onto the flapping, flying sail like frightened children holding the skirts of their mother, who fought to keep them alive. Furious ropes whipped over their heads snapping and crackling with laughter as they lashed the men into devastation and deep panic. Their blood began to freeze, their faces becoming like white marble with cold, as dead men are, without hope.

The previously calm waters of the day before now crashed on the beach. Huge waves flung themselves on the sand where the children lay sleeping. They were completely unaware of the onset of the storm. Dreaming of the mysterious and wonderful miracle of the multiplication of the loaves, and where the crowd had eaten as much as they wanted; they woke up with a start. "Where did all this come from?" yelled Jeremy as the cold waters splashed on his feet. Sleepily they each sat up, amazed at the growing, roaring fury of the wind. They still sat in the middle of their circle, protected by the power of Sam's sword. Even though they were safe, they could hear the crashing waves coming even closer towards them.

"What are we going to do, Jeremy?" yelled Sam.

"I don't know, but I do know that we can't stay here!" The boys looked further up the beach for a place of safety, as the others clung together, wondering what was going to happen next. The winds became even stronger. Blackened sticks from their dying fire landed around them. Branches from the nearby trees screeched as they were torn from their trunks; like drunken souls after a late night drinking party, furious at being woken from their self-imposed stupor.

"Is there going to be a tsunami?" cried Joel to Lydia.

Joel was now sobbing and shaking with real fear as he scrambled for Jubilee, who was white and still with shock. In the chaos of the storm,

Lydia made a brave decision; she dropped to her knees in the wet and windy storm and prayed. The little ones immediately crawled closer to her side. Lydia raised her hands to the skies, "Oh God, where are you? Save us, God. Jaycee, can you hear me?" She sobbed over the shrieking howling winds.

Joel felt the stone in his pocket move. He quickly put his hand into his pocket grabbing the stone. It was hot, and it wanted to get out! He knew that only he could do this. As he took it out of his pocket, the stone shot beneath them.

Joel screamed, "My stone, my stone, I've dropped it." Before he could do anything to get it back, they all realized that they were levitating in the air.

"We... we're going up—but how?" said Sam in surprise and bewilderment. Their feet now dangled several meters from the ground, the spray of the surf and growing waves just missing them. Below, their circle of comfort in the sand was roughly washed away.

"Wow," said Jeremy. "That was close! Lydia? Jubilee? Joel?" he cried, concerned for their safety since he couldn't see them.

Jeremy looked left and right searching for them, but the wind battered his face. The rain blurred his vision. He couldn't see anyone or anything. "Sam... Sam...?"

"Where are they?" Sam yelled back, his voice hoarse. Jeremy blinked in the dark and striking spray from the sea. He couldn't see.

"Lydia! Jubilee! Joel!" they both cried at the top of their lungs.

They heard a scream; Lydia had realized they were floating. "Aaaaaaaaaaah!" she shrieked. Sam and Jeremy felt panic in the darkness. Then, Lydia and the little ones became visible through the rain and wind.

"We are floating!" gasped Lydia in astonishment. "How!"

Looking down, they saw they were standing on a large smooth slab of stone? Jeremy and Sam threw their arms around them. They clung together, united in fear, yet somehow, cocooned in peace.

"We thought we'd lost you," they each whispered, the rain now gone, yet there was brightness surrounding them in the darkness.

Joel stopped crying as he soon realized they were still floating upwards, away from the danger of the storm. Jubilee looked around in wonder and disbelief. Then she turned to

Lydia. "Did you call to Jaycee?" she asked in a quiet voice slipping a small hand in Lydia's. She nodded, her green eyes shining with tears as they continued to rise high above the storm.

"Are we drifting into another dimension?" asked Sam. "Because I don't feel as though I'm in the storm anymore." He held out his hand to check if the storm waters from the sea had stopped.

"I'm not sure," answered Jeremy, starting to grin. "The stone seems to have some power we haven't come across before," he said beginning to grin at Joel, who looked very pleased.

"I thought I'd dropped the stone, I was so sad, but…," he said.

Blinded, the fishermen could not control their small vessel. Filled with fear, panic took their minds into the reality that they could all drown. The night was dark. The sea like shaken dense black ink. The waves raged at each other as they pounded the hull, tossing their small fishing boat back and forth as they held on—watching in desperation as the waters begin to fill the boat.

From the safety of their bubble on the stone overhead, the children watched the terrified men struggling to survive.

"What are they going to do?" asked Jubilee.

"They need a lifeboat to rescue them," said Joel with a trembling voice, "or they will die."

"This is terrible," said Lydia, looking around desperately for an answer. "Can't we do something to help them?"

"This is like a terrible dream!" said Lydia. "It reminds me of a time when we knew someone very violent." She looked down at her hands as she wrung them together. "He was the father of a friend at school."

Jubilee leaned in closer; she knew Lydia was close to tears. "And what happened?" she asked.

"There was a girl in my class called Jean. She hated me. I don't know why, but she did. She wasn't very pretty: the

221

others said she was jealous of me." "What did you do about it?" Joel asked.

"Well, she persuaded all the other girls to be horrible to me. They would pinch me or punch me when I had to walk past them. They called me terrible names and constantly texted horrible messages to me, saying I should disappear because no one at the school liked me – or would miss me. . ." She went quiet. "It was if I was in the middle of a storm, and I couldn't find a way out."

"Why didn't you tell Mum and Dad about it?"

"Her father was a terrible man. And he had a terrible temper. I think he used to beat Jean and her brother quite a lot. She was very thin and pale most of the time. I felt sorry for her. Everyone else knew her father was drunk most of the time. What could Mum and Dad do to help me?" They had enough worries of their own at the time. I just wanted them to stop being horrible to me. They said I did horrible things that I didn't do. Then they all used to gang up and wait for me after school." Lydia's voice wobbled and cracked as she began to cry.

"What a nightmare, I didn't know that," said Jeremy, moving closer to her and putting his arms around her as he wiped away her tears with his finger. "Why didn't you tell me?"

"I tried to, but you were always busy. Jean fancied you and so I didn't think you would believe me," Lydia replied.

"There must be lots of people who live through nightmares in their lives too. Perhaps a parent dying suddenly or someone becoming terminally ill. It must be horrible."

Jeremy and Sam, who stood close by, nodded in agreement.

"Everyone has a nightmare at some time in their lives," said Sam quietly.

They were all quiet for a moment. Jeremy and Sam each remembered times when they had been very afraid, too. "I remember the man a few doors away from us at home," said

Sam. "Remember him, Jeremy? The angry man who drank and swore all the time? Once we had to take a package to his house because it had come to us by mistake. Mum asked us to take it around to him— remember now?"

Jeremy nodded. "Yes, he swung the door open and was screaming in our faces. Behind him, his dogs were running frantically around the house. All skinny and bruised and barking, it was terrible." Jeremy remembered well, his gaze fell to the floor.

"Yes, and his daughter came to the door. She was skinny, too. Big black rings under her eyes, arms covered in bruises and her eyes were wide with fear." Sam remembered, his voice wobbly.

"I still have nightmares about that," Jeremy added, looking back at Sam.

The little ones had been listening. "What happened to the girl?" asked Jubilee.

"And the dogs?" asked Joel.

"Oh, that was a long time before you were born, Joel, and Jubilee was only a baby," Sam said quietly.

"What happened?" Jubilee pressed for details.

"Mum and Dad prayed for the girl; and they went to the police," Sam said simply.

"I'm not sure what happened then, but I know he was taken," Jeremy added, "and the family moved away."

"Funny the parcel going to the wrong house. It was like a divine appointment for that man," Lydia said.

"It wasn't the wrong house, was it? Because Mum and Dad found out what was going on, they prayed for the girl and took action!" Sam exclaimed.

"I suppose everyone has dark nights, like those poor men down there," said Jeremy. Joel thought he saw something. He looked over the stone and down at the boat in the storm and screamed, "Jeremy! Sam! Help!" Everyone moved towards the edge of the stone. Their eyes widened.

To their horror, they saw the demons attacking the boat, rocking it wildly as they shrieked and cackled with sickening laughter as if it was all good fun. Both babies covered their eyes.

"I can't look, I can't look!" cried Jubilee as Sam picked her up, and she gripped him in a hug. Jeremy picked up Joel and hugged him too, grabbing Lydia's hand simultaneously.

"What do we do?" asked Sam, madly looking around in the dark for somewhere to hide.

It was about four or five o'clock in the morning when they heard the loud, fearful cries of the fishermen. One man was nearly thrown overboard into the angry, evil world of huge waves of pain that were trying to swallow him alive.

"Oh God, help me," cried one man. "I don't want to die. Save me, Jaycee, where are you?"

"What's that over there?" another man yelled out, pointing toward the white figure.

Everyone turned to look where he pointed.

"Is it a ghost?" Lydia whispered.

The children were gripped with terror, for the men.

"Oh no!" cried Jubilee.

"Isn't there something we can do to help them?" asked Sam.

"No," said Jeremy. "This is something that happened; we are only here to watch."

"Something has to happen, or they will all be lost," cried Lydia.

"I know, I know," said Joel. "They need a lifeboat to come out and save them!"

"Oh, for goodness sake, they don't have lifeboats here. They just die when this kind of thing happens. They don't have anyone!" said Lydia. They watched in mounting horror as the white ghost came nearer to them.

"It's not walking," said Joel. "Ghosts don't walk— do they?"

"I...I don't know," said Jubilee, "It does look as if it is gliding."

"If it is Jaycee," said Jeremy quietly, "I don't remember any mention of him swimming to get to them, do you, Sam?"

Sam shook his head in silent agreement. His eyes glued to the moving image of the ghost. He listened to the screaming men being thrashed about in the raging waters, by the cackling, laughing evil spirits, that enjoyed the terror they caused.

"They are right out in the middle of the lake—that's three miles away from the other side," Joel added.

The children above and the fishermen below were all so afraid that no one could think clearly. Terrified, they stared at the white image, in dreadful fear, as it approached the fishermen in the midst of the dense black of the raging night.[118]

---

118 **John 8:12** *"I am the light of the world. Whoever follows me will never walk in darkness, but will have the light of life."*

Symbolic meaning: – [However terrible your problems seem, if you follow me I will bring you through into light and peace.]

Jaycee had heard them calling him and felt their fear, so he called out to calm them "It's me, take courage! Don't be afraid."[119] His voice immediately brought peace to their hearts, bringing them great relief and joy. They were so glad and relieved to see their beloved teacher, who had heard them calling him in the night, of their storm.

The fisherman called Peter shouted out, "Lord if it's you, tell me to come to you on the water."[120] "Come," said Jaycee.

Filled with joy and excitement, Peter stepped out of the boat onto the water while looking straight into the eyes of Jaycee, smiling as he went towards him. The wind howled[121] as the demons cried out in annoyance and fury. Peter heard the storm[122] and forgot to keep his eyes on Jaycee; his faith temporarily forgotten. The evil spirits taunted him, trying to stop him from walking towards Jaycee. Suddenly afraid, he began to sink into the dark waters. Before he plunged into a black abyss, he cried out, "Lord, save me!" [123]

Immediately Jaycee reached out his hand and caught him in the water, saying, "Ye of little faith... why did you doubt?"[124]

They both stepped back into the boat and the storm calmed down. The demons disappeared. The waves and the raging wind calmed.

The children were shocked.

"Did you see that?" asked Jeremy. "Look, everyone, look. The storm has gone—just like that!" "And the demons, too!" said Jubilee.

---

119 **Matthew 14:27**

120 **Matthew 14:28**

121 **Symbolic Meaning:** – [In the middle of a difficult time bad people continue to cause pain but as our faith in the Son of God begins, peace comes and our lives change forever.]

122 **Meaning:** – [He took his eyes off Jaycee and again remembered his worries and the things that made him afraid]

123 **Meaning:** – [Keep your faith and you will be saved. Fear is 'False Evidence Appears Real'].

124 **Matthew 14:31**

"That is amazing," whispered Joel.

"Yes," echoed the others beginning to grin.

As they watched from above, on their foundation stone,[125] sharing the understanding of what had happened, they saw the boat fill with light. The men greeted the one who had come to save them.

"Well, Lydia," said Jeremy, "He's a lot more than just a prophet, wouldn't you say?" Lydia did not reply.

As they watched the love the men shared, they had to blink suddenly three or four times, to refocus. Without any warning, the boat immediately reached the far shore.

Galilee, near the north end of Magdala;[126] just where they wanted to go in the first place! [127]

"I don't believe it," said an astonished Lydia. "You mean the only person who could have done that just had to be Jaycee. Their large stone slowly lowered them back to the beach where they had slept that night, and then it shrank and plopped back into Joel's pocket, just like that. They saw no sign that there had been a storm. Their campfire still burned, warming them as they sat down to watch the rising sun. Strong warm rays of pink and orange rays of light began to beam across the stage of a morning on a backdrop of pale blue mist, announcing a new play. The dark curtains of the night withdrew in obedience.

Smiling at each other, the children began to relax. Jeremy passed his golden bottle of pink living water to each one of them. As they drank, the older children wondered what adventures this new day would bring. They only had two more signs to see before they could go home and tell Mum and Dad all their adventures.

---

125 **Meaning:** – [foundation of belief in Jaycee (Jesus Christ, the Son of God).]

126 NIV study Bible. p. 1435. This place *'was considered a garden spot of Palestine, fertile and well-watered.'* [**Symbolic meaning**] Jesus had taken them to a beautiful place.

127 **Symbolic Meaning:** – [Where they wanted to go – to a new life].

Joel looked thoughtful.

"What is it, Joel? Are you alright?" Jeremy asked him.

The small boy looked up at his older brother and nodded, saying, "I've decided I want to give this stone a special name because we were all safe when we stood on it. It can do such wonderful things as well."

"Well, how about a corner-stone?" Jeremy suggested.

"This isn't a corner, and we weren't in one. We stood on it, silly!" Joel commented.

"Quite right," said Lydia, "It's more like a foundation stone, like one that a house can stand on." "And it found me!" said Joel with delight.

"That's right, it did, sweetheart," said Lydia, putting her hand on his shoulder and pulling him gently towards her.

"I'll call it my founding stone then," he smiled a sleepy smile up at Lydia.

"Have a drink before we all have a little sleep," she said, passing him Jeremy's golden glass bottle.

After drinking the refreshing water, they fell into a deep sleep, exhausted from the worry and fear of the black night and the storm they had just experienced.

When they awoke, they felt like they had had a long, peaceful, and refreshing sleep, but it could only have been a few minutes. The beams of light in the sky were still there. In fact, they seemed to be... becoming... bigger?

Sam sat up. Jeremy rubbed his eyes, and Lydia squinted as she realized that something was happening. "Look at that, Jubilee!" she said as she pointed to the sky above them. The others turned to look as well.

No one spoke for a few moments as they watched the movement of the clouds being parted by the strong sunlight.

"That one over there seems to be...bending?" said Sam. He instinctively reached out for his sword.

Joel got excited. The others just sat and watched in disbelief.

Lydia groaned, "Oh no, now what?"

Joel ran forward, shading his eyes from the sun so that he could see more clearly.

Lydia jumped up and ran towards him, but the beam of light shot down like lightning through the sky towards him, hitting him on the head. Sam and Jeremy screamed at the top of their voices as they ran towards Joel. Lydia ran to catch him. Jubilee watched in horror as he disappeared.

They stood in a circle around where Joel had been, their hands outstretched in absolute shock and dismay. Lydia turned to look at Jubilee. The beam of light changed direction. It now hovered above Jubilee's head. A piercing scream came from Lydia's lips. "Oh, no!" Lydia lunged at Jubilee but wasn't fast enough.

The boys turned to see Jubilee also disappear.

"What the…?!" yelled Jeremy.

Sam grabbed his sword. He didn't know what he could do with it, but… Right away, it lit up with a blue/white beam, which threw a circle of light on the rest of them. What on earth were they going to do now?

Chapter 15

THE MAN BORN BLIND AND THE BEAM OF LIGHT

The Sixth Sign – According to John Chapter 9

THE THREE OLDER CHILDREN, SHOCKED, turned around to see if Joel and Jubilee might be somewhere near, but there was no sign of them.

Two pink streaks circled around them.

"Don't panic! Don't panic," said Thumper. "It's our new form of transport. We've just passed our exams. And we haven't had much practice, but we thought you were getting used to incredible things happening. You should realize by now that we only have good things for you."

Bumper managed to land inside their circle of blue light.

"Thank goodness for that," he said, rubbing his behind. "I'm getting better at landing. And I haven't bumped into anyone—yet!"

Lydia was so angry that she slapped him. Feathers flew in all directions. "What has happened to my little brother and sister?" She stood over the bewildered young angel with her hands on her hips, ready to give him another swipe. "Where are they?"

Thumper just couldn't believe what she had just done.

Sam and Jeremy came to stand behind her, frowning down at Bumper.

Then they heard Joel giggle. Then Jubilee laughed. But they couldn't see them.

"It's NOT funny," said Lydia. "Where are you? Come back here this minute, do you hear me?"

So they did. They immediately appeared in the blue circle, holding hands and smiling up at their older sister and brothers.

Bumper seized the opportunity to escape the circle. Thumper grabbed him as he landed. "I told you not to touch the beam controls, didn't I? You wanted to be the first one to do it. Now look what you've done. I won't be a bit surprised if you don't pass your exams. It will serve you right, so there!"

"Will you two stop arguing and tell us what's going on!" said Jeremy, who didn't want to step outside of their safe circle.

Thumper coughed, cleared his throat, puffed out his chest. Then he said, "We thought that, since you know Jaycee quite well now; you would enjoy being transported in your dreams, this way to Jerusalem and King Solomon's temple. We used the beam because we have to move forward in time from spring here to winter there, where Jaycee is walking in the Colonnades with two of his followers, Nathaniel, and Thomas. Jaycee is about to use the beam of light as well. It's all very exciting," he said waving his arms wide with joy causing him to lift off from the ground, but he toppled over, landing on his bum and bouncing back up again.

Jeremy put his hands on his hips, shouting adamantly, "I don't care whether you think this is a good idea! Just don't touch the babies, whether in our dreams or not. Clear? And will you both stop flying around? You're making me feel sick with worry!"

Thumper nodded his head as he dropped to the floor. Bumper stood beside him, his feet, chubby hands, and wings all crossed in submission. His face was one of bewilderment and sadness.

Lydia, overjoyed to see that her brother and sister were safe, felt sorry for slapping Bumper. "Don't be too hard on them, Jeremy. They didn't mean to frighten us, did you?"

The cherubs beamed up at her, nodding their heads in agreement.

"Women!" said Sam, grinning at the scene before him. He wanted to change the subject so that everyone would calm down. And the cherubs' new information intrigued him. "So what's all this about something happening at King Solomon's Temple?"

"Well," said Thumper, puffing up his chest again. "This is your Sixth Sign. Jaycee is going to do an incredible miracle, one that proves he is the Light of the World. But... well, you have to come and see for yourselves."

"I suppose that means we have to use the beam of light to get us there?" said Sam. He was leaning his head to one side as he frowned and grinned at the same time, while also putting his fists on his hips.

Thumper nodded. Bumper stepped closer to him for protection as he watched Lydia—just in case she didn't like the idea.

"How does the beam work?" asked Jeremy.

"I know, I know," said Bumper leaping off the ground. "It's powered by faith."

"I might have guessed that was coming," said Jeremy, looking at Lydia, who seemed unsure.

"Don't worry, Lyd," said Sam, "I'll make sure that my sword is switched on to keep control of things."

The clouds above them swirled around as if they had been waiting for a decision.

"Right," said Thumper, "everyone in the circle." Then he turned to Bumper, frowning. "And this time I will activate the beam."

"All hold hands and.... We're off!" They zipped into the beam with a whoosh. Flashing images shot past their eyes so quickly that they couldn't catch anything clearly, but being inside the beam felt wonderful.

"I've never felt anything like this before," yelled Sam.

"Me, neither," replied Jeremy, as they whooshed around and around as if in a friendly whirlwind.

"I have," said Lydia. "When I was sitting in the teacup with grandma at the fair when I was a little girl. We went round and round and rou…"

"You still are a little girl!" Sam said with a cheeky grin.

"You know what I mean!" she argued, rolling her eyes.

This memory and the joy they felt traveling in faith made them all burst out laughing.

"I just knew they would like it," said Bumper, tapping the side of his nose. "I just knew."

As they landed in the colonnade of the temple, they noticed that they each now wore a warm robe. That was good because it was much colder than they had expected.

In addition to their new outfits, Lydia's hair was pulled back into a long, tight, sleek ponytail with a plated leather band. Jubilee's long wavy hair had been brushed back in a bun with an elegant silk green ribbon woven in it. Her dark hair, done that way, brought out the colour of her eyes. Jeremy wore a very dark blue toga with a brown wrap around his waist. His water-skin clipped tightly onto his belt; Sam wore a pale cream robe with a short hem, like a shepherd boy, with a coarse rope around his waist, his stick tucked through it. Lastly, Joel wore a similar robe to Sam except it was a warm brown in colour.

Lydia examined her dress, and so did Jubilee. They liked the pale creamy colour next to their pale skin.

"You are here early," whispered Thumper, "but don't worry; Lydia will be told what to do."

"Oh dear," said Lydia, "I hope that means I have my looking glass, just in case we have to ask questions about what is happening." The small glass in her pocket jumped. She smiled. "It's alright," she said quietly to Jubilee. "I just felt it jump! We need to find somewhere to sit down and ask it what we are looking for," she said looking around uncomfortably. "That'll do," said Lydia pointing. Lydia and Jubilee backed into a quiet corner in the shade of the colonnade and sat down together. As they sat down, the looking glass became very excited. It almost jumped out of Lydia's pocket. "I wonder what it will show us?" she wriggled with anticipation.

They hadn't expected to see a fierce battle taking place in a church! A name came across the mirror: 'Antiochus IV'.

"Who is that?" Jubilee asked, looking up at Lydia.

Jeremy answered, "He was a bad Roman ruler who lived a long time ago."

"Like Dad's boss, you mean?" Jubilee replied without looking up.

"Oh no. Much worse than that!" Lydia said.

More words came across the glass: 'Do not worship false idols'.

"'Do not worship false idols'?" Jubilee said out loud as she read it.

"What does that mean?" asked Joel leaning forward.

"Don't give your love to worthless things," said Lydia.

"Pardon?" said Joel, who still did not understand.

Jubilee smiled and added, "We are supposed to love people first, not things!"

He still didn't understand.

"But—why are they fighting in a church?" asked Sam looking at Jeremy, changing topic. "Everyone looks furious."

The mirror changed again. They saw a statue of Zeus, a well-known athlete, at the altar, and pigs being burned as a sacrifice to the idol.

"So what's happening now?" asked Jubilee.

Jeremy felt he knew the answer. "I think the Festival of Dedication is to remember the actions of a family who loved God. The father was a priest; his name was Mattathias, and he had five sons. They were all furious that the Greeks were trying to make them worship their man made idols instead of the God King." He explained while everyone listened to him.

"So what happened then?" asked Lydia, becoming interested in the story. They all looked at each other; no one knew for sure. Lydia was aware she could only ask three questions of her looking glass at one time, so she kept quiet and hoped that the boys knew something.

"If I remember right," said Sam, "wasn't one of the sons called Judas Maccabee. Didn't he decide to get an army of rebels together and fight off the Roman rule of this Antiochus IV."

"Yes," said Jeremy, "I've heard of them, too. They became known as the Maccabees. The Jews were thrilled that someone was fighting for them, a bit like that movie, The Magnificent Seven when the good men came to help the people in the villages. The young Jewish 'rebels' came to help the poor people. They destroyed all the evil altars the Romans had put up and then they made the temples clean again by rededicating them to God. Their religious freedom was restored."

"So that the villages were safe to talk to God and didn't have to bow down to pretend statues of something else. They could go back to church again?" said Joel.

"So," said Lydia, nodding, "This Festival of Dedication means it was the last time the Jews had been saved from evil rule." [128]

The looking glass closed itself. Quietly, Lydia placed it back in her pocket.

"But...what's this got to do with where we are now, here in the temple?" asked Jubilee.

"Maybe Jaycee is going to do something that will set the real people free again?" said Sam with a wide smile.

---

128 (Perhaps this was a sign of an even greater deliverance to come – through Jaycee?)

They began to walk along Solomon's Colonnade,[129] looking for Jaycee and his two followers.

"Over there! Over there, I can see Jaycee," said Sam. As if he heard them calling his name, he turned. They felt that Jaycee looked at each them with a soft and gentle smile. Transfixed by the love they saw, they felt he knew them.

Then Jaycee slowly turned back to the blind man, as if he was thinking. His followers knew of this blind man called Josiah. So they asked Jaycee. "Who sinned, this man or his parents that he was born blind?"[130]

They asked this because, at that time, people believed that someone somewhere must have sinned to cause this blindness.

"Neither this man nor his parents sinned," said Jaycee. "This happened so the power of God could be seen in him. We must quickly carry out the tasks assigned us by the one who sent us. The night is coming,[131] and then no one can work. While I am here in the world, I am the light of the world."[132] His voice was kind and calm, and the children became aware of a brilliant light that seemed to surround him. Instinctively they remembered the colours they had seen around themselves on the night of the storm.

"What is he doing now?" asked Sam.

"He spat on the soil," Jeremy told him.

"Why?" asked Jubilee in amazement.

"I don't know!" replied Sam.

"It looks as though he is…making mud," Jeremy observed.

"Why?" asked Joel.

---

129 John 10:23

130 NBC – p.1045. This 'assumption [of guilt] that either the man himself or his parents must have been at fault was in line with [thinking at that time] theories'. 'Some rabbis [priests] taught that it was possible to sin before birth'? c

131 NBC – (Night – the end of this time on earth?)

132 NBC – This 'shows the illuminating power of [Jaycee] Christ, not only in the physical but also in the spiritual sphere.'

"We don't know why! Stop asking questions!" said Lydia, getting exasperated.

Bewildered, they all went silent as they continued to watch. "He's making some medicine to help him...I think," Lydia said, raising an eyebrow at Joel.

"Really?" said Joel. He wanted to say that he thought that was funny, but he decided not to say anything. Still, he had to ask another question. "It's only earth and mud? How is that possible?"[133]

Then Jaycee put the mud on the blind man's eyes and told him, "Wash in the Pool of Siloam."[134]

The man's friend led him away to the pool.

"I'm glad that he is obeying Jaycee and happy to wash himself the way he told him to," said Joel.

"You don't wash the way Mum tells you to!" said Lydia. Joel pulled a face and grinned back at her.

"Hmmm," murmured Sam, guessing. "He may have agreed to go to that pool because everyone here thinks it has healing powers."

"Maybe he needs some encouragement?" concluded Lydia.

"You mean they think it is like the pool where Jaycee healed the man who couldn't walk?" Jubilee asked.

When Josiah, the blind man returned to the temple, to show everyone who knew him that he was no longer blind, not everyone believed him. They said, "No, it can't be. Josiah is blind; you must be someone else.".

The Pharisees looked furious. "Uh-oh. I think there is going to be trouble," Lydia said slowly dropping her voice to a whisper in fear.

"Are we safe?" asked Jubilee as she tugged at her brother's arm.

---

133 **Symbolic meaning:** – [medicine made of spirit and earth.]
134 **Meaning:** – [this word means 'Sent'.]

"I hope so," replied Sam, kissing her forehead. "I'm not sure that anyone here can even see us. The last time this kind of thing happened, it was our fear that helped them to see us. So we must stay calm." Sam looked at Jubilee, who had a very worried expression plastered all over her face.

Jubilee couldn't help sobbing quietly, as she saw that the men were all so angry, like the men she had seen once outside a pub. She could hear their frustration, and the loud voices made the air around them tremble with the growing anger and violence.

The colour in Joel's face drained away. He looked up at Lydia for assurance. She put her arms around both of the young ones, hugging them to her side. As they watched, one group of men argued loudly about the law.

Those who wanted to uphold their law became louder and louder, insisting on their point of view. The other, quieter crowd was bewildered by their anger. Surely they should be pleased that the blind man had been healed?

"What is happening?" asked Lydia, becoming even more concerned. "Why are they so spiteful? What's the law got to do with it? I just don't understand." She cupped her head in her hands.

The Jewish high priests demanded that the man be brought before them. They simply did not believe that the blind man they had all known for so long had been healed. It just had to be a trick.

The children had huddled closer together as the priests became even more demanding. Joel spoke, "They look like spitting thistles to me. They'll never believe anything clever that they haven't done themselves!" The others looked at him.

"He's right. That means that they are going to get very nasty," Jubilee predicted, nodding her head and crossing her arms.

"It's the mud," they heard one of the Jews say. "He must have done something to the mud!"

"That's it," said another one. "He did something with the mud we don't know about, and he did it on the Sabbath. That's against the law!"

"Uh-oh, there is going to be real trouble. They are so stubborn, what are they going to think of next?" said Jeremy very quietly. Before anyone else could speak, they heard someone saying, "Get his parents. Bring them here, at once. They will tell us the truth!"

People pushed and shoved one another as the crowds grew even bigger. Everyone wanted to see what was happening. All of them murmured about the miracle—or was it a miracle?

"I don't understand why the people seem so afraid of the priests. What will the priests do to the people if they say Jaycee did it?" asked Sam.

"They won't be allowed to go in their church ever again. And that means no one else will talk to them again, ever!" said Jeremy.

"That's horrible—and its blackmail," said Lydia.

"They are afraid that Jaycee may be the long awaited Messiah and Saviour of the Jewish people," Jeremy said.

"So?" said Sam, shrugging his shoulders. "Shouldn't they be happy?"

"If it's true, everyone will turn to Jaycee. The priests don't want that, do they?" said Jeremy. "They won't be important anymore, will they?"

A man at the back of the crowd yelled, "Give glory to God. We know He doesn't listen to sinners."

One of the supporters of the priests shouted, "We are followers of Moses. And everyone knows that God spoke to him!" [135]

---

135 NBC – a superior place was given to Moses in their thoughts than they gave to Jesus [Jaycee].

Josiah, the blind man Jaycee healed, didn't care; he kept on telling everyone what had happened. Jaycee healed him even though he never asked for the healing!

"I've had enough of all this, Jeremy," said Lydia, "It's time to get out of here. The little ones are frightened of these bullies. They are obviously never going to accept what Jaycee has done." She got both the younger ones up and collected their things.

Jubilee joined the conversation. "I think they are just like Levi. Lydia is right. They won't change their minds, ever." She dusted her toga off and shook her hair out.

"Levi!" said Sam with hope. "He's here—

remember? We saw him on the way here. All we have to do is find him and leave."

Rowdy crowds continued to gather; they were now trapped in the middle of a large, angry mob. People ran and pushed and pulled past. After being yanked this way and that, suddenly Lydia was pushed over. She fell forward over on her knees and lost her grip on Jubilee's arm. Jubilee disappeared into the crowd. Lydia scrambled to her feet, screaming, "Sam! Jeremy! Jubilee's go... She's gone!"

The children gathered together in a cluster.

Sam grabbed at his stick, it immediately became the sapphire sword, a blue beam shot across the crowd. He sliced upwards, holding it at arm's length, high in the air. The crowd immediately split in half. One part ran in all directions; they feared the power of the Jewish priests who could excommunicate those who didn't agree with them. They didn't want to be cut off from everyone else. Life was too hard already. They would be completely alone. No one they knew would speak to them.

They feared change, so they had to get away, and so they ran anywhere they could, like sheep all bunched together, darting here and there. The other half broke into two parts. One part moved slowly, but in the opposite direction from the others. But they seemed quiet and calm. The rest froze, just as they were, stopped in time.

Despite themselves, the children watched for a moment, mesmerized by what was happening.

Then they desperately scanned the crowds for any sight of Jubilee. Lydia, distraught and filled with panic, clapped a hand over her forehead, breathing heavily, drenched in anguish for her little sister. Looking left and right as she felt herself slipping into a black panic attack.

Jeremy jumped into action. "Sam! Sam, you head for the runners, you have your sword to help you get through them quickly. With so many people here—looks like hundreds— it's not going to be easy. Watch Lydia and Joel! I'll find Jubilee and get to a high place so that I can find you. Quick! Go! Go!" They never followed Jeremy's instructions. They were interrupted by a low, mournful howling sound like a forgotten donkey, or water buffalo or…alone at night crying out for his mate.

"That sounds terrible," said Lydia looking around her in the dimming evening light.

Jeremy and Sam stood alert, trying to make out what that sound was as if they somehow knew, a distant memory?

"The sun is beginning to set!" said Lydia with fear in her voice. We haven't much time left. What are we going to do? Oh, Jeremy, I'm so afraid of what might happen. We need help to find her in the middle of all these hundreds of people all doing different things." Her voice trailed away as she began to cry. Joel slipped his arm around her waist. He gulped down his fear, but couldn't stop the tears welling in his wide innocent eyes.

Then they heard the howling moan of an animal getting nearer… followed by the baying of a donkey. Joel's head shot around in the direction of the noise.

"I know who that is!" he yelled at the top of his voice. "Levi! Esther! Where are you?"

They all turned to look in the same direction. In all the mayhem, they saw the two animals galloping towards them. Levi yelled, "When I saw you earlier in the crowd, I just knew you would need our help. I get feelings about this kind of thing."

Lydia flung her arms around his neck as he stomped to a dusty halt sobbing with relief. Joel ran to Esther, who lowered her head to let him nuzzle his face into the soft mane on her neck. "Esther, Esther. How did you find us?"

Sam and Jeremy gave a sigh of relief as the extra help arrived.

Lydia turned to the others. "We need to pray to Jaycee before we do anything. We mustn't go off without his help. We'll only get it all wrong if we don't."

"I want to use my stone. I want to know if we can have helicopters," said Joel.

If they hadn't been so worried, they would have laughed at Joel's suggestion, but he looked so upset that they didn't know what to say as gazed at his frightened face. Jubilee was his best friend. They did everything together. The others realized how terrible it must be for him.

"Ask your founding stone. There must be a reason, you found it," Lydia finally said, kneeling to his level.

Joel pulled his stone out of his hip pocket. He held it in the centre of his small hand. Closed his eyes and began to talk to Jaycee. The heart of the stone began to shine. The seven 'eyes' glowed as beams of blue light shot into the darkening sky. The stone began to spin, rising above them into the darkening sky and disappeared. They all watched while Joel continued to pray in silence.

Sam knelt down beside him and smiled at Joel. He spoke softly, "What are you praying for?"

Joel gulped and said, sadly, "Helicopters. But I don't think they have them here."

"Helicopters?" asked Sam. "We'd need a time jump for that…"

"So? Jaycee can do anything, can't he?" Joel asked, upset by the heartbreak evident in his eyes.

Sam dropped his head; he couldn't argue with that.

Lydia spoke. "Let's join him in praying. Hold hands, quickly, come on everyone." They all gathered in a circle, kneeling and praying.

She reached out and held Jeremy's hand, and then she turned and Levi was standing by her side. He looked up at her with his large, sad eyes, which questioned what she was going to do. She smiled, then held onto his long straight ear, which he held high. Esther followed her lead and gently held his tail in her soft mouth. Sam realized what Lydia was doing, so he took Esther's tail in his hand, then took Joel's small hand in a strong, firm hold. Joel looked up hopefully at Jeremy. They formed a completed the circle of faith.

Each of them closed their eyes and dropped their heads as Lydia spoke. "Jaycee, we've lost Jubilee. I was so busy listening to the crowds talking about the way you healed the blind man who had been blind from birth. It was amazing. We all found it difficult to believe. I lost my grip on Jubilee for a moment, and she was pushed away by the angry, frightened people, all arguing and pushing one another. She has disappeared in the crowds." She gulped.

They all felt her pain and squeezed each other's hands in sympathy. Levi felt his ear being squeezed and winced. Esther was also biting his tail a bit too hard, but still he did nothing. He just screwed up his face and nose in pain. He had come to love Jubilee as well.

"Please, Jaycee," said Lydia softly, almost in tears but keeping control. "We need your help. We've just have to find her quickly."

Joel whispered quietly, "We need her to come back to us. She holds your 'Book of Mirrors'. Jules...please find us."

The others lifted their heads and looked at him. He always managed to say something so innocent and sincere. Now they saw tears welling up in his eyes and his mouth trembled at the thought of losing his best friend and sister forever. He said with more determination, "We do need helicopters, Lydia!"

No one knew what to say. They just stood looking around for hope.

Jeremy lifted his eyes to the sky. "What's that noise?"

They all squinted into the evening sky. There were tiny dots, a long way off, coming towards them. "There are helicopters coming!" Joel squealed with delight jumping up from the circle.

"There's three of them," said Sam. "No, four." Sam counted, pointing his finger.

"No," said Lydia, above their voices. "There're six of them."

"It just can't be," whispered Jeremy, shaking his head. He frowned. "I don't believe it."

They all stood in silence as the dots grew bigger and bigger. Then they realized that they were following a light, like a spinning star in the darkening sky.

Levi couldn't believe it, either. He stepped backwards. He had never seen anything like this before. Esther also stepped back and closer to Levi as they watched the unbelievable sight coming towards them.

"That's not helicopters. It's Gregory and Sally!" said Jeremy with delight.

Gregory landed first. The whirring sound of his wings stopped as he tucked them neatly down each side of his back. Jeremy leaped forward and reached up to slap his hand on Gregory's shoulder in greeting.

Gregory frowned, concerned. "What's the problem? We received a message from the Stone of Seven Eyes. That only happens in a real emergency."

Levi, surprised to hear the creature speak, jumped even further backwards. Esther stood her ground, figuring that it must be alright because the children all looked so pleased to see the locusts. Lydia noticed Levi's shock and fear. "It's

alright, Levi. They are old friends of ours. They have come
to help us, just as you have." She smiled.

"We've lost Jubilee!" Joel suddenly sobbed. Sally and
Esther came over to comfort him.

Again Jeremy jumped into action. "Gregory, can you circle
above around the outside edge of this crowd and make sure
that Jubilee hasn't left this area? I'll come with you. Sally, can
you and the others fly crisscross over the people—especially
the people running away? They are going in all directions;
they are confused; it won't be easy."

Even as Jeremy spoke, the locusts shot up into the sky one
by one. Jeremy turned to Lydia.

"The frozen people still haven't moved, but we don't
know how long that will last. The slow moving people can
be searched more quickly; they seem to be calmer." Lydia
nodded.

Sam interrupted Jeremy's flow. "What about me? What
am I going to do?"

"You, Sam, must get into the running crowds and use
your sword to slow them down. I don't know how you will
do it, but you will know. They are the most selfish. They
won't care about Jubilee; they are too busy thinking about
themselves. You have good instincts for how to handle that
kind of people. And the chances are that's where she will
be. You are our warrior, Sam; you can do it." He nodded
encouragement to Sam and looked at Levi.

"Take Levi; he'll get you through any crowd. We all knew
how brave and determined he is. Nothing will stop him,"
Jeremy said, handing Sam the reins. Levi puffed up his chest,
snorted, and dipped his head as if he might charge. Esther
grinned, thinking, Jeremy knows how to get the best out of
everyone. So she waited to hear what position he wanted
her to take.

"Esther, will you take care of Lydia and Joel, please?
Lydia, you check out the frozen group. But be careful; we

don't know what will happen here. Where do you think is the best place to wait and be safe?"

"Over there by the entrance to the narrow road, where it goes over the deep chasm of darkness. No one can go over it if they don't know Jaycee. Anyone who can go over it will be a friend." She nodded.

"Brilliant idea. But keep Joel away from the edge," Jeremy advised. Joel objected to that.

"I'm not going over there. I'm going with you on one of the other locusts!" He nodded his head adamantly, planted his feet and folded his arms firmly.

Lydia joined in, begging, "But, Joel, who will look after me while we wait for Jubilee? What will we do if no one finds her, and she comes looking for us? Esther and I need you to be with us. You are our guard. Please, Joel!"

Joel blinked. He suddenly realized that he wanted to the first to find Jubilee. He wouldn't be able to hug her first if he was just a 'look out' up there!

Esther came to stand beside him. "Would you like to sit on my back? You'll be able to see much more if you do."

The thought of this pleased him. Lydia saw the change on his face, so she picked him up and placed him gently on Esther's back. Esther said, "Hold on to my mane. My hair is strong; you won't hurt me, and you'll feel safer." So he did.

The sun began to sink behind the distant mountains, sending long shadows over the sands, like creeping slugs crawling to devour all life. Lydia shivered.

"We must hurry," said Sam, Jeremy had already mounted Gregory and was heading high into the sky above, already beginning to circle around the distant crowd of people, who hadn't stopped running. They were determined to travel far away from the angry Pharisees.

After all, no man had ever healed another man who had been blind from birth. This miracle had shocked them, and they couldn't find anyone to tell them how Jaycee had done it. So it must be a trick. Not even the blind man's parents knew what had happened; they just knew he could now see! But some brave people spoke up and said, "Only a good man could do such a thing. It was a wonderful thing to do, even if it was on the Sabbath." They threw their voices across the sky.

Sam and Levi charged into the running crowds. Sam's eyes searched, looking for anything. Something was wrong. He blinked. Then he realized that some of the people were beginning to...fade? As if, they were moving into another dimension? Puzzled, he pulled Levi to stop as he took in, what was happening in front of him.

"It's as if they have turned off their minds? They no longer care," Sam observed, then began to panic.

Levi frowned. "You mean they have decided to do what they want, not what they know inside they should do?"

"Something like that," Sam said, gritting his teeth and continuing his search.

"What about Jubilee?" Levi broke the tense silence.

"She won't fade. She holds The Book of Mirrors— God's word." Sam forced himself to remain calm.

"True. That will protect her. So, as the running people begin to fade into another time, we will be able to see her?" Levi wondered out loud.

"Yes. But I'm wondering how long will it take for all the remaining people to...disappear," Sam said, constantly scanning the crowd in search of his little sister.

Levi shrugged; he felt helpless.

Lydia turned to Esther. "You two stay here and keep a lookout for Jubilee. It shouldn't be too difficult to search through this frozen crowd of stubborn people. If Jubilee is in here, she'll be the only one moving." Joel and Esther nodded in agreement.

"This should be easy," they said in unison.

Lydia hurried through, looking left and right as she moved along. Soon she began to feel...different? Stiff? She forced herself to keep going. She just had to find her little sister. Then it dawned on her. Mixing with these frozen-minded people was affecting her. She was beginning to freeze too. She had to move away from here, but her resistance was weakening. She turned, forcing her legs to move, to take her back towards Joel and Esther, who waited for her. She fell to the floor and crawled. Her knees hurt, and her hands clawed at the floor, pulling her forward. Everything was going dark…

Joel stood up on Esther's back. He thought he saw something happen to Lydia, but he wasn't sure. Then a beam of light shone through the growing darkness. It showed exactly where Lydia lay, lifeless.

He yelled, "Lydia, Lydia. What's wrong? We can see you!" The beam grew larger, engulfing them as well as Lydia.

He jumped down and ran towards her. Esther followed him in the warmth of the light. "Lydia, wake up, wake up. Are you alright?" she asked, braying on her way.

Lydia did wake up, shivering, grateful to be moving. Joel rubbed her hands as he cried with relief. Sally landed quietly beside them, smiling as she too enjoyed the warmth of the beam. They looked up and saw the silver glowing stone hovering over them.

"We've spotted Jubilee. Somehow she has managed to take control of the slow moving people. They are all following her back here, and she is holding The Book of Mirrors over her head. They are all walking in a beautiful beam of light—it seems to be showing them the way back. Come on, I'll show you the way," Sally urged them. They climbed to their feet.

Gregory and the other locust joined them. "She's on the other side of the hill. Mount up; we'll take you to her."

Joel burst into tears. Lydia picked him up and held him tight as she brushed away his tears. "I wanted to find her first," he sobbed.

"She is alright; that's the most important thing," said Lydia.

"I feel sick," Joel said, holding to his stomach.

"Oh sweetheart, that's because you are so glad. We'll go straight away," promised Lydia, carrying him on her hip.

Esther went over to Levi and snuggled her head into his neck. "What happened to you two?"

"The people started to fade away. It was weird. They had seemed so selfish, and they had talked, only about how they knew all the answers. They had even thought that they knew more than the God King, calling themselves 'humanists'! They said they didn't need him; they could take care of themselves. They were so empty—blind to what was going on here. I felt very sad for them." Levi hung his head and sat down to think as his ears dropped either side of his sad face. 'Did he have it wrong as well?' He thought.

Esther looked at the children waiting to fly away with the locusts. "We'll stay here and rest a while. You go on. Give Jubilee our love. I'm sure it won't be too long before we see you all again. It's been an interesting experience. I think some people have learned a lot, don't you?" She said humbly.

Lydia smiled a tired smile, as she looked down from her saddle on Sally with Joel on her lap. "Learning to see the truth can be hard, but when we can see the truth, then we have no excuse, do we?" Lydia said, wisely.

"I want to go to Jubilee—now!" Joel wailed.

"I'll hold you tight till we get there," Lydia said, leaning in and ruffling his hair.

As they flew, the bright beam of light came upon them, taking them higher and higher.

CHAPTER 16

THE HOUSE OF HOPE – BY STILL WATERS

THE CHILDREN FOUND THEMSELVES SITTING on the soft grass. The trees were still and quiet and the air pure, with a heavy heat haze. No more confusion. No fear. No hate. No, no... The atmosphere felt...different. What was happening? Where were they? Were they all here? Were they alone? And was Jubilee with them?

A calm voice spoke. "You are all safe and in the Father's house of many rooms.[136] We are here to look after you so that you may rest. You have been through a lot."

---

136 **John** 14:2-6 *'In my Father's house are many rooms',* **Meaning:** – [many realms, places].

On hearing the calm, strong voice, everyone felt secure again. Lydia wanted to know for sure that Jubilee was with them. Her fear was immediately answered. No voice spoke, but somehow she just knew. She kept very still. So much had happened while they were away from home. So many strange things and wonderful things, but now, at least, she no longer felt the anger of the Jewish priests. She still felt they wanted to kill Jaycee—but why? And what would happen to them?

"Hello. Hello, can anyone hear me?" yelled Joel, his footsteps quite loud, as he patrolled a nearby track.

"Yes, I can hear you," said Lydia, standing up wondering if she was dreaming. A dense mist surrounded her, where were the others? She could only see a few meters in front of her.

"I can hear you as well," said the others in unison.

Lydia waved her hands about trying to clear the mist around her, but the clouds remained. She sighed. "Joel? Jubilee?" she called, though she didn't expect any reply. To her surprise, she heard Joel's voice again.

"Lydia? Where are you?" he called. She waited. Just as she was about to speak, she heard Jubilee.

"L-Lydia?" she called out. Lydia stood, bolt upright as if electricity had struck her and looked around frantically.

"Jubilee! Jubilee! Are you okay? Listen to my voice, walk towards me," she called, smiling with relief.

The clouds that surrounded them disappeared slowly, and they could see one another. A wave of relief swept over them, making everyone smile. Jubilee stood there, her sandals missing. She was now wearing her tee shirt and skirt that she had worn from the beginning of their adventures in this strange world. Her hair was a little untidy with wisps of curly hair straggling down, but all in one piece. Seeing the others, she relaxed pushing a lock of hair behind her ear. It was a relief to see her brothers and big sister.

"Jubilee!" everyone cried and ran to her. They threw themselves at her, their arms entangling in a big group hug.

"We're so glad that you're safe," Lydia said sweeping her into her arms.

Then, when the hug was over, Joel smiled at her and squeezed her hand again. Jeremy ruffled her hair, and Sam knelt to look her in the eyes, holding her other hand. After a pause, Lydia stood up, sighing and looking around.

"I wonder where we are this time. I don't like all this change?" she wailed, feeling weak after so much worry about Jubilee. "I just hope this time it's going to be more peaceful."

They looked at one another. "Are there any Pharisees here?" asked Jubilee quietly.

"I'd like to know that," said Sam. "I'm fed up with that lot as well. They wanted everyone to think how they did about their laws!"

"I agree," said Jeremy. "They caused a lot of troubles, and it looks as though they are going to cause a lot more, too."

A tall, slim man all in white slowly appeared before them. They stared up at him. He was magnificent. As tall as Neph, he had large, beautiful white wings. Joel gulped. Jubilee and Lydia smiled up at him. Jeremy and Sam relaxed but wondered what on earth was going on.

"This is not the earth," he said, smiling at the boys, "and the only thing going on is that we have brought you here to have a good rest."

Sam nudged Jeremy. "He knows what we are thinking— that's spooky."

The angel laughed. Joel wondered if he knew Neph. He'd love to see him again. Then he realized that the angel had understood. He winked at Joel and nodded.

"We can get him to come and visit you if you'd like. He's also in this realm," the Angel said softly.

"Oh yes," they all said together, exchanging excited looks. "That would be great."

"What do you mean by the same realm?" asked Lydia, wanting to make sure they were prepared. "Where exactly are we and I want to know now what is going to happen to us this time?" she said stamping her foot on the soft grass. She wasn't going to stand for any more nonsense, even if he was an angel.

He looked startled at her, his eyebrows rising in complete surprise.

"Nothing is going to 'happen'. You are here for a good rest," he said spreading out his arms for them to see where they were.

"Hoh!" was all she could say.

They found themselves standing on a beautifully manicured soft emerald lawn by a shimmering opal lake, which seemed to ripple and laugh at her as graceful swans sailed by completely ignoring her. She frowned. Jeremy wondered if babies were swimming in it.

The angel laughed. "No, no babies in here. This place is called the House of Hope, a place of rest with many rooms. The God King's house where the perfume of his presence is felt by all. Here we can help those who suffer from the black nights of their lives. We bring them here by the still waters of God's love. Sadly, some souls find life on earth too much for them, and they don't want to live anymore. The valley of death has filled them with despair,' and they can't see a way out," the angel said, his voice turning solemn.

"The valley of death?" asked Jubilee. "Where is that?"

"I think he means earth, where Mum and Dad are," said Sam under his breath.

Jubilee looked at Joel; her face crumpled then Joel burst into tears.

"Oh dear, now look what you have done. You've reminded them of home," Lydia said.

"Don't worry," said the angel. "We can assure you that they are well. To them, you haven't been away for too long. You see, here in God's house of rest, time is very different.

You humans live by the hours and days; we live by something like cycles of time, only not quite. It's just a different dimension, that's all," he said with a reassuring smile.

Lydia turned to look back at the large house.

"It looks like a manor house to me," she said as the others turned their attention towards the elegant red brick building.

"You mean a bit like 'Downton Abbey'?" asked Jubilee. "But it's pink."

"Yes, only a square one."

The others laughed, but they knew what she meant. The pale red bricks were looking pink in the bright sunlight that surrounded it. The front entrance had a big white wooden door that looked strong. On either side of the door was an even number of windows.

Jeremy thought its size and height resembled half of a cube. Lydia couldn't help thinking that it looked a bit like somewhere that would lead on to a much bigger place between here and there, but she decided that was silly, nowhere could be halfway! Could it?

A grey stone church with a square tower stood to one side that was as tall as the house. The church gave the distinct impression that it had been there for a very long time and given hope to many who had passed through its doors.

"Saxon, isn't it?" asked Sam. They all felt there was something special about this place, and the church seemed to be protecting the house. The beautiful green silken lawns laid out before the house felt like an invitation to walk inside it and have a look around. Surrounding the house were many mature trees, perhaps some hundred years old. They stood regally, as if they were a 'guard of honour' in full ceremonial dress; their high branches heavy. The full bloom of summer was decorating their broad shoulders in splendour, and resembling an antique frame holding a living picture of the 'House of Hope'.

"Can we go into the church?" asked Sam in hope.

the table sat many obviously ill people in wheelchairs with angels attending them. They all turned to face the children.

"Oh splendid, visitors," said one man, laughing hospitably. "There's room for you next to me."

"That's Tom," said the angel. "He's always joking."

The sight of him clearly upset Lydia. He jerked very badly when he spoke, and saliva dripped from the corner of his mouth. She wasn't sure what to do. Then, she saw his brilliant blue eyes. They were bright and sparkling as they looked at her from under his bent brow. For a moment, she forgot how she felt and was drawn to sit next to him, just as he had a spasm and jerked violently with excitement.

Another voice came from across the table. "The little girl can come and sit next to me; I'll move my chair over a bit," said a young man in a wheelchair, half way down the long table.

Jubilee didn't know what to do. Then she saw that he struggled to lift the lower part of his arms to move his chair. His wore a stiff body jacket, which was a shiny brown colour and looked like leather. His arms and legs were very thin, making his head seem too big as it hung to one side. Then she saw his smile; his eyes lit up. He wanted so much for her to sit next to him. She felt sad and good. Instinctively she walked over to sit in the chair the angels had provided.

"Hello, my name is Brian. What's your name?"

"Jubilee. I think we are just visiting, but I'm not sure," she said, nervously.

A woman's voice said, "I'll take the tall one."

Another angel behind her moved a chair into place for Jeremy and then moved away. He stared at her. She was fat, elderly, and stiff, but her face was nicely made up, and she had an air of elegance about her. Jeremy couldn't help thinking that she must have been very exquisite when she was young. She smiled at him and said sweetly, "My name is Edna."

Everyone tittered with laughter. Jeremy wondered why. Joel stepped closer to Sam, taking his hand nervously. Was he going to be next?

"Don't be afraid, love," said a tiny lady with knobbly, bent fingers. She perched on the edge of her small wheelchair, which looked much too big for her. She smiled shyly at Joel and said, "My name is Vera. I had Spanish parents. Can you speak Spanish?" Joel shook his head.

"Ola!" she whispered, smiling as she tilted her pretty head to one side as she winked at him. He grinned. Her dark hair was beautifully groomed, but her straight teeth seemed enormous when she smiled. Her tiny body sat up straight; her crooked hands were folded in her lap.

"I can teach you how to say other words in Spanish if you like?" she offered.

Joel thought this was a brilliant idea, and she seemed quite nice. So he let go of Sam's hand and ran over to her. Sam looked around at the rest of the table. There was a young woman lying on a bed, to one side of the room. Her skin covered in ugly lumps that looked like warts, all over her body. She just looked at him anxiously, yet her bright blues eyes sparkled as if they were laughing at his apprehension.

Sam suddenly laughed, throwing his handsome head backwards; then he walked over to her. As he leaned on the side of her cot with his elbows he said, "Hello, my name is Sam. What's yours?"

"Kathy. And I'm Irish." She smiled, her black locks resting loosely on her shoulders.

The whole table relaxed and settled into a cacophony of joyous banter. Jokes flew back and forth. They all tucked into the delicious meal of fresh bread, cheeses, fish, and lots of fruits.

"Golly," said Sam, "I hadn't realized how hungry I was." He had balanced his plate on the edge of Kathy's bed while he talked to her. She held his plate when he went to get more fresh baked bread.

"I could eat a horse," said Joel rubbing his tummy. Bursts of laughter filled the room at this remark.

"What a thing to say," said Tom through his spluttering. "Let's hope he wouldn't mind... the horse I mean!" Another burst of laughter spluttered around the table. The banter was obviously great fun for all of them.

Before the children had realized it, they became blind to the disabilities and disfigurement of the people. There were a few moments when someone, suddenly shook violently, or food came flying across the table from a jerking hand or arm. Sometimes food just couldn't go down and had to be scooped up from their chins and spooned back in by the angels. The silence gave Tom the chance to make several funnier remarks, about the cook or the need to interview new management.

"He writes poetry; you know?" said someone from the other end of the table.

"Really. Can I read some of it?" asked Lydia to Tom's absolute delight. Then Lydia wondered how he could do that because of his severe jerking. An angel answered her thoughts.

"He uses a typewriter. He waits until he is still, and then he punches one letter, then he waits to be calm again before he can punch another letter."

"Golly, that must take an awfully long time," remarked Jubilee as she tried to image having the patience to do this.

"It does," said Vera, "but his poems are beautiful." Everyone agreed, delighting Tom once more.

None of the children realized how their attitudes were changing. They started to look past the physical illnesses of the people with whom they were sharing a meal. The angels smiled as they glided in and out, as if this was all quite normal. Light and joy filled the room from the tall windows that faced the calm lake beyond the green lawns. The children ate until they were full, both in their stomachs and in their souls.

Lydia admired Tom's wit and his looks. He was quite handsome really. His dark hair had a slight wave in it, and his eyes were a striking silver grey. She thought his smooth, slim hands were perfect for a writer.

Jubilee was enjoying Brian's company; he felt like an older brother. He was so patient and spoke so softly. He was much stronger that she first thought and taller, too. She thought he might have been in the air force; she could imagine him in uniform, so handsome. Most of all she liked talking with him.

Joel had forgotten Vera's knobbly hands. Despite her striking appearance, she spoke gently with much patience, repeating the Spanish words he wanted to learn. Her mouth now seemed beautiful and glamourous. She'd make an excellent sister, he thought.

Jeremy seemed to be flirting with Edna. She laughed girlishly as if she was quite young, not much older than himself he thought. He liked the way she dressed. She had style.

Sam had helped Kathy to sit up; now he could look into her lovely face. Her curly jet black hair fell in little ringlets over her forehead, bobbing up and down when she laughed. He hadn't realized how charming she was and not old at all.

Suddenly the doorbell rang, loud and clear.

Jeremy blinked. So did Lydia. Sam looked around. Joel and Jubilee carried on talking as if nothing had happened. They simply didn't notice that Vera and Brian were returning to their bodies as if they were slipping, into their coats to go outside. Both children were still looking into the eyes of their beautiful new friends, Vera and Brian.

"What's happening?" asked Lydia.

"The outside world has knocked at our door. They don't see us as we are. They are still blind," said Edna.

"The outside world?" Sam asked.

"Yes, someone who doesn't believe in God and His world. Perhaps a new member of staff in the earthly realm," an angel replied.

SHE WHISPERED 'REMEMBER ME, WE'LL MEET AGAIN
ONE DAY.'

He grinned, saying "I will have other work to do, but
thank you for wanting me." She looked again at his strong
frame. He stood so tall and handsome. His sleeping body
waited for him in the chair. His smile told her that he was
glad that had seen him the way he was. And as she watched,
he slowly floated back into his physical, broken form.

Sam was saddened to see Kathy's vibrant girlish form
re-enter her sleeping tormented body. She lay again in the
hospital bed, where she had been for many, many years
since she was a teenager. She whispered to him, "Remember

263

me; we'll meet again one day." As he heard these words, a lump came in his throat. He had to swallow hard to get rid of the pain he felt. He also felt joy at the picture he had in his mind of the beautiful girl from Ireland, someone special he had come to know. He imagined himself as a soldier in a wartime going back into battle and leaving his sweetheart behind.

A stout man stomped into the dining room.

"Hello, everyone. Having a nice meal, are we?" he bellowed. No one spoke. They knew what he was thinking, and it wasn't nice. The angels stayed by their loved ones.

"Why is he here?" Lydia asked the angel. "He doesn't fit in here at all."

The angel whispered back, "He desperately needs our help, but he's stubborn, which probably means he is afraid. I think he comes here without planning to come as if he knows he needs our help, but he just can't bring himself to admit it."

"You mean like people who go to church but just can't accept Jaycee as being real?" The angel nodded.

"Hmm, Levi is like that." Said Lydia, "He's stubborn, too, but he has a big heart and means well."

A funny little angel, a little like Thumper and Bumper, swept into the room.

"Hello," he said, hovering in mid-air over the table, making a point of looking for Joel and Jubilee. "You have a visitor. He's waiting for you in the Hall of Transit."

"Hall of where?" Lydia asked.

"Oh, sorry. I mean in the church. He has to wait there until the all-clear is given," the angel reported.

"All clear?" said Sam. "That horrid man who came into the dining hall wasn't nice—and no one checked him out?"

"No, you don't understand. No evil spirits are allowed in this valley. That man isn't evil. He has a good heart, but he is, well, confused and not a stable unit, that's all."

"Unit?" Jeremy asked the angel. "Now we are units?"

"Whatever we are, we need to walk to the church, don't we?" said Lydia showing authority.

Joel grabbed Jubilee's hand.

"It must be Neph; we did say we would like to see him again. Come on, Jubilee, while they are talking, let's get over to the church," said Jeremy.

"Yes, it must be Neph because he was in this same realm," Lydia agreed.

Joel and Jubilee slipped out of the main hall and began to run across the green grass, when a powerful voice said, "And where do you two think you are going—hmmm?" That voice sounded familiar. They spun around to see Neph grinning down at them.

"Neph! Neph, it is you. How did you see us and know where we were?" Jubilee asked.

Throwing his head back, with his hands on his hips Neph roared with laughter. "How did I see you? You can't sneak past me, little ones! I have been given permission to see you anytime I think you need me."

"Really?" said Jubilee, who suddenly burst into tears. "Really?" she asked again.

Neph bent down and swept her up into his arms to comfort her. He was touched by her love for him. Joel just grinned at their large friend.

"Are you always going to be our best friend?" she asked.

"Oh, little one. Jaycee is your best friend. I am just one of his many angels who love him too. He guides me and all the others to do the right things for you. He has sent his very own Holy Spirit in Jaycee's name to be your counsellor and guide while you are on the earth,[139] didn't you know that?"

---

139 **John 14:16- 17** NIV. *"I will ask the Father and he will give you another Counsellor to be with you forever – the Spirit of truth." "The world cannot accept him, because it neither sees him nor knows him. But you know him, for he lives with you and will be in you."*

John 14: 26 *"The Counsellor, the Holy Spirit, whom the Father will send in my name, will teach you all things.'*

Neph put Jubilee down and picked up Joel putting him on his shoulders then he bent his strong knees and scooped Jubilee into his arms. "Let's walk down by the still waters,"[140] he suggested.

Without speaking, they all strolled down to the edge of the lake where the wild birds played, ruffling the waters, making circles of sparkling ripples from their wings. The circles were knitting together on the surface of the silver water making delicate patterns of swirling lace. It was so peaceful there as they sat on the grass enjoying the silence for a few moments.

Jubilee spoke first. "Neph, did Jaycee have a best friend while he was on earth?"

Neph smiled. "Yes, as a matter of fact, he did. His name was Lazarus.[141] He loved him dearly and his sisters Mary and Martha. They all lived near Jerusalem in Bethany."

"Is he still living, too, like you?" asked Joel.

Neph answered their simplistic understanding of life. "Yes, that is the last sign you have come to see and experience."

"Why are you frowning?" she asked.

Neph spoke seriously, "Because this is the most incredible sign. It is painful and joyful all at the same time. This climactic seventh sign proves Jaycee's identity as the God King's son beyond any doubt, and it shows the growing conflict between the Jews."[142] ———————————

"They were horrible when Jaycee healed the man born blind," said Joel.

---

140 **Psalm 23** – American Standard Version (1901). '*He maketh me to lie down in green pastures; He leadeth me beside still waters.*'

Psalm 23: NIV. '*Green pastures.*' [all that makes life flourish – beside quiet waters -resting places – that provides refreshment and well-being – see **Isaiah 49:10**].

141 **A.J. Köstenberger** p.130. 'We realize our indebtedness to John for his inclusion of material not found in the Synoptic Gospels... [which] appear to be of a much more private and nature personal nature'

142 **A.J. Köstenberger cf.** p.130

"Yes, we were there. The Pharisees became really angry, not just with Jaycee, but with everyone else too; I began to cry I was so frightened," said Jubilee.

"I did, too," said Joel. "We were saved from all the hatred and anger by a beam of light that came down from Joel's stone, you know, the one with seven eyes."

"You mean the foundation stone?"

Joel was taken by complete surprise. "How did you know I called it that? It's mine," he said with glee. It chose me, didn't it, Jubilee?"

She nodded in agreement.

"It belongs to all those who want to know the truth... but you have been honoured with holding its symbol." And he nodded at Joel then touching him on his chest with his finger as if that was a wonderful thing. Joel didn't answer; he was still thinking about it.

"We were frightened," said Jubilee. "It looked as though the Pharisees were determined to put someone in jail or even kill them. I just hope it wasn't Jaycee, that's all..." she finished.

Joel leaned on Neph saying, "It was so-so good to wake up here—and to see you again,"

Someone was shouting from the Hall.

They heard Jeremy and Sam calling, "Joel, Jubilee, where are you? Lydia is having a dickie fit. She's worried stiff," Sam babbled.

The little ones jumped up and started waving their arms in the air. Neph stood up as well.

Lydia cried out, "I can see them. They are down there, by the water." They started to run, then suddenly found themselves next to the Joel and Jubilee and Neph.

"Hey, how did you do that?" said Joel. "They were still a long way away?"

"I can do lots of things, you know. That's an easy one. Watch this," he said, holding his hands out like a performer.

Jeremy, Sam and Lydia were now standing about six feet up in the air! "Put me down this minute!" shouted Lydia indignantly.

"Whoops," said Neph. "That wasn't a very good idea was it?"

"You'd better watch out, Neph, she might give you a good slap like she did Bumper," laughed Joel. Jubilee wasn't so sure. Sam grinned; he had enjoyed that. Jeremy stood between Neph and Lydia, just in case.

"Why did you run away like that? You must tell me before you do anything, do you hear? I'm still upset from last time," Lydia scolded, pulling Jubilee and Joel to their feet.

"Sorry, Lyd," said Jubilee, pleading. "We really wanted to see Neph again. We were only going to the church to meet him."

Neph said, "I'm sorry, Lydia. I should have made sure that you knew where we were. We all get so used to knowing things telepathically, I forget that you still have to speak to one another."

"Well, we won't be if this happens again," Lydia said, smiling slightly as she looked up at him.

"What does teli...pa...tic mean?" asked Joel.

"It means thinking and sending thoughts to one another, instead of speaking," Neph explained.

"Oh, I forgot; they can read our minds, but we can't read theirs," Jubilee pondered, not sure if that was a good idea or not.

"Something like that," grinned Jeremy.

"How long are we going to be here?" asked Sam looking up at his angel friend.

Neph looked down at their innocence.

Slowly he said, "As I was telling the little ones just now about their best friend of Jaycee, but you have to travel forward in time to see the last sign. The seventh sign.

268

"This is the event that brought about the end and the beginning." He hesitated before continuing. "Jaycee's best friend died while he was away," Neph said, his voice echoing.

"Ho no! That must have been horrible for him."

"Yes it was – but you have to look in the Book of Mirrors to find out what happened." He looked at Lydia. "You will be able to ask questions from your looking glass – now that it is whole again."

He looked at Joel who sitting listening very carefully to every word that Neph had spoken.

"You, little man, must take great care of the stone with seven eyes." Joel's eyes lit up, was he going to be used this time? Neph continued, "You have the stone which can carry you into the future – as far as the end times. You still need to learn how to handle this gift."

"Oh, why?"

"Because it is very powerful. The one substance that has the power of the created universe.[143] It is the power and greatness of God's son – Jaycee. He is the stone."

They were all shocked, why did this gift go to such a young boy? Surely he would lose it or break it or... Neph smiled and answered their thoughts.

Jaycee said, "Let the little children come to me, and do not [stop] them, for the kingdom of heaven belongs to such as these."[144] Joel represents the innocence of the world. The stone can't be broken, destroyed or lost – because it is the

---

143 **John 1:1-3**; John confirms that Jesus was the divine Word through whom God created the universe: *"All things were made through Him, and without Him nothing was made that was* [had been previously] *made"*

Ephesians 3:9 Paul states quite clearly that *"God ...created all things through Jesus Christ"*. He Paul writes of Jesus: *"For by Him all things were created that are in heaven and that are on earth, visible and invisible, whether thrones or dominions or principalities or powers. All things were created through Him and for Him"*

144 **Matthew 19:14** NIV.

foundation stone on which we all should stand and put our hope in."

"Golly," said Joel. "We did, we did, didn't we, Lydia? He said looking up at her with delight on his face. "We stood on it."

He took it out of his pocket and stared at it. It was bigger than the palm of his small hand, his fingers struggled to clutch the edges of the stone, to keep it safe. He whispered "This is amazing..."

"Grandma!" said the others quietly smiling down at their little brother.

"Before I can take you to the place of dreams," said Neph, "you will have to be prepared. Only the pure in heart can travel inside the Corridor of time. No evil can enter. But first, read God's Book and find the truth." And he disappeared before their very eyes.

They remained sitting beside the still waters, Jubilee prayed and the Book of Mirrors came into her hands. Lydia took out her looking glass and waited for the book to tell them of their last journey to see the seventh sign. The book showed a huge crowd of angels gathering to see Jaycee perform a truly wonderful and significant, event. It had never been done before and it would never be done again on earth.

They saw a tomb with a large stone rolled in front of it. It had been sealed. The people were sobbing and crying as if in great pain of sorrow. They had lost someone who was very dear to them all. Who could it be? As they watched tears came to their eyes as they felt the pain of someone lost to them – forever.

Lydia felt she should open her looking glass. They saw joy on the faces of the angels – but how could that be? Lazarus had died? What was going on?

Neph led them quietly to the church. A crowd of angels hovered outside to witness this event being allowed for the children. Inside, the church was filled with smoke from the glory of God's presence. No one could enter the temple until the seven angels had completed their preparations.[145]

As they watched in stunned silence they saw a swirling blue white beam begin to come down through the grey stone tower. They waited. The beam grew stronger and stronger bringing with it a powerful presence in the light. The angels moved to form a circle around them, as they did so they raised their arms out wide, yet their hands did not touch.

'It looks scary,' thought Jubilee.

"Don't be afraid," said Neph quietly. "Your guardian angels will travel with you."

One angel in the circle then raised his head, stepped back, smiled and nodded at Joel to step forward – into the light. He didn't hesitate. With a confident grin on his face he stepped forward, his arm outstretched in front of him with the stone sitting in his palm. He felt so proud and honoured. Lydia thought about grabbing him and pulling him back, she wasn't sure about all this. The last time it was Jubilee who disappeared. The others immediately knew what she had thought. Jeremy was standing next to her. He placed his hand on hers and gave it a quick squeeze of comfort. Everyone knew it was her love for her little brother that caused her concern. No-one moved.

Telepathically they thought, 'We must pray, clear our minds of anything other than Jaycee.' As they did so the beam began to get bigger and bigger, slowly enveloping all of them, including the seven angels.

'Their spirits were carried away to a great and high mountain.'[146] They saw seven golden lamps lighting the way, standing on seven hills. Before them 'there was what looked like a sea of glass, clear as crystal.'[147] They saw the 'holy

---

145 **Revelation 15:8 cf.** NIV.

146 **Revelation 21:10 cf.**

147 **Revelation 4:6** *"there was what looked like a sea of glass, clear as crystal".*

city... coming down out of heaven from God... Its brilliance was like that of a very precious jewel, like jasper, clear as crystal. It had a great and high wall, with twelve gates, with twelve angels at the gates.'[148] 'The wall was made of jasper, and the city of pure gold, as pure as glass. The foundations of the city walls were decorated with every kind of precious stone. The first foundation was jasper, the second sapphire, the third agate, the fourth emerald'[149] also with many other precious stones. This city does not need the sun or the moon to shine on it, for God gives it light and Jaycee is the lamp to light the way.[150]

There was no fear, no pain just perfect love and contentment as if someone had opened their arms to them. They awoke in bright sunshine, on the outskirts of Bethany. The people were waiting for Jaycee, because Lazarus had been very ill.

---

148 **Revelation 21:10-12** *It had a great and high wall, with twelve gates, and at the gates twelve angels; and names were written on them, which are the names of the twelve tribes of the sons of Israel.*

149 **Revelation 21:18-19.**

150 **Revelation 21:23 cf.**

Chapter 17

RESURRECTION—FROM DEATH TO LIFE

The Seventh Sign: Jaycee's Best Friend, Lazarus, had died, According to John 11:1-11

– Four days later –

Jaycee and his followers walked one and a half miles to Jerusalem on the southeast slope of the Mount of Olives, crossing over the river Jordan to go to Bethany and see Lazarus, who was sick.

Only a few moments ago, all the children had been in relative comfort. Now the children found themselves standing in the middle of grief-stricken crowds, all sobbing loudly and falling on the ground, with sadness, beside the closed tomb. Then the groups of crying people heard shouting, someone important was coming. The children turned to see who it was. They gasped as they saw Jaycee arriving with his followers.

"At last, he's here!" shouted a man standing near them. Everyone looked towards the group of men coming their way.

A disciple standing in the crowd said confidently, "Don't worry, this sickness will not end in death! Jaycee promised!" People stared at each other with tears of joy, fear and hope.

"But he's been dead for four days—it's too late! Everyone knows that it takes three days for the spirit to leave the body. It's too late, do you hear? It's too late!" said a man in the crowd. Hushed arguing broke out in the crowd and whisperings of disbelief continued.

Mary fell to her knees in front of Jaycee. "If you had been here, my brother would not have died," she said. Her voice was breaking in her throat, as she looked up at him with desperation, yet with longing; her tears continued to flow.

The children were amazed to see Jaycee begin to cry with her.

"He must have loved Lazarus a lot," whispered Jubilee, wiping away her tears and focusing intently on what Jaycee would do to resolve this problem. They watched as he walked slowly and gracefully towards the cave where Lazarus had been laid. The crowds fell silent in anticipation. As enemies, the trouble making Pharisees stood apart from the crowds.

Jaycee turned to look at her with much pain in his eyes. "If you believe, then you will see the glory of my Father," he said, his voice barely a whisper.

"What does he mean by glory?" asked Joel.

"I suppose he means that God has power over death," Sam answered, standing himself next to Joel.

"That's amazing," said Joel under his breath, as he reached out to hold Jubilee's hand. The crowd stopped sobbing. Everyone went very quiet. They were all watching Jaycee.

"Those who know me will live with me and my Father". Jaycee approached the tomb, father in heaven, "Father, I thank you that you always hear me."[151] The people heard him say this, and they began to believe in him.

---

151 **John 11:42** Jaycee said to his father God, '*I knew that you always hear me, but I said this for the benefit of the people standing here, that they may believe that you sent me*' [to be with them].

In a strong voice, he was heard by all to say, "Take away the stone."[152]

Without hesitation, several men rushed forward. They stood to one side and began to push, heaving and struggling to roll the stone away.

"He's not going in there, is he?" asked Joel insensitively, nudging Sam and Jeremy, who stood beside him.

"We don't know; just be quiet," said Lydia impatiently putting her hand on his shoulder to quieten him.

No one could make themselves look away. Everyone was transfixed by Jaycee's command. The Pharisees would not allow this, surely?

No one moved or spoke, except Joel couldn't be quiet. "Err, Lazarus's body will stink. He'll be full of maggots crawling out of his—"

"Be quiet, for goodness sake!" whispered Jubilee under her breath, making Joel clamp his lips into a tight thin line.

"It has been four days, Lydia," whispered Sam as he almost stopped breathing not wanting to miss every moment.

The whole situation fascinated Jeremy. "Nothing is impossible for Jaycee to do," he said thinking scientifically.

"That must be true," Jubilee suggested. "Because he healed a man blind from birth and made a man walk again after years and years lying on his back by the pool. So, why not again!" she insisted with such faith for her young age.

"That was different; they were all alive," insisted Jeremy, beginning to wonder and rethink everything through logically, shaking his head in wonder and disbelief.

"I know, but... well, he is the son of God, isn't he?" Jubilee argued quietly, trusting in Jaycee and watching eagerly without a doubt of disbelief.

The stone was rolled away. Everyone gasped in disbelief as Jaycee began to walk towards the open tomb.

---

152 **Meaning:** – [The rock of doubt.]

"What is he going to do"? asked Mary. Lazarus's sister, Martha, said, "But Lord, there is a bad smell; he has been there for four days—it's too late."[153]

Jaycee smiled, and then commanded, "Lazarus, come out!"

Silence froze the moment. Only Lazarus moved. The crowds waited, in disbelief to see if Jaycee was about to do the most impossible of all miracles. Then, in the shade of the tomb, a man still wrapped in bandages that were beginning to fall off, walked out into the warmth of the sun.

Jaycee held out his arms to his dear friend Lazarus in welcome. People gasped and women screamed. Many fell to the floor weak with shock at what they had just witnessed, their hands over their open mouths as they fought denial, their minds swimming in turmoil trying to accept the truth of who Jaycee was. Truly the Messiah, the Son of God.

"Golly, look, he's still wrapped up in bandages, and over his eyes. How can he see where he is going?" asked Joel, breaking the beautiful moment.

"For goodness sake, Joel sweetheart, be quiet, please. This is just unbelievable!" Jeremy said hardly breathing. Like the others who were all astounded as they watched this amazing event.

Jaycee said to them, "Take off the grave clothes and let him go."[154]

The sisters of Lazarus and others rush forward to help take off the bandages.

Lazarus stood there, strong and well, his flesh fresh and smooth as he began to smile at those who loved him as they gathered around touching him in disbelief and wonder. Others who had been mourning gasped and wiped their eyes. After a few moments of absolute silence and disbelief,

---

153 **Meaning:** – [It is never too late!]
154 **John 11:44**

276

everyone burst into joyful talk, all at the same time, each one describing the miracle they had just witnessed.

Lazarus truly lived; they could see him; others touched him but those who doubted, murmured to each other because they were very afraid.

The children looked at one another in amazement. Blinking, they shared the moment of wonder, disbelief, and joy. What they had seen, was the most amazing thing they had ever witnessed.

"What does this mean for the future?" asked Sam.

LAZARUS APPEARS

"Are you asking if something else will happen to amaze everyone, perhaps everyone in the whole world?" Jeremy replied.

"Hmmm. It's just that Jaycee gave him his life back, even when it wasn't possible. How can he do that?" Sam asked, trying to accept the reality of it."

"If he can bring Lazarus back to life after four days, stone dead and stinking rotten, then he really must be the giver of life! Right?" Jeremy concluded.

Sam thought about this for a long moment; he knew that this was true. "This was a resurrection of an earthly man – to carry on living on earth!" he said looking into the eyes of his admired older brother who nodded.

The others had stopped talking and were now listening to the two older boys were talking.

"Do you know what I am trying to say?" Sam continued. "So if he can do this, then... then... it's true what the Bible says about Jaycee. That if his Father the God-King, is so powerful, he can do this, then ... then... the evil spirit king of the Apollyon locust scouts, and all his devils will be beaten in a mighty battle in heaven – probably very soon. Because we now know that Jaycee can and will be able to live on earth in spirit AND live in Heaven at the same time!

"Because he's going to beat the horrible king of evil, isn't he in a whopping battle," said Joel. "I want to be here when that happens, and next time I am going to have a locust horse of my own, so there!" he said stamping his little foot.

"Was this what our friends in the Hall of Hope were trying to tell us, that they were still alive when they left their sick and tired bodies—perhaps they just had to wait for their time to continue?" Joel pondered out loud, asking both his older brothers.

"I think I will see Kathy again, one day," Sam said quietly.

Lydia had been listening to them. She put her hand on Sam's shoulder, "Yes, we will see them all, especially those who know how real Jaycee is and that he is definitely God's son," she said. She smiled, then directed their attention towards Jaycee and Lazarus, whose hearts were filled with joy.

As they watched the amazing scene, Joel and Jubilee noticed what looked like thousands of angels singing all together in a huge choir in the skies.

"Listen, can you hear that? It's beautiful, isn't it?" Jubilee admired, pointing to the sky. She closed her eyes and listened with her heart.

"And that perfume I can smell. What is it? It must be very expensive; it smells like a billion dollars," Lydia said, looking across at Jubilee.

"Maybe its myrrh," replied Jubilee with a smile, as beautiful golden sunlight shone across her upturned face.

Jeremy and Sam nodded in agreement. Jubilee, looking up to the blue skies, noticed small puffs of white clouds appearing. "That's everyone's tears floating away," she said quietly. Lydia and the others turned their eyes to the skies. "Yes, perhaps the clouds are their tears being washed away. "

"Can you hear the music, Lydia?" asked Jubilee stepping lightly over to her.

"I can!" said Joel, jumping up and down, laughing, and waving his arms. He looked ready to conduct the choir. Jubilee giggled and threw arms around him in a big hug. They both tumbled down onto the thick green grass, tumbling down a slope where they sat laughing.

Lydia and the boys enjoyed watching the little ones as they relaxed in the happy atmosphere. Then Lydia stopped, touched her ear and said to the boys, "Just keep still and listen for a minute. I think Jubilee is right, I can hear the angels singing." She smiled as they turned their faces towards the skies, everything slowly faded…

Chapter 18

THE CHARIOT OF GOLDEN LIGHT AND 'THE FOUR CREATURES OF MANY EYES'

'THERE WAS WHAT LOOKED LIKE a sea of glass, clear as crystal… In the centre, around the throne were four living creatures, and they were covered with eyes, in front and back'.[155]

Two pink streaks buzzed past them heading for the celebration in the skies.

"Come on, Bumper. We have to hurry; everyone is waiting. It's time to go!" Thumper pushed. "And don't make a mess of landing this time! Everyone will be watching us! So please, get it right!" Bumper caught up with him.

"I know, I know. If this all goes well, we will get to Grade 3. Whoopee! And then we can go up to 3 1/4," Bumper said excitedly, not watching where he was going yet again.

The children found themselves in the garden of the living waters, where the babies played and swam in the pool. They saw the spot where they had seen Jaycee on the green, grassy bank with the lamb and the lion sitting together. They soon became aware of others talking and laughing as they sat on the soft grass beside the sparkling bubbling water.

"Hello!" someone shouted over to them making them looked across. "We have come to see the chariot that is

---

155 **Revelation 4;6**

going to take you to on your final journey home. Well, home to your place in the third dimension," the man said—or so they thought.

Jeremy couldn't believe his eyes. "Levi? Esther? What—where are we? And what are you two doing here?" he asked, greeting them with joy.

"Hello," smiled Gregory. "We wouldn't have missed this for the world, either—would we, Sally?" Sally shook her head adamantly.

Sam and Lydia stood up and rushed over to them, first hugging Levi and then Gregory.

"How's your leg? Is it working normally?"

They grinned at one another. "It was a good fight for right, wasn't it?" they said, exchanging smiles.

Sally added, "And scary, too."

Joel leaped to his feet and ran to hug her; Jubilee joined him and threw her arms around Esther's soft furry neck. Sam ambled over casually grinning at Levi, who seemed to frown at him.

"Hello, stubborn mule. Are you here to take us safely on our next journey?" he asked. Levi brayed as if laughing.

Before he could reply, Lydia spotted the haughty camels, Maureen, and Hazel.

"Uh-oh, what are they doing here?" she asked, gritting her teeth and looking at Jubilee, who gave her a confident nod.

Maureen dropped her eyes in embarrassment, then looked up slowly, her nose in the air, and said, "Actually, we liked you all and enjoyed our time with you. Hazel here hasn't stopped talking about the happy times we had together—but I still don't like to carry!" she said sheepishly smiling when Jubilee approached them both.

This honest comment broke the uncertainty. Even Lydia smiled.

"It was fun, wasn't it?" Maureen said, lowering her head for Jubilee to stroke.

Then a deep and gravelly voice interrupted. "Hello, Joel. I see you haven't managed to break your silk thread yet, little man!"

Joel's eyes widened, and he whipped around to see Bomby.

"Bomby! What are you doing here?" asked Joel. "Are we going to do another jump and skydive?"

Bomby threw his head back wheezing with laughter then wobbling as he nearly fell over.

"No. You are not!" said Lydia sternly. She gave Joel a serious look. "I couldn't cope with that again!"

Everyone giggled, remembering the first time. Then they all realized that this was a special meeting of old friends.

Jeremy took the lead with Sam by his side. "Why are you all here?" he asked, looking at the crowd of friends they had met on their journey.

At that moment, Thumper and Bumper rushed down to join them. "So sorry we are late. It's been such a rush with all the celebrations, but we wouldn't have missed this for the world!" said Thumper, tumbling in.

"No, we weren't going to miss this," Bumper said as he landed successfully.

They landed in the middle of the group and stood before the children. Bumper had his legs crossed; his wings were neatly folded down, but his feathers drooped. He doodled a circle on the grass with his foot. They both looked sad.

Gregory came forward and said quietly, "It's time for you to go home."

"Home!" they all repeated in unison, trying to think back to home as they exchanged glances.

"Yes," Gregory confirmed.

"But... but...," Jubilee rubbed her eyes as tears began to swell making her eyes shine. "We...we'll miss you all."

Lydia stepped forward. "Well, it's a relief to be going home," she almost smiled but she had a lump in her throat which stopped her.

Joel didn't know what to say – for a change. He looked at Jeremy; Jeremy and Sam looked back at each other.

"Mum and Dad need to know the truth about Jaycee, especially now we know that he always hears our prayers," Sam said, grabbing his little brothers hand giving it a light squeeze.

"That we will live with Jaycee forever when the time comes for us, too," said Sam. "Like our friends we met at the House of Rest." He thought about Kathy and everyone they had met who had blessed them in any such way.

Joel's face crumpled letting out a little whimper, followed by a loud cry. "I want my Mum and Dad!" he wailed holding out his arms to Lydia to be picked up.

"Of course you do, dear!" she said, lifting him up to place him on her hip. "But I don't want to go, either—I can't choose!" he screamed aloud with tears now streaming down his red cheeks.

Jubilee came to stand beside Lydia. "Me neither, but... but I miss Mum and Dad, too. They will be so worried about us, and we should tell them what we have learned," she said, looking out at the crowd, whose hearts were clearly touched.

Gregory sniffed as he fluffed his bronzed wings slightly. Sally stood close to him, her silver-green wings touching his golden brown body for comfort at this sad parting with their friends from the third dimension on earth. Esther's eyes glazed over as she too sniffed back her tears. Levi snorted to hide the pain of having to let them go.

Then, Bomby humped himself clumsily forward. Grinning, he said, "Don't worry, I'll keep the silk thread of life linked to you, and I'll make sure it won't get broken. That's my job for Jaycee, you know." He smiled encouragingly.

Suddenly, in a flash of light and a puff of sparkling mist Neph stood beside them; as he looked at them, they saw love in his eyes. The children were so thrilled to see him that they momentarily forgot their sadness. With squeals of delight, they rushed over to him. Immediately he swept the little ones up into his arms hugging them as his large snowy wings folded gracefully behind him.

"I won't forget you two. Nor your brothers and big sister, Lydia, with her green eyes," he said winking at her. Then he said, "God's chariot is waiting for you. The same chariot that took Jaycee to all men."

He gently put Joel and Jubilee down as Neph turned to point towards the sky. A gentle breeze carried a perfume through the air as the chariot appeared in a sphere of golden light. Four large creatures covered in eyes floated beside it. The eyes swivelled without blinking looking in all directions. They each had six wings so that they could fly in any direction. Everyone stood in awe at the sight. None of them had ever seen anything like this before.

Neph whispered, "They can see all things, but don't be afraid, little ones. You are being honoured. They are high messengers of the God King. Let me introduce you."

He held out his hand towards the beasts, as they floated gracefully down with the chariot between them. The golden chariot floated just above the ground. It looked like glass as if made of pure sunlight without blemish; a diamond of magnificent brilliance with all the colours of the rainbow sparkling from it in all directions. There were no doors, no windows, no wheels. It moved on its own as if it knew everything. It was from where the perfume came. It was the reason time had stopped.

They were all aware and were frozen in a moment of time in this garden of beauty, by the silver lake of living water. The only thing that moved was the chariot. They all watched in awe without breathing.

As the warmth emanating from this sun chariot touched them, they became aware that one of the creatures had the head of a lion. He was floating just above the ground and, was coming towards Jeremy. His long golden mane swayed in rhythm with his movements; his six wings fluttered without making a sound. Solemnly, he handed Jeremy a bowl containing five pieces of fruit. "This will help you all to be noble in character, so you may always choose the right and honourable action." His voice sounded strong like a roar, yet it was also soft, spoken as if he was thoughtful. He handed the bowl to Jeremy, who accepted it graciously while the others came to stand beside him.

Another beast floated over, his six wings also moving without noise. He was magnificent, with a head of a strong young ox, yet he looked humble. He extended his strong, big arms and held out five scrolls of parchment.

"These are from the God King. They have your names on them, for you are now special children, heirs who will serve his son, Jaycee. These words will give you strength in your hearts to help others in need—for him." His raspy, rough voice sent a shiver down Joel's back.

The third creature came slowly forward. He had the face of an eagle. His many eyes glistened as he carefully turned his head to each one of them. They held their breath in awe. He held out five olive branches. The tone of his voice reminded them of a bird calling in the night from far away. "These are symbols of the divine words of God. They are the swiftest way to understand the greatness of Jaycee as you live in his world today." He took his time delivering them, gently and carefully to each one of the children.

Last came a softly spoken creature with the face of a man. They knew that he understood them; the man smiled a familiar smile as he gave them five caskets of words. "These hold the wisdom you'll need to live happy lives on earth. With your new wisdom, you will find peace and joy. Hold them close to your hearts for they are the treasure you keep in your jars of clay." He then winked, which surprised and calmed them. "These four gifts are the symbols of universal love for humanity. Take care of them." He joined the three other creatures whose eyes had seen everything that had happened.

FOUR CREATURES COVERED IN EYES
Revelations 4:8

While each creature spoke to the children, their many friends watched. The choir of angels in the skies around them were singing glorious songs to the God King and his son, Jaycee. The children had stood in complete awe of the powerful love that came from these amazing creatures, with their many eyes recording every moment. Joel's head kept swivelling around so that he could see them all clearly, to remember them, blinking as if photographing moments with his eyes.

Then the creatures turned to look at Neph, who seemed to understand something because he slowly nodded his head in grateful acceptance. He turned to the children. "Don't worry. We will never lose contact with you as long as you keep these things in your hearts."

The transparent golden chariot became bigger as it hovered between the beasts. Neph bent down to pick up Lydia first; he knew she would want to make sure that it was safe for her brother and sister. She disappeared. Jubilee gasped and threw a hand over her mouth. "She is still there. Don't worry," he said picking her up. He passed her into the golden cloud. She disappeared. Jeremy picked up Joel and handed him to Neph. Joel threw his arms around Neph's neck and clung to him with his eyes squeezed tightly shut as if not wanting to lose his strong and good friend. Then he turned with a huge grin, and nearly jumped out of Neph's hands into the chariot with excitement, at this last adventure of going home. Sam went next, and then Jeremy.

When they had entered the chariot, they realized that their gifts had disappeared. The jar of living water on Jeremy's shoulder had gone. Lydia's looking glass melted away into the perfume of the air. Jubilee's Book of Mirrors remained in her heart though she didn't know it. Sam's sword could not be seen. Only Joel's stone remained. He took it out of his pocket and held it in the palm of his hand. Then another hand came into view. Jaycee appeared before them.

He took the stone, saying, "This stone is symbolic of me, for the seven eyes are me. My father engraved on it a message, that 'he will remove the sin of man in a single day'."[156] Then he smiled and reminded them, "I will be with you always. You can pray and talk to me whenever you wish."

"Thank you," Jeremy spoke for them all. They nodded enthusiastically.

With a flash of blue lightning, they swished away as their friends below waved and wept.

"I do hope that they will come back some day, don't you?" said Sally to Esther. She nodded, as Levi came to share their sadness at the loss of their friends.

"They'll be back," said Neph, a single tear sliding down his cheek.

---

156 **Zechariah 3:9** *'There are seven on that one stone, and I will engrave an inscription on it', says the Lord Almighty, 'and I will remove the sin of this land in a single day.'*

Epilogue

THEY LANDED WITH A THUMP as the lightning flashed and the windows crackled. Their bodies felt warm and very heavy, but the room seemed filled with light and the brightness lingered as they fell asleep. By the morning, the wind had stopped and so had the rain. Jubilee dashed over to the window, placing her hands on the sill; she looked out at the grey street below.

Lydia sat up in bed. "What's it like out there?" she asked, rubbing her head as though she had just woken up from a long dream.

"Horrible. I had expected the sky to be blue and the air warm. Funny. It seems odd here this morning," Jubilee pondered walking away from the window slowly and thoughtfully.

Their mother Jane quietly opened the bedroom door. "Oh, you're awake. My goodness, you were all so sound asleep when we got home last night. You all looked peaceful, so we crept out. Aunty Joan is much better; perhaps you can go and see her today, after school." She spoke endearingly, stroking Jubilee's long fringe gently.

Jeremy and Sam staggered into their room, still looking half-asleep.

"Funny, I thought we were with you last night, during the storm."

Jane laughed. "Dad and I walked you two sleepy heads back to your room. It was a bit crowded in here with the girls." She looked around.

"Hmm. I don't remember that," Jeremy said, giving Lydia a sideways look.

"I don't either," said Sam looking puzzled.

"What's that you have in your hand, Joel?" asked their mother, kneeling and prying open his fingers. He clutched the shining pale brown stone in his hot little fist.

"It's a stone with seven marks that look like eyes on it," Joel explained.

"Where did you find it? In the garden?" she asked, looking into his eyes.

"I don't remember…well, I'm not sure. Something like that, but I think I'll keep it safe. It makes me feel good." Joel grinned at his mother; he did love her.

The others came to look down at the unusual stone in his small, still hot, hand. Slowly with one mind, they all began to grin.

"That is a good idea, Joel, keep it safe," said Jeremy, ruffling his hair gently with affection.

"It looks as though it could be precious," said Sam, nodding.

Two pink streaks flashed across the room.

"What was that?" asked Joel as they whipped around, looking in all directions. They exchanged puzzled glances.

"Come on," said their mother leaving the room, who hadn't seen anything. "You'll be late for school. I'll give you all five minutes to get downstairs for breakfast." "Mummy?" said Joel.

Jane stopped and turned around in the doorway, "Yes?"

"Will you say my prayers with me tonight when I go to bed?" he asked, sweetly.

She paused for a moment of thought. "Of course I will, sweetheart," she said, smiling with an inquisitive frown.

"We all will," said Lydia with a smile, "Won't we?"

THE BOOK OF MIRRORS:
Afterword

This book acts as a stepping stone to the mysteries of the Bible. It forms an allegory based on the *Seven Signs of John*, as scholars have named them. Footnotes provide meanings, references and straightforward explanations for those who wish to refer to their Bible for more understanding.

I felt called to write, with humour, through the eyes of five children, who experience life between the worlds of earth and spirit; in the fourth dimension, time. The children travel back to the days of the New Testament, to the life and times of Jesus; they have further adventures witnessing Old Testament incidents and finally move forward to End Times, thus bringing the Bible together as one story. The various experiences enable them to relate to things from the two worlds, and consequently ask many questions from a child's point of view. Only 'the little ones' can indeed see the angels and the glory of the Son of God, because their minds are not yet cluttered by the influences of the material, physical world. Their simple questions will help us to see and understand more clearly the truth of the mission of JC – Jesus Christ.

The main references I have used for the academic aspect of this work –

Baker. Kenneth L; & Kohlenberger. John R. III (eds) *NIV Bible Commentary Vol 2*: Zondervan Publishing House, Grand Rapids, 1994.

Carson. D.A ; France ; R.T. J.A. Motyer J.A; & G.J. Wenham, *The New Bible Commentary*, 2010.

Köstenberger. A.J, *Encountering John*, Baker Barker Book House Co, Grand Rapids, Michigan. 49516, 2003

NIV Study Bible, Hodder & Stoughton/The Zondervan Corp. (for all Bible quotes), 1991.

Wright Tom, *John for Everyone*, Part 1, WJK

Westminster, John Knox Press, Louisville, Kentucky. 2010

About the Author

Penny was blessed with a happy childhood with her older brother and younger sister. Their home was filled with love and laughter, whilst living in both England and South Africa. Sadly, she had to leave school at 15 years to support her family, due to her father's illness.

She married and has two children, Jane and Martin. Penny's adult life was tough, but through the years she persevered starting many businesses, mainly in property development. Whilst living in Spain Penny experienced a chance meeting with someone who changed her life. She was invited to a New Year's Eve party on a private yacht in Purto Banus, Costa del Sol. After admiring the owner's boat he told her, "If God says I can have it, I will. If he says I can't, I won't." Her ensuing discussions with him that evening changed her life. She never saw him again. No one else seemed to know him…

In 2004 she met Keith, a retired Royal Naval officer, in Normandy, France, where she now lives. They married in France in 2006. He became her rock. On the 10th June 2007 Penny experienced a call from God. He told her, "You will be used." Stunned, Penny argued, "Why now? It's too late, I'm too old." Yet she understood that she would have to study theology and achieve a degree! Impossible, as she had never studied academically. Nine years later, Penny is in her final months for a BA at the London school of Theology and Middlesex university – by distance learning. During the last three years she began writing her allegorical book, *The Seven Signs of John*, written in three levels: for children, adults and the wise. This is the first book in a series of *The Book of Mirrors*.